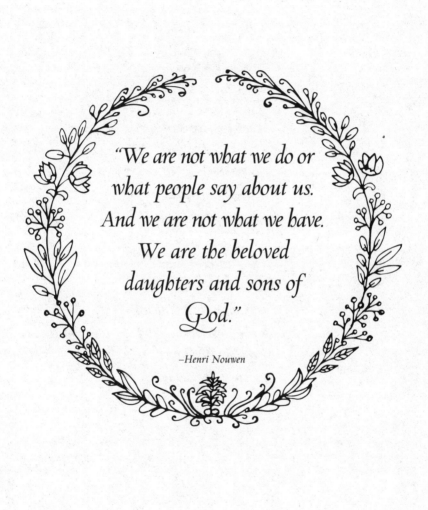

"We are not what we do or what people say about us. And we are not what we have. We are the beloved daughters and sons of God."

–Henri Nouwen

MYSTERIES *of* LANCASTER COUNTY

BY ANY OTHER NAME

MYSTERIES *of* LANCASTER COUNTY

Beth Adams

Guideposts

Danbury, Connecticut

Mysteries of Lancaster County is a trademark of Guideposts.

Published by Guideposts Books & Inspirational Media
100 Reserve Road, Suite E200
Danbury, CT 06810
Guideposts.org

Cover and interior design by Müllerhaus
Cover illustration by Bob Kayganich, represented by Deborah Wolfe, LTD.
Typeset by Aptara, Inc.

Printed and bound in the United States of America
10 9 8 7 6 5 4 3 2 1

BY ANY
OTHER NAME

CHAPTER ONE

The phone on the counter rang as Martha carried her plate to the sink.

"Just let it go to voice mail." Elizabeth balanced the bowl of leftover asparagus and the plate of ham with her own plate as she walked toward the sink. "It's always robocalls at this hour."

Martha was tempted, but she set her plate down and leaned over so she could see the name that popped up on the screen. If it was an unidentified caller, she would let it go. But the name that showed up on the screen was *Silas Fischer*. She set her plate in the soapy water and then picked up the phone.

"Hello?"

"This is Ephraim. Is this Mrs. Watts?"

It was their Amish neighbors' sixteen-year-old son. He sounded out of breath. He must have run to the phone shanty that stood at the end of the family's driveway. Martha knew right away that something was wrong. It was the only way Ephraim would have forgotten to start with a greeting of some sort. Those Fischer children were the most polite children Martha had ever met.

"Yes, this is Martha. What's wrong?"

"There are police here. They say Adam is lying about who he is. *Maam* asked if you or your sisters could come over and explain that he was on your land all day."

What in the world? Adam was Rachel and Silas's twenty-two-year-old son, who was married and had a baby on the way. He farmed the Classen sisters' land. None of what Ephraim had said made sense. But Martha knew there was only one answer.

"Of course. We'll be right over." They would figure out what was going on when they got there.

"*Danki.*"

She set the phone down and found both Elizabeth and Mary looking at her.

"That was Ephraim. He said the police are there, saying that Adam is not who he says he is, or something. We need to vouch that he was here this afternoon."

Mary's eyes narrowed, and Elizabeth just looked confused.

"I don't know. It wasn't exactly clear what's going on. But Rachel is asking us if we can come."

"Of course." Mary set down the water glasses she was carrying.

"Let's go." Elizabeth was already heading toward the door.

Martha glanced at all the dishes waiting to be dealt with, but then she shook her head. The dishes would wait. Their friend needed them.

The sisters pulled on coats and piled into Elizabeth's car. The drive to the neighboring farm took only minutes. Daylight Savings Time had recently begun, and the sky was still light when they pulled into the driveway. They saw that the horses were in the paddock and several buggies were lined up against the fence. Through the open barn door, Martha could see Ephraim, as well as twins Matthew and Thomas, tending to the animals. A police car was parked in front of the house. It looked incongruous in this peaceful setting.

"Let's go see what this is all about," Mary said, pushing her door open. The three sisters walked across the yard to the side door. Before they even got there, the door opened and Luke, Rachel and Silas's eighteen-year-old son, was ushering them inside.

"Thank you for coming," Luke said. "My parents do not know how what they are saying could be true." He closed the door after they all stepped inside and led them through the kitchen, with its wooden cabinets and propane-powered appliances.

"How *what* could be true?" Mary asked. "What happened exactly?"

"Maam and *Daed* and the police will tell you," Luke said and showed them to the living room, where Rachel and her husband Silas sat on wooden chairs. Martha was glad to see that one of the police officers was John Marks. John was a close friend of Elizabeth's, and he was a fair and good man. He sat on a couch against one wall and smiled when Elizabeth walked in the room. There was also another police officer, one she hadn't met before, and Adam Fischer sat on a wooden bench across from him. Even under the full Amish beard, Adam looked so young and scared. Adam's wife, Leah, sat in a rocking chair, cradling her growing belly. It wouldn't be long now— probably only a month or so left.

"*Hallo*," Rachel said. She and Silas rose as the sisters entered the room. "Please, sit." She gestured for Adam to move from the bench, and he stood so the three sisters could sit down. Both police officers watched them settle into the seats, and they looked uncertain.

"What brings the three of you here?" John asked, though he was smiling, as if he already knew. Rachel explained that Ephraim had called them. John introduced the other officer as Officer Hooper, and he nodded, though he seemed confused by their appearance.

"Thank you so much for coming," Silas said, and then he turned to the officers. "Adam was working on the Classen land this afternoon," he said to them. "They can tell you. He could not have done this thing."

"He was," Mary said. "Adam leases our land, and he was out there plowing today." Martha and Elizabeth nodded along with her, but Martha was bewildered. What was all this about?

"What is going on?" Elizabeth asked.

Officer Hooper spoke first. "There was a hit-and-run accident this afternoon over on Cherry Hill Road, out by Oak Hill Road. A car was driving far too fast and hit a buggy as it came over the rise."

"Oh dear," Mary said.

Elizabeth felt her stomach drop. Accidents like this were becoming far too common. Cars drove too quickly over these rural roads and often didn't see the slow-moving buggies until it was too late. The Amish buggies didn't stand a chance against thousands of pounds of metal, and there had been several fatal crashes in recent years.

"It was the Mast family," Rachel said. "Abner and Miriam and their three-year-old son, Abel. Coming back from a visit to see her sister's new baby."

Martha didn't even need to ask how Rachel knew this. She had never understood how news spread so quickly in the Amish community, but it always did.

"Are they all right?" Elizabeth asked, echoing the question that was in Martha's own mind.

"They were taken to Lancaster General Hospital," Officer Hooper said. "We do not know their condition at this time."

"The car sustained substantial damage and was abandoned at the scene," John said. "It was registered to Adam Fischer at this address."

Elizabeth and Mary looked as confused as Martha felt. "But Adam doesn't have a car," she said.

"He's Amish," Mary added, as if the officers hadn't figured that out already.

"Nevertheless, the car was registered in his name," Officer Hooper said. "And this was listed as the address."

"But Adam does not even live here," Silas said quietly. "He has not for several years."

"He lives on another piece of the property, on Herr Road," Rachel explained to the officers. "Since he got married. He has a different address."

"That may well be." Officer Hooper had the thin, wiry build of a long-distance runner and thinning gray hair. He had a small notebook open on his lap, and he made a note before looking up. "But when we ran his name through the system, we came up with a laundry list of other offenses committed by Adam, including public intoxication and a DUI."

"As well as a restraining order taken out against him," John added.

"This came up as his most recent address," Officer Hooper said.

Martha wanted to laugh. It was ludicrous to imagine Adam, with his horse and buggy and his suspenders, drinking and driving a car. But the officers weren't laughing, so Martha held it in.

"It wasn't him," she said. "That's obvious, right?" Neither of the officers gave anything away. "If what you're saying is true—"

"It is," Officer Hooper said, with no trace of humor.

"—then it was someone pretending to be Adam," Martha finished. "There's no way it could have been him. He doesn't drink. He doesn't drive. And he certainly doesn't need a restraining order."

"Plus, as we said, he was working in the fields this afternoon," Elizabeth said. "I can vouch for the fact that he was out there all afternoon."

"I saw him out there too," Martha added.

"Have you ever been to State College?" Officer Hooper asked Adam.

Adam shook his head. "No, sir. That is quite far from here."

It was only a two-hour drive, but it would take all day or longer in a buggy.

"What's in State College?" Elizabeth asked.

Neither officer answered the question. Officer Hooper wrote something down in his notebook.

Martha knew the borough of State College was the home of Penn State, a huge university with a football team and a party culture. The officers had to see how funny it was to imagine Adam there. The Amish were only educated through eighth grade, so he hadn't exactly gone on a college tour.

"This is crazy," Mary said. "There's no way Adam could have caused that crash."

Martha glanced at Rachel and saw that her lips were pressed together, and her face was pale. Silas's shoulders were hitched, and his knuckles were white where they gripped the arm of the couch.

The two police officers glanced at one another, then Officer Hooper said to Adam, "And you don't own a car that you loaned to someone else to use?"

"No, sir," Adam replied, shaking his head.

"Well then, it appears as though you aren't the one responsible for this crime," John said slowly.

Martha heard Elizabeth let out a breath. Rachel's face relaxed, but only a little.

"If this is Adam Fischer—" Officer Hooper started.

"This *is* Adam Fischer," Rachel said.

"—then it seems pretty unlikely to us that he was behind the crash, or the other offenses," John continued.

"Which begs the question, who *was* behind them?" Martha asked.

"And why was he using Adam's name and address?" Mary asked.

"And how?" Elizabeth added.

"That just about sums it up." Officer Hooper closed his notebook. "I guess that's what we'll be looking into."

"Do you have any idea at all how someone could have stolen your identity?" John asked.

"No," Adam said. "I did not even know this was possible."

"Someone must have gotten a driver's license in your name."

"And you need a social security number to get a driver's license," Officer Hooper said. "But you don't have one of those either, correct?"

"Actually, I have both a social security number and a driver's license," Adam said.

Officer Hooper's face registered surprise, but John seemed to understand.

"I thought you were against those kinds of things," Officer Hooper said. "Government registration, taxes, and all that."

"We are not against cooperating with our government," Silas said. "We pay taxes just like everybody else. What we do not approve of is insurance, like social security."

Officer Hooper looked confused, so Martha jumped in.

"The Amish don't use insurance. They believe it's up to their community to provide for one another in times of need. And social security is a form of insurance, right?"

"I guess so," Officer Hooper said.

"So in their community, they opt out of social security."

"I didn't know you could do that," Officer Hooper said.

"Most people can't," Elizabeth said. "The Amish have a special exemption through the courts."

"But you must register for a social security number to be able to say you do not want to take part in it," Silas said. "So most of us have these numbers."

Officer Hooper still looked confused. "Did you say you have a driver's license?"

"That is right." Adam nodded. "I did, in any case. I do not drive anymore. Not since I joined the church."

"When was that?" John asked.

"More than two years ago." Adam looked at Leah and smiled.

"You got it while you were on *rumspringa*?" John asked.

"Yes."

Even Officer Hooper was nodding now. Everyone around these parts knew about rumspringa, or the teenage years, when Amish youth were allowed to experience the Englisch world before deciding whether they wanted to join the Amish church and commit to the lifestyle for good.

"That's quite unusual, isn't it?" John asked. "To get a driver's license?"

"I suppose it is," Adam said.

"He works very hard. He is very responsible," Rachel added.

"How does an Amish person even get a driver's license?" Officer Hooper asked. "How is that possible?"

"Before they join the church, the Amish are allowed to learn to drive," Mary explained.

"But it's unusual because of the work and cost involved in learning to drive a car," Martha said. "Adam is a very determined young man."

"What made you want to drive?" Officer Hooper asked Adam. Martha thought it was a silly question. What teenage boy didn't want to get behind the wheel of a car? But Adam's answer surprised her.

"Back then, I was thinking I might become a veterinarian," he said.

"Really?" Mary looked as surprised as Martha felt. Becoming a veterinarian would mean years of schooling beyond the eighth-grade education most Amish received. Martha wasn't even sure you could be Amish and have an advanced degree like that.

"I was not sure if I was going to join the church and farm or become a veterinarian and help animals," Adam said. "I thought I might be able to do more good helping many people's animals than I could by staying here and raising my own."

"That's admirable," Mary said.

"So I got a job helping out at a clinic in Lancaster to see what it was like. And I wanted a car for an easy way to get there regularly, rather than use the family's horse and buggy all the time."

It showed a tremendous amount of initiative on Adam's part, Martha thought. Not many young men in his position would even know where to start, even if they had the desire to get themselves jobs and cars to get them there.

"But you decided to join the church instead," Officer Hooper said incredulously.

"Yes. In the end I could not leave my family and my church," Adam said. Martha wasn't sure, but she thought she detected a bit of uncertainty in his voice. She wondered if there was ever a small part of him that regretted his choice, but knew that she could never ask. "And I wanted to marry Leah." He glanced again at his wife, who let a slow smile spread across her face.

Ah. There it was. He'd made his decision for love, as so many young people did. Well, you couldn't fault him for that. Martha had chosen to marry Chuck and have children over the possibility of opening her own restaurant.

"And what happened to your driver's license when you joined the church?" Officer Hooper asked.

"I do not know," Adam said. "I had lost the card a few weeks earlier, but I figured it did not matter, since I would not be driving anyway."

Martha couldn't imagine losing such an important piece of documentation and not doing anything about it. Once, many years ago, she'd lost her wallet, and within hours she'd canceled every credit card, reported her license lost, and had a replacement on the way. How could you not take something like that seriously? But then, maybe Adam hadn't realized what could happen if his identification got into the wrong hands.

"You lost it?" John's eyes met Officer Hooper's. "Where?"

"I do not know," Adam said. "If I knew, it would not be lost."

Martha couldn't help laughing at that, though Officer Hooper seemed stunned. Many people underestimated the Amish sense of humor, she knew, and this seemed to be the case for this police officer. John was fighting back a smile.

"How could someone else be using his license?" Leah asked from the corner. Her dark hair was combed back under her *kapp*, and her brown eyes were sleepy. "I thought the whole point was that it tells who you are."

"That's true," John said. "But in this case, I'm guessing there was no photo?" He looked at Adam, who nodded.

Martha knew that the Amish church did not allow its members to be photographed, and the Commonwealth of Pennsylvania had granted a special exemption to members of the Amish community who got licenses and state-issued identification cards. The corner where the photo usually went was just a white square.

"In that case, it wouldn't be hard for whoever took the ID to put his own photo on your card and start using it as his own," John said.

"So it could be anyone," Mary said.

"Just about," Officer Hooper said. "Anyone who could pass for a man around Adam's age, that is."

That's a whole lot of people, Martha thought.

"Do you have any ideas where you might have lost the physical license?" Officer Hooper asked. "Given what we know so far, I'm guessing that whoever is calling himself Adam Fischer is using your lost license. If we can find out where you might have lost it, we might be able to figure out who has it."

"I do not know," Adam said.

It had been over two years ago. How could he possibly know at this point?

But Adam continued. "Though I do not think there could have been too many places. I did not go very many places when I was driving."

"Let's start by thinking about places you went regularly," Officer Hooper said, opening his notebook again. "Where did you go?"

"There was the veterinary clinic," Adam said.

"And the racetrack," Silas said.

"The...what?" Officer Hooper's eyes were wide.

"Lancaster Speedway," Adam said reluctantly. "I liked to watch the car races."

Martha wasn't sure she'd heard correctly. She'd never heard of an Amish person who went to watch car races. "Seriously?"

"Seriously," Adam said. "I was on rumspringa, and I got to experience the Englisch world. And I had always been fascinated by fast cars."

Maybe she shouldn't have been surprised. Her own sons, Craig and Kyle, had both been into cars. Maybe it was a genetic thing, something about that Y chromosome. But she had never thought about Amish men having the same fascination.

"That's unusual, isn't it?" Officer Hooper asked.

"I suppose," Adam said. "Then again, if you spent as much time in a slow-moving buggy as I have, being passed by cars right and left, you might find yourself dreaming of racing cars someday too."

John laughed, though Officer Hooper still just seemed incredulous.

"It does not mean that he was driving that car today," Rachel added. "He does not drive anymore."

"I understand," John said with a smile. "Is there anywhere else you went regularly?"

Adam looked around the room, his eyes darting from the officers to his wife and then back at the officers. Leah cleared her throat, and Rachel shifted in her seat and looked down. There was a pause, just a fraction of a second too long, and then he continued. "That's it, really. The vet clinic and the racetrack."

Something had passed between the Amish people in the room, something that they all understood and didn't want to say. Martha wanted to ask what it was but decided she would follow up with Rachel about it later. Right now, John was asking Adam about where the vet's office was, and what his address was and how long he'd lived there, and then, after a few more questions, he and his partner promised to look into the matter.

"You will find the man who is pretending to be Adam?" Silas asked.

"We will do our absolute best," Officer Hooper said. He tucked his notebook into his pocket and stood. "We'll find him and bring him to justice."

Silas stood and walked the police officers to the door. John cast a glance back at Elizabeth then stepped out. Adam and Leah also stood. Leah looked exhausted, as most women did at this point in their pregnancies.

Rachel hugged them both, and after they'd left, she turned to the sisters. "Thank you for coming. I appreciate your help."

"Of course," Elizabeth said, pushing herself up. "I'm just sorry about this awful situation."

"It's ridiculous," Mary agreed, also standing up to go.

"I'm sure they'll figure out who is pretending to be Adam very quickly," Martha said.

"I hope they will," Rachel said with a sigh. She looked like she wanted to say more, but she didn't.

"If there's anything else we can do to help, please let us know," Martha said.

"I will," Rachel said. Again, there was a look on her face like she wanted to say something more, but she simply ushered the sisters to the door.

Neither of Martha's sisters said a word as they crossed the yard. Night had fallen while they were inside, and she could see

Luke in the barn, silhouetted against the light from a lantern. He'd led the horses into their stalls and was tossing hay in for them. Martha pulled her coat closed around herself. The days may have been getting longer, but winter had not let go of its grasp completely yet.

"So," Mary said, as soon as they were all buckled into Elizabeth's car, heat pouring out of the vents, "are we going to figure out who stole Adam's identity?"

"I was just about to ask the same thing," Elizabeth said as she put the car in REVERSE.

"The police are looking into it," Martha said. She was crammed into the back seat, and she tried to shift to find more space for her legs. "I'm sure they'll find him."

"But what if they don't?" Mary asked. "What if he gets away with it, whoever he is?"

"I think we should do our own investigation," Elizabeth said. "We won't interfere with the police. Just do some digging on the side."

Martha knew her sisters loved mysteries, and she had also enjoyed solving several puzzling situations since she'd moved home last year. But this seemed like a clear case when their help wasn't needed.

"Look, girls. I'm sure there's an established protocol for looking into identity theft," she said. "And I'm pretty sure it doesn't involve the victim's friends figuring it out on their own."

"I think this is probably a pretty unique case," Elizabeth said. "I can't imagine there are many times when the identity theft victim is Amish."

"Officer Hooper didn't seem to know a whole lot about the Amish," Mary said. "He might not see some things that would be clear to someone who grew up around here."

"But John knows this world well," Martha argued. "He'll make sure to clarify anything Officer Hooper doesn't understand."

"It's not like this is some victimless crime," Elizabeth said. "Whoever the man using Adam's identity is, he landed a family in the hospital. He crashed into a buggy, and then he left. He needs to be found and brought to justice."

"I agree with you, of course," Martha said. "I'm just not sure we need to get involved in this." But even as the words came out of her mouth, she knew they were futile. Her sisters had already made up their minds that they were going to "help" in this case, she could already see that. Well, for her part, Martha was going to do her best to stay out of it and let the police do their job. Maybe there was something she could do to help the Mast family. She didn't know how badly they were injured, but they would no doubt have significant hospital bills at any rate, and she knew they didn't have insurance. Martha would talk to Rachel about how she could help with that.

Still, as they pulled into their own driveway just a moment later, she couldn't help but wonder who was behind the crash and the stolen identity. She prayed that whoever it was would be found sooner rather than later.

CHAPTER TWO

Elizabeth lay in bed Friday night, but she couldn't make her mind stop spinning around in circles. How had someone stolen an Amish man's identity? Who would do such a thing? Would the Amish family in the buggy survive?

She was already thinking through possibilities for finding out who had taken the license. Yes, she knew John and Officer Hooper were investigating, and she was sure they would find the answer soon enough, but Elizabeth had known the Fischer family her whole life. They had been such good neighbors to the Classen family, and she couldn't help but think of ways to help her friends.

Finally, she switched on the light and pulled back the covers. She shivered as she stepped out of bed. Spring was coming, but the nights were definitely still chilly. She slipped her robe on and tied it and then crouched down in front of a stack of plastic boxes she'd dug up from the basement. Elizabeth had learned to quilt a few months back, and she'd decided to start a project before the rush of the summer months really set in. Last week she'd gone to the fabric shop and picked out a selection of fabrics that all had a dusty rose color uniting them, but when she'd been in the basement earlier this week, she'd spotted the boxes of Daddy's old clothes, and she'd had an idea.

She opened the top of one box and pulled out a blue checked short-sleeved shirt. It was an old work shirt that Elizabeth remembered him wearing when she was a kid, and it was faded from the sun and several sizes smaller than those he'd worn later in life. The fabric was soft from many washings. It would do perfectly.

These old clothes were just sitting down there in boxes, not doing anyone any good, so Elizabeth had asked her sisters if she could use them to make a quilt. Martha had thought it would be more efficient to simply sell the clothes in the resale shop, and Mary had wondered if she should practice on a few more projects before diving into these, but Elizabeth had convinced them to let her take a stab at it.

She reached in again and pulled out a pair of thick brown work pants. The fabric was probably too heavy for a quilt, but it was good quality. Beneath that were a few long-sleeved church shirts and his one good suit, reserved for weddings and funerals, and a plaid flannel that he'd worn around the house often.

She set aside the first box and opened the second, pulling out nearly a dozen work shirts in various shades of blues and browns. They would make an attractive palette. She'd keep the pattern simple, maybe a Log Cabin or a Four Patch, and let the colors of the shirts create contrast. At the bottom of the second box were a few shirts Elizabeth didn't remember seeing before. She held up one in a soft minty green. It was hard to imagine Daddy in a shirt that color, but it was slim enough that he had to have worn it when he was a young man. There was some fine stitching around the pocket, and pearlized buttons. She wished she could have seen him in it. Beneath that was a slim-fitting suit coat made of fine gray wool along with the matching pants. Elizabeth held the coat up and shook it out. It was handmade, with neat, even stitches. By Grandma? Elizabeth guessed so, but it was hard to say. It appeared, again based on the sizing, to be from the same era as the green shirt. She hated to cut this up. It was too precious. She folded the suit back up, but as she set it down, she felt something in the inside pocket. She lifted the jacket back up again, reached into the interior pocket of the satin lining, and pulled out a faded yellow envelope.

Elizabeth turned the envelope over. Daddy's name—Henry—was written on the front in blue ink, but that was all. No address, no stamp, no return address.

Elizabeth slipped her finger under the flap and opened the envelope. The note inside was written on thin, plain white paper in scrawling blue cursive letters. She read the short note quickly, and then over again, more slowly. But it didn't become any clearer after the second reading.

Elizabeth didn't know for sure what the short note meant, but if it meant what she thought it might mean…

Well, if she understood correctly, this pretty much changed everything.

CHAPTER THREE

Mary was the first one to come downstairs Saturday morning, Tink, their little dachshund, trailing down behind her. The house was quiet, and there was a chill in the air. She knotted the tie on her robe and turned the coffeepot on, and then she wandered over to the back door and opened it. Tink ran out and sniffed the barren rosebushes, the coiled hose, and the picnic table, wet with dew.

While Tink sniffed around, Mary let her gaze turn toward the patch of overgrown weeds that had once been her mother's garden. Things had been so crazy last year, with her and Martha moving home and reopening Secondhand Blessings, that she had never gotten around to getting the garden in shape. But Mary had big dreams for the garden this year. She would clear out the weeds, first of all. Then she would put in beans, tomatoes, squash, and greens of all kinds. Maybe some eggplants and carrots too, and even potatoes. And there would be a section for flowers, of course. Mary envisioned having fresh-cut flowers in vases all throughout the summer—peonies and bluebells in the spring, asters, daylilies, goldenrod, black-eyed Susans, and lupines in the summer; mums through the fall. Mary wasn't an expert gardener like Mama had been, but she would do her best to get Mama's garden back into shape this summer.

"Come on, Tink," Mary called, and the dog stopped chewing on a weed by the fence post and hurried back on her stubby little legs. Mary had gotten the rescue dog after Brian had left. Her friends had joked that she'd traded one dog for another, but Mary tried not to think unkindly about her ex, no matter how much he deserved it. Tink climbed the steps and went inside for her breakfast. Mary patted the dog on the head and tossed some dry food in her bowl, and Tink wolfed it down in a few bites.

Mary pulled a mug down and poured herself a cup of coffee, and then she settled at the table with an old church cookbook and flipped through it, trying to decide on a recipe for a birthday cake for Martha. Her birthday was Thursday, and Mary wanted to surprise her with a lavish cake to make her feel special. She settled on a German chocolate cake and made a shopping list, and then she turned to the seed catalog that had arrived in the mail the day before. Sipping her coffee, she flipped to the pages of tomatoes. She'd had no idea there were so many varieties. It wasn't just a choice between heirloom and beefsteak and cherry tomatoes. Her mouth watered as she read the names of the varieties—Lavender Lake and Black Beauty and Brandywine, Chocolate Amazon and Pink Opal and Sweet Scarlet. And the greens—there were dozens of varieties of butterheads and romaines and raddichio. There were more than ten kinds of green beans and more varieties of radishes than she'd known existed. Mary didn't even like radishes, but she was excited by the images of the glistening red vegetables.

"Find anything you like?"

Mary looked up and saw Martha coming into the kitchen.

"Just one or two things," Mary said with a smile.

"I'm glad you're going to get the garden back in order," Martha said as she poured coffee into a mug. "It'll be nice to see that producing again."

Martha took a long sip then set the coffee down on the counter and pulled a large mixing bowl from the shelf. Mary flipped the page, gazing at the dozens of varieties of peppers. They were so beautiful. Her garden could look like a rainbow.

Martha took out the bins for flour and sugar.

"What are you making?"

"I'm just going to keep it simple this morning, since I didn't get my baking done last night," Martha said. Martha baked treats to sell in the shop, and they were always a hit. "Iced chocolate chip bread, and maybe some pumpkin bread if there's any of that canned pumpkin left."

It didn't sound simple to Mary at all, but she nodded. "That sounds delicious."

Mary got up and poured herself a second cup of coffee while Martha started to sift the flour in Mama's old metal hand sifter. Mary flipped past the pages of fruits and vegetables and into the section that advertised stakes and fertilizers, and her mind began to wander, thinking back to what had happened the night before. How had someone stolen Adam's identity? It was so ridiculous it was almost funny, really, except that it was very serious. Who'd ever heard of an Amish person having their identity stolen? And yet it had happened. Mary thought about how the police had assumed someone had been using Adam's missing driver's license. If the thief had his picture professionally placed into the spot where Adam's should have gone, he could have used that instead of his own actual identification when he'd gotten stopped by the cops for public intoxication, and even for the arrest for driving under the influence. The restraining order was harder to explain, though. How thoroughly had this other man taken on Adam's life for a restraining order to have been taken out against him in Adam's name? It was chilling. Well, Mary agreed with the cops that the first step was finding out where Adam had lost the license.

Mary looked up as Elizabeth came down the stairs. "Good morning," she called. Both of her sisters said good morning as Elizabeth poured herself coffee. She was already dressed in slacks and a sweater, and her hair was pulled back into a low ponytail.

"How did you sleep?" Martha asked, leveling off the flour precisely in the measuring cup. Mary didn't have the patience to bake like Martha did. What was the point of sifting, anyway? And an extra pinch of sugar or butter never hurt anyone.

"Not well, unfortunately." Elizabeth added milk and sugar and stirred. "I couldn't stop thinking."

"It's just so terrible," Martha said. "Who would do such a thing? I hope the police find out who stole Adam's identity right away."

Elizabeth took a long, deep drink of her coffee. She looked like she was going to say something, and then she changed her mind.

"What is it?" Mary asked.

Again, Elizabeth started to say something then sighed. "I had an idea."

Both Mary and Martha looked at her and waited. Whatever she was about to say, it wasn't what had initially popped into her head, Mary was sure of it. What was going on with her?

"Do you guys remember last year when hackers got into the state's computers?" Elizabeth asked.

Martha narrowed her eyes. "Vaguely."

Mary tried to think back, but nothing came to mind. "Not really."

"It was last summer, probably. I heard about it on the news at first. Hackers got into the state's computers and got access to all kinds of records. I got a letter in the mail saying that my data might have been compromised. Did either of you get a similar letter?"

Mary was sure she would have remembered if she had. "I remember when something like that happened at Target and Home Depot, but I don't remember anyone breaking into the state's computers."

"It sounds like it wasn't too long after Mary and I moved back home," Martha said. "We might not have been in the system long enough to have much data to steal."

Mary supposed that was possible.

"You might be right." Elizabeth sat down at the table next to Mary. "Well, I got a letter, so I remember it. It was all over the news. Hackers—they think maybe from Russia or China, but I don't know if they ever found out for sure—got into the state's computers and accessed all kinds of personal data. They never came out and said it, but I assumed that meant birthdays, social security numbers, that kind of thing."

"And you think Adam's information might have been among the information taken?" Mary asked.

"But even if it was, how could someone have stolen a driver's license that way?" Martha asked.

"My thought is that whoever broke into the state computers got ahold of Adam's file, which would have had his birthdate, social security number, and address," Elizabeth said. "He then could have used that to apply for another driver's license in Adam's name, using his information."

"Ohhh…kay. I see now." Martha pursed her lips as she thought it through. "But what about the license Adam lost?"

"It doesn't really matter what happened to it, if the hacking idea is right," Elizabeth said. "I guess we assume no one found it or it got thrown away or whatever. Because this idea assumes that the license was generated with information taken from the state's computers."

"So you're saying that the missing license might not be how someone stole his identity after all," Martha said.

"Right. It's one possibility, but I wondered if it might not be the only possibility."

"It's worth looking into." Mary hoped she sounded more confident than she felt. It seemed tenuous to her.

But Elizabeth smiled and said, "I'm going to do some research today to see what I can find out about that data breach."

"That sounds like a good plan," Mary said, again trying to project more confidence than she felt. "And I was thinking I might head over to the vet clinic where Adam worked and see if they have any ideas."

She could predict what Martha was going to say before she said it.

"The police were going to do that." Martha dumped a carefully leveled scoop of sugar into a bowl. "Is it really necessary?"

Mary knew her sister better than anyone, and she knew that what sometimes came across as callousness was simply Martha's practical, efficient nature. It was how she was able to get so much done in a day and keep the farm and the store running. Mary was grateful for it, most of the time. But for now, she bit back her frustration and did her best to answer sweetly.

"I thought I might have a different take on it than the police do," she said. "I might be able to find out something they missed." She took another sip of her coffee and tried to find the right words. "And besides, I can't just sit here and do nothing. I want to help. And that seems like the most likely option, so I thought I'd start there."

Martha dumped a stick of softened butter into the mixing bowl. "Okay."

Martha still didn't see the point, Mary knew, but she was acknowledging that it was important to Mary. That might be as close as it would come to agreement for Martha.

"I spent a good part of the night trying to think of how we could help the Amish family that was hit by the car," Martha said.

There it was. It wasn't that Martha didn't care. She was just focused on practical ways to help.

"Have you heard any update on their condition?" Elizabeth asked.

"Not this morning," Martha continued. "But I was thinking that if they spent any time in the hospital without insurance, their medical bills are going to be ridiculous."

"You're right about that," Elizabeth said. "It's crazy how much it all costs these days."

"So I was trying to figure out how to help." Martha turned the mixer on, and the low motor hummed in the background.

"Were you thinking about another fundraiser?" Mary asked. They had all helped out with a fundraiser last fall to raise money for Rachel's grandnephew, who had been diagnosed with leukemia.

"Maybe," Martha said. "For starters, I was thinking we could take up a collection at our church. I'm sure people in our community would be happy to help out."

Mary agreed, as did Elizabeth. The people at their Mennonite church were so generous, and they would certainly want to help this family.

"And then I was thinking I would talk to Rachel about what their community is doing and how we can help."

"That makes a lot of sense," Mary said. Best to see what the Amish were already doing and how they could help with that before going too far down this road.

"I was also wondering if it might make sense to host a bake sale," Martha said. "That's something pretty simple we could do, and I bet we could make some money that way."

"If you're baking, I'm certain we could," Elizabeth said. Mary agreed. Martha's treats were gathering quite a following among their customers at the shop. Some people had even started coming into the shop just for the baked goods Martha sold there.

"I'll talk to Rachel," Martha said.

Mary drained the last bit of coffee in her cup and stood. "Good. It sounds like we all have a plan." Mary's own plan started with a shower and then heading over to the shop to get things ready for the day.

"Let's get to it." Elizabeth finished her own coffee and pushed herself up. "This mystery isn't going to solve itself."

Martha had just finished setting the freshly baked chocolate chip bread in the display case at Secondhand Blessings when Rachel Fischer walked through the door.

"Good morning," Martha said.

"*Guten morgen.*" The strings on Rachel's kapp bounced as she walked toward the back of the shop. She had a large basket draped over one arm.

"How are you this morning?" Mary called from the counter, where she was setting up the cash register. Elizabeth was finishing up feeding the goats and chickens and would be over shortly. "How is Adam?"

"Adam is all right," Rachel said. "And we are doing well. Silas is worried, but I told him we do not have to worry, because *Gott* is in control, and the Classen sisters are going to help us."

Martha laughed. "I think the first part of that is probably most important."

"Yes, of course," Rachel said. "But I do not discount the second part."

"I'm going to head over to the vet clinic later this morning," Mary said. "To see if anyone there can tell me anything about where Adam lost his license."

"Oh good. I am so glad to hear that," Rachel said. "I believe the police were going to do the same, but... Well, I think you will find out things they cannot."

Martha didn't necessarily agree, but she wasn't surprised to hear Rachel say it. The Amish were often reticent to allow the police to get involved in their affairs. And the Classen sisters had helped the Amish in their community before, even when the police couldn't find answers.

"And I was hoping we could find a way to help the Mast family," Martha said.

"Oh, that is very good," Rachel said. "I know they would appreciate that. In fact, that is why I am here. I was hoping to ask for a favor."

"Of course." Martha was glad to help. "Anything."

"I wondered if one of you could give me a ride. I am going to the home of the Mast family to bring food, but Silas needs one buggy, and the axel is broken on the other. Allie Hinchcliffe is not available this morning." Allie Hinchliffe was a local "Yoder Toter"—an Englisch lady who gave rides to the Amish when they were going farther than their horses could reasonably go, or when they needed to get there faster than a horse and buggy would allow.

"I'd be happy to give you a ride." Martha looked around and saw that Mary had finished setting up the register.

Saturday was usually a busy day at the shop, but it was quiet now.

"I've got it under control," Mary said. "And Elizabeth will be over shortly. You go ahead."

"Just let me grab my purse," Martha said, and a minute later Rachel was buckling herself into the passenger seat of Martha's car. She gave Martha directions to the Mast farm. The basket was resting in the back seat, filling the car with the aroma of baked beans and ham.

"It's nice of you to bring the Masts a meal," Martha said as she pulled out onto the road.

"It is the least I can do. They will have a difficult time, I am afraid. They hope Abner will be released from the hospital today, but Miriam and Abel will stay."

"Is Abner..." Martha wasn't sure who was who.

"The father. He was the one driving the buggy. Miriam and little Abel were on the side the car hit. I am told Abel will be all right, but they are not so sure about Miriam."

"Oh goodness. I'm so sorry. I'll be praying for their family."

"I am sure they will appreciate it."

Martha let a moment pass, with only the hum of the engine filling the car, and then she said, "I was trying to think of a way to help them, and I thought of a bake sale. If we hosted a big bake sale at the shop and donated the profits to the Mast family, do you think that's something the Amish community would support?"

"A bake sale?" Rachel repeated the words. "That is not traditional for us, but I do not see why it could not work." She was quiet for another moment and then said, "I will ask

BY ANY OTHER NAME | 31

a few people and see what they say. But I think it is a nice idea."

"Oh good. I'm glad to hear that." Martha decided that she would do a bake sale regardless. If the Amish community didn't want to participate, that was fine. In any case, she would bake some extra goodies to sell at the shop and donate the profits to the Mast family. "It's such an awful thing to happen."

"It is scary," Rachel said. "These accidents are happening more and more, and this was particularly bad because the driver left."

"And was using Adam's identity," Martha added.

"Yes," Rachel said. "That is a puzzle. I still do not understand how that is possible. Could someone really have taken Adam's identification and stolen his name? How can that be?"

"I suppose it's possible, but it is a terrible thing to do," Martha said.

"I am glad to hear that Mary is going to the veterinarian's office," Rachel said. "It will be a relief to Adam to know who has done this thing in his name."

"Yes, I'm sure it will." Martha was still not sure they would turn up anything that the police wouldn't, but hearing Rachel's faith in them was encouraging. "I hope you're not putting too much trust in us, though. The police will investigate thoroughly, I'm sure."

"I am sure that you are right," Rachel said. "But I have more trust in my friends than in the law. You will help, won't you?"

Martha didn't know what to say. How could they turn up anything the police wouldn't? But of course, there was only one thing to say. "Of course. All of us want to help however we can."

"Oh good." Rachel nodded. "Thank you. I cannot say how much we appreciate it."

Martha thought about what they knew about the identity theft. The thief had used Adam's license—or a license taken out in his name—as proof of identity. He had registered a car in Adam's name. He'd had a string of brushes with the law, during all of which he'd used Adam's identity as his own. He had been in the Bird-in-Hand area yesterday. And the police officers had asked Adam whether he'd ever been to State College. Why had they asked that? The logical conclusion was that at least one of his earlier brushes with the law had occurred there. If she was going to help Rachel figure out who this man pretending to be Adam really was, she needed to find out more about that. Weren't arrest records public record? Martha wasn't sure.

But there was something else that was bothering her.

"Rachel?"

Rachel looked her way, and Martha noticed that she had dark circles under her eyes. She must not have slept well the night before either.

"As I said, Mary is going to go to the vet clinic to ask if anyone there remembers Adam or has any idea what might have happened to his driver's license. But last night, when we were discussing the places Adam might have lost his license, there was a kind of a strange moment. An awkward pause, I guess."

She saw that Rachel was nodding, just slightly, but she wasn't saying anything.

"I got the impression that there was something no one was saying. Was there somewhere else Adam went when he was driving? Someplace other than the veterinarian clinic and the racetrack?"

Rachel didn't answer for a moment. This wasn't unusual—the Amish tended to think before they spoke, which led to pauses in conversation that often felt awkward to the Englisch—but the length of time this pause went on told Martha what she needed to know. Finally, Rachel spoke.

"It is not for me to say. You will need to ask Adam about that."

Martha felt frustration rise up. If Rachel wanted help figuring out what was going on, she couldn't keep information back from them. But Martha took a deep breath and tried to understand. Rachel was honoring Adam's privacy, she knew, and it was admirable, no matter how frustrating Martha found it in the moment. Besides, the vagueness of her answer still told Martha something. She understood that the answer to her question was yes. There was definitely more to this story, but for some reason Rachel didn't feel it was her place to talk about it. This just made Martha more curious.

Well, if Rachel wanted their help investigating this mystery, they were certainly going to have to ask Adam about that. If there was another place he frequented, some place where he might have lost his license, they would need to check it out. She would need to talk to Adam and get the real story.

"Adam's running-around years were challenging," Rachel said.

"How so?" Martha imagined the threat of Adam's leaving his church to join the Englisch would have been difficult for his parents, but she didn't know the specifics. Martha had only moved home to Bird-in-Hand less than eighteen months ago, and Adam had been married and a member of the church by then.

"It is a difficult time for many families," Rachel said. "Children are allowed the chance to experience the world outside of our community, and some find the freedom difficult to adjust to after a lifetime of rules."

"It's an interesting idea," Martha said. "To let the kids get a taste of Englisch life so they know what the world is like before they decide whether to join the church." Privately, Martha had wondered if Englisch churches and families should adopt the tradition. She and Chuck had maintained high standards of behavior for their children all through their teen years, and that had led to many fights and more than a little rebellion. And, well, she wasn't totally sure it had all been worth it, if she was honest. Craig had gotten Molly pregnant in college and didn't go to church anymore, and Kyle had distanced himself from the church he'd grown up in as well. She wasn't sure where Trish stood spiritually. Martha loved her children with her whole heart, and she had honestly believed she had been doing the right thing by them in maintaining strict rules, but a small part of her couldn't help but wonder if anything would have been different if she and Chuck had allowed the kids to explore their questions and doubts when they were younger.

"Rumspringa is a good idea," Rachel said. "And despite what you see on those Englisch television shows, most kids do not go crazy. They might test the boundaries now and again, and many get a cell phone or dress Englisch sometimes, but many do not. Most kids stay pretty well within the world they know."

"But Adam didn't." The fact that he'd gotten a driver's license was proof of that.

"Adam did not."

"That must have been very hard." Martha knew that an Amish person who left before joining the church would not be shunned, but the Amish life was so insular that anyone who was not part of the church could never really be part of the community. It would be a difficult thing for a mother to lose that connection with her oldest child.

Rachel nodded. "He needed to explore. Adam is so smart. He is always reading and learning new things. He thought he might want to go to college. Plus, he has always loved animals. He thought being a veterinarian would allow him to help animals and people too."

"He must have been very determined," Martha said.

"He has always been that," Rachel said. "And also very determined to give his mother a heart condition."

"Does this have anything to do with his fascination with race cars?"

"That was part of it," Rachel said. "He has always been interested in cars, from the time he was little. I do not understand it, personally."

"My boys were also into cars."

"He would spend whole afternoons at the racetrack, watching cars go around and around in a circle. What is the point of that?"

"I don't understand it myself," Martha admitted.

"And then he started driving as if he were a race car driver."

"How did he manage to get a car?"

"He saved up his money for many years. It was not a nice car, but to a boy who was used to traveling at the speed of horses, it was heaven." Rachel adjusted the air vent in front of her. "He liked to drive fast, and he got more than one speeding ticket. I am so thankful he did not hit anyone, like the man who was using his identification did."

"That was very lucky," Martha said.

"The Lord protected him," Rachel corrected.

"Of course." Martha felt silly. Of course she was right.

"He was also caught shoplifting once," Rachel said. "It was so silly. He wanted some headphones, and he did not have enough money, so he decided to simply take them. He was not as smooth as he thought he was, and the store owner saw it and stopped him. We were grateful that he did not feel the need to call the police, but he did call us and tell us."

"That must have been difficult."

"I have never seen Silas so angry," Rachel said. "The other things, those were hard, but stealing?" She shook her head. "We do not believe that is ever okay. Adam had extra chores for many months after that. I have never seen the barn so clean as it was during that time." And then she added, "It is just up here."

It took Martha a moment to realize that Rachel was indicating that the Mast house was just up ahead. Rachel pointed to a small wooden house set back from the road and surrounded by fields. Martha flipped on her blinker and turned in to the driveway. She thought about what Rachel had told her. It seemed that Adam wasn't the saint she'd assumed he was. But then again, just because he had gone through a rough patch before he'd joined the church didn't mean he would do anything like that now.

Martha shook her head. Adam was the victim here. But still, a tiny part of her couldn't unhear what Rachel had said.

Rachel hoisted the basket and climbed out of the car. Martha smelled something musty in the air and heard several dogs barking somewhere on the property. Who was feeding the family's animals, she wondered.

Rachel walked to the front door of the house and found the key that was hidden under the mat. She unlocked the door, opened it, and went inside. Martha followed just a step behind.

"Oh dear," Rachel said as she stepped into the living room. Clothes were in piles on the couch. It was as if someone had been doing laundry and given up halfway through. Dirty dishes were piled in the sink in the kitchen, just beyond, and the floor could use a good sweeping. The house was messy, which wasn't really so strange, considering the young couple had a small child. But it was a stark difference from the neat, efficient appearance of most Amish homes Martha had been inside. Rachel walked into the kitchen and set the basket down on a counter. "Poor Miriam. She must be so overwhelmed."

"I remember what it's like to have young children," Martha said. Those had been hard years, with Chuck working overtime to help make ends meet, leaving Martha to raise three kids mostly on her own. It had been exhausting, and it had been a constant battle to keep the house neat and the children in clean clothes. "I'm pretty sure my house looked like this every day."

"It can feel overwhelming," Rachel agreed. "And Miriam does not have family in the area." She lifted a container packed with ham from the basket and opened the door of the propane-powered refrigerator. Aside from a few containers of leftovers, it was largely empty. Martha was suddenly very grateful Rachel had brought food over for this family. When they were released from the hospital, it would be nice to have something to get them through a meal or two. Judging by the state of the fridge, Martha should probably bring a meal over as well.

"All right," Rachel said. "New plan. Would you be willing to come back and get me in a few hours?"

"Of course," Martha said. "What are you planning to do?"

Rachel was already walking toward a door that was cracked open, revealing shelves of dried pastas and beans, as well as cleaning supplies. "I would hate to have them come home to a mess when they are released," Rachel said. "I will do some cleaning."

Martha was touched by her thoughtfulness. "That is such a nice idea."

"Can you come back around one?" Rachel was already pulling a broom from the closet. "That should give me time to get this place in better shape."

"I certainly can," Martha said. "Or would it be better if I stay and help too?"

"Oh no. You have a shop to run. And if you and your sisters can figure out who did this to Adam, that would be such a gift."

"Okay then," Martha said. "I'll come back in a few hours."

"Thank you." Rachel was already running the broom around the edge of the wooden floor. Martha knew she shouldn't be surprised. The Amish took care of one another. But it was still nice to see love in action.

Martha would be back to get Rachel in a few hours. And hopefully by then, she'd have some answers.

Elizabeth had spent the morning in the shop, there but not really present. Her mind was still running through possibilities for what had happened to Adam, in between trying to make sense of the note she'd read the night before. She knew she needed to talk to her sisters about it, but she didn't know when would be the right time. How could she just drop a bombshell like this into their day? Elizabeth didn't know, but trusted that the right moment would come.

She had just finished ringing up an Amish woman who'd come in looking for some new books to read when the door opened, and her Saturday morning garage sale crew came into the shop.

"Hello, Elizabeth," Della Bradford called. Nancy VanSlyke and Beverly Stout trailed in just behind her. All three had bags hanging from their arms.

"Where's Linda this morning?" Elizabeth asked. They were missing one quarter of their crew.

"She's got a bad cold," Nancy said. Her long brown hair, which was threaded with gray, was showing from under her knit cap. "It seems to be going around."

"Thank goodness it's starting to get a bit warmer," Beverly said. "This winter has just been brutal."

"You say that every year," Della said.

"And it's true every year. Winter is just awful," Beverly said. "Every year, about mid-February, I start to wonder why I don't just move to Florida."

"You would miss us," Nancy said. "Besides, you change your tune every year when garage sale season starts up again."

"'Garage sale season.'" Della smiled. "What most people refer to as 'spring.'"

"Did you find anything good today?" Elizabeth asked. The garage sales had largely tapered off over the winter, and the foursome was forced to resort to estate sales and online auctions for their bargain hunting. But Elizabeth had seen a few sales advertised for this weekend, and it looked like, in true form, these ladies had been there when they opened to get the best deals.

"Check this out." Della was the first to start unpacking her bags. "I found these tablecloths." She set a stack of lacy linens on the counter. "They look like they're in pretty good condition."

Elizabeth unfolded one and held it up. It was lacy, worked in tiny precise stitches. The yarn was good quality and very fine. "This is lovely."

"I thought so." Della pulled a large book out of the bag and set it next to the tablecloths. The spine was broken, and the pages were falling out. "And look at this. This is in bad shape, obviously, but look at these pages." She opened the cover, and Elizabeth saw that it was a book about architecture, with prints showing famous structures like the Duomo in Florence and St. Peter's in Rome. "I thought someone could take the pages and frame them, and they would look great on the wall of the right house."

"That would be lovely," Elizabeth agreed. It would take someone with vision to see it, or she could frame the pictures herself and sell them for more right here in the store. That might be the better option, she realized. She worked out a price with Della and then looked over the finds Nancy and Beverly had brought in, including a silver serving spoon, a hand-stitched quilt, and half a dozen records. They would be able to resell them all. She handed the women cash for their finds, and they walked away smiling.

After they left, Elizabeth set the items aside for inventory and pricing, and while she straightened the book section, the door opened, and Martha came in.

"How's it going?" Martha asked. A gust of cold wind swept in behind her.

"Just fine," Elizabeth said. "Della, Nancy, and Beverly were here, and we've had a few other customers, but there was a lull, so I decided to do some cleaning." She pushed up a stack of books that had fallen over. "How did it go with Rachel?"

"She decided to stay and clean for the Masts so they would come home from the hospital to a clean home." Martha sighed. "It's really beautiful how the Amish take care of each other, isn't it?"

"It is." Elizabeth loved that they looked out for one another. "Did you talk to her about the idea of a bake sale?"

"I did. She said she would ask around and let me know what they thought. But I think I want to do it anyway, even if it's just selling a few extra goodies here at the shop."

"I think that's lovely," Elizabeth said. She loved to see Martha really step up to help the Amish family.

"I'll go tackle that mountain of invoices that need to be paid," Martha said and headed toward the back. But she stopped and turned when the door opened, and the way she stopped made Elizabeth turn and look too.

Elizabeth's stomach flipped when she saw John Marks walk into the shop. John was wearing the blue uniform of the East Lampeter Township police, and he smiled when he saw her.

"Hi there," he said. Elizabeth loved the way the skin around his eyes crinkled when he smiled.

"Hello, John," Martha called, and he waved as he crossed the floor in long strides.

John gave Elizabeth another warm smile, and Elizabeth's stomach flipped again. It felt silly that she was reacting to him like a lovestruck teenager, but she couldn't help it.

"I did some digging," John said.

"Did you find anything?" Elizabeth had called him that morning to ask if he could help her figure out whether there was any chance the hack of the state computers was behind Adam's identity theft. Elizabeth tried not to rely on John for inside information too often, but she couldn't deny that having a senior member of the police force as a close friend sometimes had its advantages.

"Well, first of all, I'm supposed to tell you that you don't need to investigate this matter, because the police are going to be investigating thoroughly," John said.

"Did Chief Bender tell you to say that?" Martha asked. She had turned and had stepped closer to listen.

"Got it in one." John laughed. "And even though he's right, I know better than to assume that saying something like that is going to keep you three from trying to help your friends."

"You're exactly right," Elizabeth said. The Fischer family had been such a help to Elizabeth over the years as she had cared for her aging parents. After Daddy passed, Rachel had quietly sent her sons over to clear the Classen driveway whenever it snowed, and she had brought so many meals and given so much support when Mama was sick. Elizabeth would have tried to help them through this awful situation even if Rachel hadn't asked, but since she had, Elizabeth was even more determined to help figure out who had done this to her friends. "Rachel asked us to help, so obviously we're going to."

John laughed again and shook his head. "That's what I thought. But if my boss asks, you can tell him I did pass the message along."

"Absolutely," Martha said. "Message received. And promptly ignored."

Elizabeth wasn't sure what had made Martha change her mind about investigating, but she was glad to see it.

"I didn't hear that," John said.

"So what did you find out?" Elizabeth asked.

"I looked into that computer hack, like you asked me to," John said. "It was a good idea, but I'm afraid it seems unlikely that whoever is posing as Adam was able to do it based on information from the computer hack."

"How do you know?" Elizabeth asked.

"According to his records, Adam—or, I suppose, the person pretending to be Adam—was picked up for public intoxication a year and a half ago, in October. That's when he first showed Adam's identification as his own, at least as far as the police are concerned. But the computer hack that exposed the state's data didn't happen until November of that year. So whoever this Adam impersonator is, he couldn't have gotten the real Adam's information from the hack."

Elizabeth blew out a breath. "Well, I suppose that settles that."

"Not so fast. It *does* mean that the computer hacker probably isn't responsible for impersonating Adam. But that didn't seem very likely in any case, as the information security team at the capital is pretty sure hackers in Russia are responsible for the attack—"

"How can they tell that?" Martha cocked her head.

"I'm not going to pretend to understand it," John said with a smile. "Something about the channels they used to get into the system matching patterns of other hacks or something like that. But whoever is responsible is likely thousands of miles away, not getting stopped for having a few too many drinks in State College."

"So we're back to focusing on figuring out who took Adam's license and started using it as his own," Elizabeth said. It probably made more sense, anyway, she supposed.

"Yes and no," John said.

They both looked at him, waiting for him to go on.

"Officer Hooper did more research on 'Adam'"—he made air quotes at this— "and he discovered that several credit cards have been taken out in his name."

"Credit cards?" Martha asked.

"The Amish don't use credit cards," Elizabeth said.

"I know. And unless your friend Adam has developed a taste for expensive Englisch men's clothing and electronics, it seems unlikely that he's the one who opened these cards."

"I definitely don't think it was," Elizabeth said. "Neither of those sounds like Adam at all."

"That's what we thought too," John said. "The thing is, to open up a credit card, you need a social security number, which you wouldn't get from just looking at a driver's license."

"So whoever we're dealing with, he didn't just find Adam's license lying around somewhere," Martha said.

"He might have," John said. "But then he also managed to get ahold of Adam's social security number, and used that to open up credit cards in Adam's name."

"Did the person responsible at least pay the bills on those credit cards?" It was the least he could do.

"Oh, no." John shook his head. "It doesn't appear that he ever paid a penny on the things he bought with the cards taken out in Adam's name. They're all in collections at this point."

Martha shook her head.

Elizabeth doubted Martha had ever missed a due date on a payment in her life.

"So you're saying that the person impersonating Adam is ruining his credit score in addition to everything else," Martha said.

Elizabeth wanted to laugh. The Amish borrowed money only very rarely, generally only to buy a farm, but she suspected that most of the time evaluating credit scores was not part of the process, since the Amish didn't use credit cards to build credit history.

"On the plus side, the credit card companies take identity theft very seriously, and the real Adam very likely won't have to pay for any of the fraudulent charges made in his name," John said.

Elizabeth was glad to hear it. But she had already had another thought.

"If we know where the fake 'Adam' used those credit cards, we could go talk to the people at those stores and see if they remember him," Elizabeth said. "That could give us information about the guy we're looking for."

"That's right." John was nodding. "We could. But I feel obligated to remind you that the police are planning to investigate this line of inquiry."

"Noted." Martha's face showed that she planned to ignore his reminder.

"They can't say I didn't try," John said.

"If we were interested in finding out the names of the stores where these credit cards were used, where would we be able to find that information?" Elizabeth asked.

"I'm afraid I can't help you there," John said. "Our officers are still trying to get that actual information themselves."

Elizabeth turned her head and met Martha's eye. She had an idea.

CHAPTER FOUR

Mary pulled into the parking lot and scanned the names of the stores on the signs. There was a vacuum repair shop, a dry cleaner, a dollar store...ah. There. Eden Heights Veterinarian Clinic.

Mary parked in front of the store and made her way inside. There was a small waiting area with wooden floors and bright white walls. Shelves of pet shampoos and foods lined one wall, and a row of sturdy wooden chairs was lined up against the big plate-glass windows. The whole place had an earthy, musty smell tinged with the tang of disinfectant. A woman had a cat carrier on her lap, and a man sat against the far wall with a dog that had a cast on its leg. Mary made her way to the reception desk where a woman with short white hair sat.

"Welcome. What can I do for you?" The woman had thick bifocals and a wide smile. She reminded Mary of Mrs. Claus, though she was wearing a sweatshirt that said HAPPINESS IS BEING A GRANDMA rather than a red suit. The skin around her nose was pink, and she held a crumpled tissue in her hands.

"Hi there. My name is Mary Baxter, and I have a strange question."

"I'm Edna Foster, and I'm sure I've heard worse. Go for it." The woman's nose seemed to be stuffy, and her voice was scratchy. Mary kept a few steps back from her.

"I'm trying to find out about an Amish boy who worked here for a while a few years ago," Mary said.

"Adam?" The woman's face lit up.

"That's right."

"He's the only Amish kid I know who's ever worked here, so that wasn't hard to guess," she said. "How is he?"

Mary decided to gloss over his present trouble for the moment. "He's married now and has a little one on the way."

"He joined the Amish church, then?" Edna asked.

Mary nodded.

"That's wonderful. He was such a nice kid. So smart and driven."

"He is great," Mary said. "And he's doing really well."

"I'm so glad to hear it." Edna sneezed and wiped her nose with a tissue, which she then threw in the trash can under her desk.

"The only thing is, it seems that during the time he worked here, he lost his driver's license," Mary said. "I know it's not likely that you have it, since we're talking about something that happened more than two years ago, but I wanted to see if anyone here might have found it."

"Now that's a funny thing for an Amish man to lose." Edna laughed. "I guess I never asked how he got here. You're telling me he drove a car?"

"That's right." Mary noticed five framed school pictures—grandchildren, she guessed—and there were stacks of papers piled on Edna's desk that were in danger of toppling over. "He had to give it up after he joined the church, but when he worked here, he did drive."

"Well, I don't know about a lost license. Let me see." Edna looked around her desk, like she was searching for something. Was she looking for the license on her desk?

"Is there a Lost and Found around here anywhere?"

"Not really." Edna paused and then reared her head back and let out another sneeze. Mary took another step back. "Usually people just bring things to me when they find them. And I will admit my memory is not what it used to be, but I think I would remember if someone brought me an Amish man's driver's license."

Mary had known it was a long shot, but she still felt a pang of disappointment.

"I can ask around, though, to see if anyone here remembers seeing it." The hesitation in her voice made it clear how unlikely she thought it was. And that was fair, Mary knew.

"I'd appreciate that," Mary said. "And is there any way to ask employees who might have worked here at the time who don't now?"

"Of course," Edna said. "Now let me think. There was an intern from over at the college for a while. But that was... Well, that was just last year, because he gave Eden a stuffed kitty for her fifth birthday. Isn't she just precious?" She picked up one of the framed photos and held it out. It showed a girl with brown braids and freckles. She was missing one of her front teeth.

"She's beautiful," Mary said. She was a grandmother too. She knew what to say. "You must be so proud."

"Oh, I am. Of course, I'm proud of all my grandchildren."

"As you should be," Mary said. She had to get this back on track. "So, if the intern was here last year, he wouldn't have overlapped with Adam."

"No, I suppose he wouldn't have."

"Is there anyone else who might have found it?"

"Well, this is a small clinic. Family run, you know? It's just my son-in-law—he's the vet—and my daughter, who does the cleaning and handles things like billing. I've tried to convince her to let me take over that part of things to free up more of her time, but she insists she can handle it." She shrugged. "Women these days think they have to do everything, don't they? It wasn't like that in our day."

Mary wasn't sure how she felt about being lumped into the same age group as Edna, but she nodded anyway.

"So there isn't anyone else who might have found the license if Adam dropped it?" *Or taken it out of his wallet when he wasn't looking,* Mary added in her mind.

"Not that I can think of. But then, like I said, my memory isn't what it used to be."

Mary wondered if she should come back another time and speak to Edna's daughter or son-in-law.

"I mean, of course we have people in and out of here all day, so I guess it's possible that one of the patients found it— the owners, I mean, not the actual patients. Can you imagine a dog with a driver's license?" Edna laughed, and the laugh somehow turned into a sneeze. She blew her nose again and tossed the tissue in the trash.

"If one of the patients—owners had found the license, would they have turned it in?"

"You would hope so, wouldn't you? Or just left it there. But you never know with people these days."

Mary nodded again because she wasn't sure what else to do. She didn't know that people were any worse now than they'd ever been, but she didn't want to open that can of worms with Edna.

Edna's eyes widened, and she said, "You know, we probably do have a photocopy of the license in the personnel files," she said. "Those are all kept in the back office. Would that be what you need?"

"No, I'm afraid not," Mary said. "We're just trying to figure out what happened to the actual, physical license."

"I'm sorry." Edna blew her nose once, twice, and then looked back up at Mary. "I don't know. But I'll be sure to ask around. If anyone knows where it is, how can I get in touch with you?"

Mary gave her a business card for the shop, and Edna promised to be in contact if she heard anything. She sounded dubious, but Mary wasn't ready to give up yet. The answer was out there somewhere.

Martha stepped inside the Mast home a little while later, and she felt her jaw fall open. "Is this the same house?"

"It looks different, *ja*?" Rachel was rinsing out the sink using water from a bucket.

"I'll say." The laundry had vanished from the couch, and the floor had been swept and mopped. The dishes were put away, the counters cleared, and Rachel had wiped down every surface. It smelled clean and fresh. "You got a lot done in two hours."

"If I had had more time, I would have done more laundry for them, as there is plenty to do." Rachel dunked the rag in the bucket and wrung it out over the sink. "But it is not as simple as throwing a load into the washing machine for us, so that will have to wait for another time."

"This is going to mean so much for them when they get out of the hospital."

"There is good news on that front." Rachel set the rag on the edge of the sink and hoisted the bucket. "I have heard that Abner will indeed be released from the hospital today."

"That's great." Wait. Martha looked around, and sure enough, there was no telephone in sight. "How did you hear that?"

"You did not know that we are all able to communicate with one another with our minds?"

Martha laughed.

"Anna Mast stopped by with a casserole while you were gone. Her husband is Abner Mast's brother, so he had been to see them at the hospital."

"Oh." Martha laughed again. "Got it."

Rachel put away the cleaning supplies, and a few minutes later they were in Martha's car, heading back toward home, and Martha was updating Rachel on what John had told them.

"Apparently, there have been credit cards taken out in Adam's name." Martha slowed as they came over the rise just before Ronks Road. You never knew when there was going to be a buggy on the other side. "So we're hoping to try to figure out where the man impersonating Adam used those cards to see if the people at those stores can tell us anything about him."

"That is good," Rachel said. "I mean, it is not good that someone ran up debt in Adam's name. But it is a good idea for how to find him."

Martha heard something strange in her friend's voice. She turned her head and saw that Rachel was pressing her lips together.

"Do you have any of the bills?"

There was a pause, and then Rachel said, "Oh dear."

"What?"

"I think I have just understood something," Rachel said quietly.

"What do you mean?"

"We have gotten some mail from a credit card company. But I thought it was junk mail. One of those tricks to make you open the envelope."

Martha could see where this was going now. "Did the mail say things like 'Final Notice'?"

Rachel nodded. "I did not think it was for real. None of us use credit cards, so how could it be real?"

"I can definitely understand how you would think that," Martha said. It seemed to make Rachel feel a little bit better.

"That also explains the messages," Rachel said.

"What messages?"

Rachel sighed. "Now that I know what really happened, I feel so silly for not figuring it out before this. But I did not have any idea."

"What do you mean?"

"There were some messages on our answering machine."

Martha knew that there was an answering machine in the phone shanty at the end of the Fischers' driveway. They only checked it every few days, so if you left a message there, someone would hear it eventually.

"What did the messages say?"

"They were very aggressive, saying we had to pay up or bad things would happen."

"Oh dear. It sounds like the Amish Mafia or something."

"The Amish Mafia is not real. That was just a television show," Rachel said, shaking her head. "We assumed the messages were just someone trying to get money from us."

"I suppose in a sense you were right," Martha said. "But they were probably from the collections agency."

"The what?"

"The people that the credit card company hires to harass you until you pay what you owe."

"That sounds like a terrible job."

"I suppose it beats the Amish Mafia."

Rachel laughed, and Martha watched her for a moment. Part of her didn't understand how they could have gotten all those threatening messages and seen the bills come to the house and not picked up on the fact that something was wrong. If they'd realized the bills were authentic, they might have known about the identity theft sooner, and the Mast family might not be in the hospital right now. But Martha knew that her friends did not have any experience with credit cards and were distrustful of the outside world in general, and maybe with good reason. There were plenty of people out there looking to make money from the Amish, believing they were an easy target. There had been plenty of scams exposed over the years. But still.

"Do you by any chance still have any of the mail from the credit card companies?" Martha asked.

"I will have to check."

When they got to the Fischer farm a few minutes later, Silas was walking across the yard, trailed by Luke and Ephraim, no doubt coming in from the fields for lunch. The younger kids were still at school, so Phoebe would have prepared the meal in Rachel's absence.

"Come in. I will go see if we have any of the mail from the credit card companies here."

The house smelled like freshly baked bread and some kind of meat, and Martha's stomach growled.

"Hi, Martha." Phoebe's sweet face radiated happiness at seeing her friend. "Will you join us for lunch?"

"I would love to. It smells delicious. But I'm afraid I need to get back to the shop."

"Are you sure? I made turkey and cheese sandwiches, and they are delicious," Phoebe said. Martha laughed. Phoebe had Down syndrome, and Martha loved to see her proud of her work.

"I am sorry to have to say no," Martha said. "Though, believe me, I would love to stay."

The back door opened, and Silas and the older boys came tromping in. They had left their boots by the door, but somehow they made as much noise as if they hadn't as they made a beeline for the table.

"I had better go get the food on the table," Phoebe said, and smiled before she turned toward the kitchen. Silas, Luke, and Ephraim said hello before reaching for their sandwiches, each pausing for a private prayer of thanks. Then they dug in. Teenage boys really were all the same, Martha thought. Her sons Craig and Kyle had both been bottomless pits when they were teenagers. She'd load up at the grocery store each week, sure she'd bought way too much, and then watch as it all vanished in the first few days. Still, even though she spent far less on groceries now, she missed those days.

"Here is what I found." Rachel appeared next to her, holding a few unopened envelopes with the credit card company's logo in the corner. The first one had FINAL NOTICE written in red on the front.

"Thank you," Martha said. "I'll take a look and see if we can find any clues here."

"Are you sure you will not stay for lunch?" Rachel asked.

"I wish I could. But I really do need to get back."

Phoebe was just settling down at the table, and had set a plate at Rachel's place.

"All right. But thank you for your help this morning," Rachel said.

"I'm so glad you asked. We're always happy to help." Martha took the envelopes, said goodbye, and headed out to the car. She backed out of the driveway and started the short drive toward home, but instead of turning right, which would bring her to her own driveway, she made a last-minute decision to turn left, and then she turned again at the corner and drove the short distance to the small farmhouse where Adam and

Leah lived, at the southern edge of the Fischer family's property. Martha knew that the youngest son was the one who inherited the family farm in Amish communities—which meant that nine-year-old twins Thomas and Matthew would have to figure out how to divide it up—but Martha loved how Amish parents usually helped older sons get on their feet. Adam and Leah had lived in the *dawdy haus* behind the main house for nearly a year while they were building this one, and she knew Adam was saving for his own land from what he made working the Classen farmland.

She pulled up in front of the white two-story house and walked to the front door. Before she even knocked, the door opened, and Leah gestured for her to step inside.

"Hallo, Martha. Please, come in." Wisps of curly hair were coming loose from her bun and escaping her kapp. "How are you?"

"I'm doing fine. How are you?"

The living room was a good size but sparsely furnished. Aside from a worn couch—probably a hand-me-down, Martha assumed—and a table lamp with a propane tank at the base, there were only a few mismatched wooden chairs. It reminded Martha of her own first married apartment. They'd fill this place up soon enough.

"I am all right." Leah blew out a breath. "I am ready for this baby to come."

"It's getting close, isn't it?"

"Just two more months."

"It will be here before you know it." And though she knew it was true, she also knew how endless those last few weeks of pregnancy felt, and how uncomfortable they were. "Enjoy the peace while you can."

"That is what people keep telling me. But how can I enjoy these weeks when I feel so miserable?"

"I know. I always felt the same way." But no matter how uncomfortable the last few weeks of pregnancy were, they had nothing on the misery of sleep deprivation with a newborn. But best not to mention that now. Leah would find out soon enough.

"Is Adam here?" Martha asked, looking around. "I was hoping to talk to him." She knew there was a good chance he was over at their place, working in the fields, but thought she should try here first.

"He is out by the barn." Leah gestured toward the wooden structure beyond the house. "One of the ewes is about to give birth, and you know how Adam loves animals. He has been paying special attention to her, monitoring her carefully." Leah smiled. "I think he is almost more excited about the birth of the lamb than the birth of his child."

Martha could see that Leah was joking but suspected this was a bit of a sore spot for her.

"He will be a good father," she said. "Many men are afraid they won't know what to do with a baby. But I know he will fall in love with that baby when it comes. And I'll pray that happens sooner rather than later."

"Thank you. I am sure you are right." Leah let out a breath and blew a curl from her face. "In any case, you can find him out in the barn."

"Thank you." Martha gave her an encouraging smile, and then she headed out to the barn. The sun had burned off the morning chill, and the air held a slight hint of warmth as she crossed the yard and stepped inside the open door of the barn.

"Hello?" she called. "Adam?"

This barn wasn't nearly as large as the main barn on the Fischer property but was large enough to hold a few horses and smaller animals. The sweet scent of hay greeted her as she stepped through the door. It was cold inside, maybe only a few degrees warmer than the air outside.

"I am over here," Adam called back. Martha followed the sound and found him in a stall with a very pregnant ewe. "Hallo, Martha."

"Hi, Adam. I'm sorry to disturb your work."

"It is all right. I am just making sure Rosie is comfortable," he said, stroking her gently. "She will have her lamb any day now." He paused. "What is going on?"

"My sisters and I have been doing some investigating into the man who is using your identification as his own, and I was wondering if I could ask you a question."

"Of course."

"Last night, you said the vet clinic and the racetrack were the only places you went regularly when you had your driver's license." When Mary had come back from the vet clinic earlier, she'd told them that the people there didn't know what had happened to his license, and though they still needed to visit the racetrack, Martha had a gut feeling that the answer lay elsewhere. And there was a secret here, she was sure about that. "But there was a moment when my sisters and I felt sure there was something no one was saying. I asked your mother about it this morning, and she told me I would need to ask you."

Adam hadn't stopped stroking the sheep. He was listening, but he didn't look up or change his behavior in any way.

"Is there another place we should be checking out?" Martha asked gently.

Martha was used to uncomfortable pauses when speaking to the Amish, but this one stretched on long enough that she was sure there was something Adam didn't want to say. Her instinct was to rush in and fill the silence, but she bit her tongue, forcing herself to let him be the one to speak.

"I did go to a coffee shop near the clinic sometimes," he finally said.

"Great. Can you tell me the name of the coffee shop?"

Another pause. Martha heard the sheep in the next pen moving around and the pig snuffling.

"It was called Joanna's," he said.

"Joanna's. That can't be too hard to find."

He nodded but didn't go on. There was more to this story, Martha was sure of it, or else why hadn't he just told her about Joanna's before?

"Is there anyone in particular we should talk to at Joanna's?" she asked. "Anyone who might remember you?"

He continued to stroke Rosie. An orange-and-white barn kitten jumped up on the gate of the pen and looked at Martha.

"I do not know if she still works there," he finally said. "It has been a while. But if she does, you could talk to Felicity."

"Felicity," Martha repeated. Not Amish, then. "And she worked at the coffee shop?" Martha reached out and petted the kitten, which stretched its back and leaned in toward her.

"Yes," he said.

Once again, her instinct was to press him, ask for more information, but she made herself wait. He would tell her when he was ready. Pushing him would only make him nervous. Based on what Rachel had told her about how challenging Adam's running around years had been, she suspected there was a story here. Finally, he stopped stroking Rosie and looked up. He seemed to have made some kind of decision.

"As you already know, I was flirting with the idea of leaving the church to become Englisch while I was on rumspringa."

She nodded again, afraid to speak and cause Adam to stop.

"I was also flirting with an Englisch girl," he said.

"Felicity?"

"Yes." He used one hand to push his hat back on his head. "I did not intend to. I simply stopped in for coffee one day before my shift because I had been up all night with an injured horse. But I met Felicity, and she was... Well, she was pretty, and she asked me questions about being Amish, and she seemed genuinely interested in the answers. I was dressing Englisch then, and she asked about that, and, well, we just kind of hit it off."

Martha tried to picture what Adam might have looked like during this phase, though of course there were no photographs to use for reference. He had big, warm brown eyes, and his hair was a deep chestnut color. It was hard to tell beneath the beard, but it looked like he had a strong jawline. He wouldn't have had the beard at that point, and Martha realized that he was probably quite handsome. And he was strong from so many farm chores. If he'd been dressing Englisch, it wouldn't have been hard for Felicity to take notice of him.

"So you went back to the coffee shop after that?" Martha asked.

"Yes. Many times." He seemed a bit ashamed of the answer, though Martha wasn't sure why. "And we started texting. I had a cell phone then too, and she would send me little notes throughout the day."

"That must have felt good," Martha said. The little cat was rubbing its cheek against the wooden post, and she stroked its head gently. Kittens, even of the wild barn cat variety, had to be among the cutest creatures God ever made.

"It was fun," Adam admitted. "The only problem was Leah."

"How so?" The kitten started purring and moved closer to Martha, nudging her hand with its head.

"We had been courting for some time. I knew she was hoping I would join the church and we would marry. I had told her that was what I was hoping for before I started this job at the vet clinic. And I knew it must have been torture for her to see me coming so close to leaving my faith and pursuing worldly goals."

Martha tried not to judge. The Amish culture was different from her own, and that was okay. But she still struggled to see how Adam pursuing more education to do greater good in the world was a bad thing.

"So she was waiting around at home while I was spending time with Felicity," Adam said. "I would go to the coffee shop every time I was in Lancaster, and sometimes I would go there when I did not have to work. We even went out a few times, to movies, you know, and just hanging out. I even took her to watch a car race one time. I knew Leah would never agree to come with me there, but Felicity enjoyed it."

"Did Leah know?" Judging by the silent messages that had been passed around last night, Martha felt sure Leah must have learned about Felicity at some point, but Martha didn't know if Leah had known at the time.

"She could tell my heart was divided, but she did not know why," Adam said. "I am afraid I did not treat her very well during this time. I am a lucky man that she forgave me and married me anyway. But at the time, I began to think maybe I did not want to be Amish after all."

Looking at him now, it was clear what he had decided in the end. But Martha didn't know why.

"What made you finally choose?"

"It was not any one thing," Adam said. "It was many things. Of course, I knew what my family wanted. And I knew what Leah wanted. But for a good long while, I did not know what I wanted. I had really started to think that the way I could do the most good in the world was to leave and help more people and more animals among the Englisch." The ewe in the next pen bleated, and Adam said something to it in Pennsylvania Dutch and then turned back to Martha. "But then the vet, Dr. Beaty, spoke to me after a shift one day. He told me he would love it if I got my schooling and joined his team. But he also said that I could also do much good in the world by caring for a farm and a family, and that there was just as much value in raising a family and serving the Lord simply as there was in what he did."

Bless that vet, Martha thought. He was right—Martha believed whatever work the Lord gave you, it was honoring to Him if you did it faithfully.

"And by this time, I had seen enough of the Englisch world to know that it is all about oneself. It is not about the community. I hope that does not offend you, but it is true."

"No offense taken."

"In our world, what is good for the community is more important than what is good for any one person, and I could not stop believing that. But I knew it would be difficult to live this way among the Englisch."

A breeze stirred the air, and Martha pulled her jacket tighter around herself.

"And then, of course, Felicity stopped returning my texts."

"She did?"

Adam nodded. "A new guy had caught her attention, and she was not interested in me anymore."

"I'm sorry." She meant it, but she was also thinking of the implications of this. Had Felicity just met someone she liked better than Adam? Had the cultural differences been too much? Maybe it had seemed exotic to flirt with an Amish man, but not as much fun as she'd hoped in the end. Or maybe, Martha couldn't help thinking, Felicity had gotten what she wanted and had no more need for Adam. Obviously Felicity wasn't the one posing as Adam, but perhaps she'd gotten her hands on Adam's license and passed it along to some young man to use.

"I am not. It stopped me from making a terrible mistake. And I realized that the way the Englisch world works, the way people think about things—it was never going to be a good fit for me. It was too different. I just could not see spending my life that way."

"That makes a lot of sense," Martha said. That was no doubt why an overwhelming majority of people raised in the Amish tradition joined the church. It wasn't that they were brainwashed or backward or any of the awful things she'd heard people say about them. It had a lot to do with the fact that it was very hard to walk away from everything you'd ever known and start over among people with strange customs. "And judging by the uncomfortable silence last night, I am assuming Leah knows about Felicity?"

"Yes, I told her. I did not want to start off our marriage with anything but the truth."

"How did she react when you told her?"

"I suppose as well as she could have," Adam said. "But she was not happy, for obvious reasons."

"Of course she wouldn't be," Martha said. The little cat was rubbing against her hand now, purring madly.

"She forgave me," Adam said. "But it is still something of a sore spot for her, I am afraid. Which is why it was so uncomfortable when we were discussing places I went last night. I did not want to remind her of that time, and I believe she did not want to bring it up."

"That makes sense." Knowing that background, Martha saw the whole encounter last night in a different light. "So, if we were looking into places you went regularly and people you knew, we should probably check out Joanna's and talk to Felicity," she said.

"Yes, that is probably the case," Adam said, nodding. "I do not know if she still works there or not, but it is one of the places I could have lost the license."

"We'll check it out, then," Martha said.

"Thank you," Adam said. "To you and your sisters. Thank you for helping me with this."

"Of course," Martha said. "We're glad to help, and we'll let you know what we find out."

She gave the little cat one last pat, and then she turned to go. The kitten jumped down and followed her as she walked toward the barn door.

"Sorry, little guy," Martha said. "I'm afraid you can't come with me. Butterscotch would not approve." The old tabby wasn't good at sharing. The cat let out a little mew, and Martha laughed and climbed into her car.

They were still a long way from finding answers, Martha knew. But after what she'd just learned, she was at least one step closer.

CHAPTER FIVE

Martha was just tucking the last of the dinner dishes into the dishwasher when the phone rang. She and Elizabeth had eaten baked chicken, while Mary had gone out for dinner with a friend. Martha couldn't keep up with her sister's active social life. Martha glanced at the phone. SILAS FISCHER, the caller ID read. Martha's mind flashed back to the previous night, when Ephraim had called to say that the police were at the house.

"Hello?"

"Hallo, Martha, this is Rachel."

"Oh, Rachel. How is everything?" It had only been a few hours since they'd spoken, but Martha's stomach clenched, fearing something else had happened.

"We are all right," Rachel said. "I wanted to let you know that I talked with some of the other women, and we agreed that it would be very nice to hold a bake sale to raise money for the Mast family."

"That's great to hear," Martha said. "In that case, I'll get started on planning right away. Do you think next Saturday would work? That gives us one week to plan."

"That should probably be all right," Rachel said. "There is no Singing that evening."

"Great." Martha flipped to a new page in the little notebook they kept near the phone. "We'd be happy to host it here at the shop."

"That will not be necessary," Rachel said. "Ruth Yutzy has asked if we can host it here in our barn, and I said yes. Abner Mast is her husband's cousin, after all."

"Oh." It wasn't that Martha really wanted the extra work involved in cleaning for and hosting a big event. But it would be so much more practical to host it at Secondhand Blessings. "But it will be cold. Here at the shop, we have heaters, and lights in case it goes late."

"You are right," Rachel said. "But we can set up propane heaters, and there are lanterns. Ruth would really like us to host the event, and I think that makes the most sense."

Martha wasn't sure that it did, but she bit her tongue. This wasn't about her. If Ruth Yutzy wanted Rachel to host, they couldn't really argue, she guessed. Could they? They would still raise plenty of money for the Mast family, even if they didn't do it exactly the way Martha would have.

"Okay," Martha said. "That sounds great." She took a moment to think, and then she continued. "So when can we get together to talk about advertising and coordinating who is bringing what? And we'll need to assign jobs. I think probably a spreadsheet would be best."

"I do not think we need to worry about those things," Rachel said. "I do not have a way to make a spreadsheet, but in any case it is not necessary. It will come together. People will find their roles. You will see."

"But…" Sure, people might figure out what to do, but it would be chaos. Much simpler to just assign jobs. But she decided to address the bigger question first. "I do think we'll need some advertising to get the word out about the sale.

Otherwise no one will know to come. I was thinking we could make up posters, and we can take out ads in the local papers, and maybe some online ads."

"People will come."

"Right." She bit back her frustration. "But we want *lots* of people to come, so we need to get the word out."

"If you want to do advertising, I fully support that."

Martha saw what Rachel had just done. She'd expertly just placed it all on Martha.

"That's fine," Martha said. "I can handle that aspect. Now, we'll need to discuss logistics, like equipment rental and set up and clean up—"

"Oh dear. Dorcas is crying. I have to go to. We will talk more about this soon."

"But—"

But Rachel had already hung up, no doubt rushing off to see about her little girl.

Just as well, Martha thought. There were a lot of details to organize, but they would wait until the morning. She gazed at the stack of credit card bills she'd gotten from Rachel earlier that day. For now, she had plenty of work to do.

Martha was hunched over a pile of papers when Elizabeth went down to the basement that evening. Bills of some kind, it looked like. Probably balancing her checkbook. Martha always had kept meticulous records of every penny she spent. Elizabeth wished she could be as diligent, but she just couldn't make herself spend so much time keeping track of where every penny went.

It didn't take long for Elizabeth to find what she needed, and she carried the cardboard boxes back up the stairs.

"What is all that?" Martha asked as Elizabeth came up from the basement. Elizabeth braced one of the boxes against the door and pushed it closed.

"Boxes." Elizabeth dumped the boxes on the table, where they landed with a thud. A puff of dust flew up.

"Really?" Martha cocked an eyebrow.

"Boxes full of old books." Elizabeth opened the flap of the top one.

"I thought we went through all that stuff last year," Martha said.

"We did. I was looking for the old photo albums. I knew they were down here somewhere."

"From when we were young? Those are on the bookshelf in the living room."

"No. From earlier." Elizabeth pulled out a few musty theological tomes her father had earmarked and underlined, as well as a thick history of the Mennonites in America. The pages were golden brown, and the spine was cracked.

"He had rather dry taste in books, didn't he?" Martha asked.

"I suppose if you were having trouble sleeping, these might just be the thing." Elizabeth set them aside and pulled out a few old cookbooks as well as a biography of Harry Truman. Then, at the bottom, she finally found what she was looking for.

"When is that from?"

Elizabeth set the old photo album down on the table. It was bound in brown leather. She carefully opened the cover and looked at the first page, black, with black-and-white images tacked on with photo corners.

"This is Grandma Classen's photo album," Elizabeth said. She had seen other photo albums of her father's relatives, but this one was new to her. She looked down at an image of her grandparents and Daddy, who couldn't have been more than eight, with his siblings. They were all wearing formal clothes, the girls in dresses and the boys in shorts and jackets, Grandpa in a suit with an elaborate collar and a pocket square. Grandma wore a low-waisted dress that dated this photo to the thirties.

"What is it doing in the basement?" Martha moved over so she could see the photos more clearly. "These are precious. They should be up here with the other albums."

"I'm not sure why they're downstairs," Elizabeth answered. "Let's move them up." She flipped past formal portraits and weddings of aunts and uncles and then, as the years advanced and photographs became less costly and more common, there were a few candid shots mixed in with the portraits.

"Here's Aunt Pearl's wedding." Elizabeth pointed to her aunt's face, so young looking, in a slim-fitting white gown. She stood on the stage at Mount Zion Mennonite Church. It still had those same unadorned wooden slats on the back wall today. As a child, Elizabeth had never understood why they didn't do something to dress it up a bit, make the place feel a little special, but now she appreciated the beautiful simplicity of the church her family had attended for generations.

"And Mama and Daddy's wedding is here." Martha flipped the page, and there they were, impossibly young and fresh-faced, standing on that same stage. Martha had also gotten married there, many years later.

"She looks so beautiful, doesn't she?" Elizabeth took in her mother's dark hair, gathered up under a simple veil, and her beautifully full gown. Grandma Bolton had made that dress by hand, Elizabeth knew, and it had taken months just to save up the money to buy the fabric, let alone cut and sew the dress.

"Oh, look at this!" Martha had found a picture of herself as a baby, sitting in a formal studio. Elizabeth nodded, but her mind had already moved on.

Susannah wasn't here. She hadn't expected her to be, really, but… Well, if she was honest, she had hoped there would be something that would make that letter to Daddy make more sense.

"What is it?" Martha was staring at her.

"What do you mean?"

"Why are you looking lost like that?"

Elizabeth sighed. She supposed this was as good a time as any to share what she'd found.

"Last night I was going through some of Daddy's old clothes to sew for a quilt, and I found this." She had tucked the letter into her purse, so she retrieved it and held it out for Martha to read. Martha took it, and then she looked down at the tissue-thin paper and read it carefully.

"Who is Susannah?" Martha looked up.

"That's what I'm trying to figure out."

"'Dear Henry,'" Martha read from the letter. "'I hope this finds you well. I hope you are enjoying college. I miss you desperately already, and I can't imagine how I am going to survive until you come home. Sometimes I sit under the dogwood where we carved our initials last year, and I remember how we used to play together in that tree when we were kids. It all seems so long ago now. It's hard to be here without you.

"'I am feeling much better, much less tired, but I won't be able to hide our secret for very much longer. I think my mother has begun to suspect. As much as I wish things were different, every kick and flutter reminds me of you. I pray for you every day. Know that I love you and will wait for you. Yours, Susannah.'"

"This was written in 1950," Elizabeth said. "Daddy graduated from college the next year."

"He and Mom weren't married until 1957," Martha said. "Did Daddy love someone before Mama?"

"It sure sounds like he did," Elizabeth said.

"And it sounds like…" Martha couldn't seem to bring herself to say the words.

"It sounds like she was pregnant, doesn't it?" Elizabeth asked.

"Wow." Martha lowered herself down into her chair. "It sounds like they were in love, and she was pregnant when he was off at college."

Martha didn't say anything else for a moment, and Elizabeth let her have some time. Elizabeth had had a full day to absorb and think about this, but it would take Martha a while before she would be able to process it.

"So that means we have a sibling," she finally said.

"A half sibling, but yes." Elizabeth sat down in the chair across from her. "But Daddy was always so…"

"He kept a close eye on us, didn't he?" Martha asked. "Even when Chuck and I were engaged, he tried to make sure we weren't alone together. Not that he could do anything while we were at college, but still. Why would he be so adamant about keeping us safe if he had…" She let her voice trail off.

"Maybe because he knew how easy it is to fall into temptation," Elizabeth said quietly. "And how real the consequences can be."

Martha didn't say anything for a moment. And then, softly, "But who was she? I've never heard of this Susannah."

"I haven't either. That's why I was looking through this old photo album. I was hoping there would be some photograph, some mention of her…or the baby."

Martha let out a long breath. "If you think Grandma would have put something like that in the family photo album, you don't remember Grandma Classen very well."

"You're right." Grandmas Classen was very formal and proper. If there had been a baby born out of wedlock, she would have done whatever she could to keep it quiet. "But I don't know how else to find out more about Susannah."

"And about the baby," Martha said. "Wow." She leaned back in the chair. "How long have you known about this?"

"I just found the letter last night."

"And you kept it from us all day?"

"There didn't seem to be a good time to say, 'Hey, fun news, I just found out we have a brother or sister that no one ever told us about.'"

Martha nodded, considering. "Do you think Mama knew?"

"I don't know." Elizabeth sighed. "It's hard to see how she would know something like that and not say anything about it. But at the same time, it's hard to see how he wouldn't have told her."

"I don't know." Martha sighed. "It's going to take me a while to process this. Part of me wishes I'd never found out."

Elizabeth closed the photo book with a thud.

"What were you doing before I came up here?" Elizabeth looked over and saw that Martha had been looking at bills. She had highlighted various lines with different colors, and she had made notes in several places. Her laptop was open in front of her, and a local yellow pages sat nearby. This was more intense than even her usual checkbook balancing session. "What are you working on?"

"These are the credit card bills for the cards taken out in Adam's name." Martha neatened the stacks in front of her. "I'm trying to figure out a list of the places that the cards were used."

"Wait. Really?" Elizabeth came around the counter and sat down next to Martha at the table. "Where did you get those?"

"Rachel gave them to me," Martha said. "Apparently they'd been coming to their house, but Rachel ignored them."

Elizabeth reached for an envelope and turned it over. FINAL NOTICE was written in red on the front.

"She ignored this?" Elizabeth might not balance her checkbook down to the penny like her sister, but even she knew you couldn't ignore things like this.

"I guess she didn't know what it was." Martha shrugged. "She thought it was junk mail."

"Oh dear." She pushed the envelope back toward Martha. "So what are the highlights?"

"These pink lines are charges made in State College," Martha said. "At least, the ones I could figure out. Those charges started in the fall. This one is a charge at a J. Crew store in State College in November."

Elizabeth leaned in and took a look at the line on the bill Martha was pointing at.

"How can you tell where the store is located?" Elizabeth could see the name of the store, but not an address.

"This is the store number," Martha said, pointing to a five-digit number after the words J. Crew. "Once I had that, I just googled it, and it turned up an address in State College."

Elizabeth was impressed. She wouldn't have figured that out herself. She looked down at the line again and studied it. "Whoa." She couldn't be seeing that number at the end of the row correctly. "That's how much he spent?"

"Whoever this guy impersonating Adam is, he's apparently never heard of a sale rack."

"When you're spending other people's money, why would you?" Elizabeth asked.

"I suppose you're right."

"Where else did he shop?"

"I'm pretty sure this is a liquor store near the college." Martha was pointing at an entry for a purchase at Discount Liquors. "And this is an electronics store at the local mall. He appears to have loaded up there."

Elizabeth was shocked at the total he'd rung up. She couldn't imagine spending that much in one store.

"And these are a couple of other clothing stores, also near the college."

"He has a taste for nice clothes," Elizabeth said.

"And cheap alcohol, apparently."

"Sounds like a college kid to me," Elizabeth said. "But we'd already suspected that."

"That's right," Martha said. "And we'd also suspected that he was from this area originally, and it turns out that he used the card in this area plenty as well. Here's a restaurant in Lancaster, and a bar near there." Martha pointed out two rows she'd highlighted in blue. "And several charges at the mall outside Lancaster. These charges were both around Thanksgiving, and these two were at Christmastime."

"Times when college kids would be visiting home," Elizabeth said. "When was the card taken out?"

"It looks like the first charges were made in August." Martha was peering at the bill.

"And were there ever any payments made?" Elizabeth asked.

Martha shook her head. "It doesn't look like it. The balance grew each month, and it looks like this card was finally shut off in December, after thousands of dollars in charges and fees. This one wasn't shut off until January."

Elizabeth pursed her lips. "Okay then. So we have a few new pieces of information. We know where he likes to shop."

"And when he shopped," Martha added.

"Right," Elizabeth said. "So we can go visit the stores and talk to the employees and see if anyone remembers him."

"It seems like kind of a long shot, but it's worth trying," Martha said.

"We also have good reason to believe that whoever this guy is, he's a local kid who now goes to school at Penn State," Elizabeth said.

"Too bad there are forty thousand students at Penn State," Martha said. "I think we'll need to narrow it down a bit more."

Elizabeth sighed. Penn State was one of the largest colleges in the country. Without more information, they'd never be able to figure out who the imposter was.

"If he's from the area, he probably graduated from one of the local high schools," she said. "Maybe we could look at some of the yearbooks of the local high schools and see all the people who graduated in the past few years."

"That's a good suggestion," Martha said.

"We can check that out tomorrow," Elizabeth said. She felt a yawn rise up. "For now, I think I need to head to bed." It had been a long day.

"I'm not far behind you," Martha said. "As soon as I clean this stuff up, I'm headed up as well. We have a lot of leads to pursue tomorrow."

CHAPTER SIX

After church on Sunday, Mary ate a quick sandwich before she headed out to the garden. The sun was shining, and there was just a hint of warmth in the air, and she figured this was a great time to get the soil prepared. She had her eye on a raised-bed garden like the one she'd seen in the seed catalog, but she would need to pull out the weeds and level the ground in the patch Mama had used before one could be built. She put on a thin wool sweater and zipped on her fleece jacket, and then she stopped in the shed for Mama's old gardening gloves and a few shovels in various sizes before heading out to the patch of garden. The shop wasn't open on Sundays, so she had the whole afternoon ahead of her, and she was looking forward to getting her hands dirty.

She walked across the yard and through the little gate Daddy had strung in the chicken wire fence he'd put up around the garden beds to keep the rabbits out. This had been Mama's domain, but Daddy had built her whatever she asked for because the whole family enjoyed the fruit of her labor all summer long. Mama had been a diligent gardener, and she turned out neat rows of green beans and tomatoes and corn and zucchini and lettuces of all kinds. In the fall, there was butternut squash and potatoes, and the spring always brought ramps and leeks and scallions and garlics so flavorful you only needed the smallest bit. Mary was getting hungry just thinking about it.

She closed the gate behind her and looked around. Well, it didn't look quite like it had when Mama was in charge. The soil was completely overgrown, choked with weeds. A vine of some kind had wrapped its way around the fence and threatened to pull the whole thing down. Had this all happened just since Mama had died? But then, Mama had been sick for a few years before that, Mary remembered, and poor Elizabeth had been completely overwhelmed trying to care for her. She hadn't had time to worry about the garden in those days.

Well, Mary was here to care for it now. She stepped in, set her shovels down, and looked around. Where to begin? She decided to start with the biggest weeds, and she got to work with her shovel, digging out the roots. She was sweating when she finally managed to uproot a nasty weed, and she yanked it out and tossed it aside. Then she moved on to the next one. As she worked, she let her mind wander, from the sermon at church this morning, which had been about the parable of the sower—perfect for her task for the afternoon, she'd thought— to the movie she'd seen last night, to the mystery of who stole Adam's identity. She hadn't had much luck at the vet clinic yesterday, but the answer was out there somewhere, she knew. Martha was planning to go to the coffee shop that Adam had mentioned to her, and she and Elizabeth were going to team up and visit some of the stores where "Adam" had used the credit card, and the racetrack. Hopefully they would find some answers at one of those places.

Then Mary thought about the car registered in Adam's name, and the accident that had landed the Mast family in the hospital. She realized she didn't know what kind of car it was, or what happened to it. There were probably clues in the car itself. You could tell so much about a person by the car they drove. Martha's car was always pristine, for instance, and she kept up the maintenance religiously. Mary's car was usually exploding with art supplies and half-finished projects and scraps of things she'd thought interesting to pick up but had never figured out what to do with. There was probably old mail in there too, and all kinds of things that had her name on them. If they could take a look at the car, surely they'd be able to learn more about the man who had been driving it, but how would they find it?

She looked up as a police car pulled into the driveway. She watched as the car parked, and saw that it was John who stepped out. He must have some news, since she wasn't aware of any plans he and Elizabeth had for today. She looked over the garden. It looked better, but it still needed work, that was for sure. But she was thirsty, and she could take a break to get something to drink and hear what John had to say. She set her shovel down and hurried across the yard, walking into the kitchen just as Elizabeth handed John a cup of coffee.

"Hi there, Mary," he said as he sat down at the table. Elizabeth and Martha had both changed out of their church clothes, and Martha had a fresh-baked cookie in front of her at the table. "Enjoying the sunshine?"

"Hello." Mary kicked off her muddy shoes at the door and walked to the sink to wash her hands. "It feels like spring," she said. "Cold, but there's the promise of better days ahead."

There was always the promise of better things to come as a Christian, Mary thought, but she forced herself to stop short of saying the words. John had made it clear he wasn't interested in attending church, and she knew it was a sore spot for Elizabeth, so she decided not to make things worse.

"I figured you must have news," Mary said instead. "And I wanted to see what it was."

"I suppose I do," John said. He had a cookie and a cup of coffee in front of him. "I wanted to let you know that we visited the vet clinic, and the woman there didn't know how Adam could have lost his license."

"Yes, that's what they told me too," Mary said.

John shook his head. "I should have known you'd beat us to it. The receptionist seemed to already know the answers to our questions."

"Well, I didn't have any more luck than you did."

"And the people at the racetrack had no idea who Adam was," John continued. "They let us look though a bin of lost and found items, but none of them was a driver's license."

"We haven't made it there yet," Mary said. "But maybe we'll get lucky."

"Maybe you will." John laughed.

"Do you have any other news?" Martha asked.

"There was one other thing," John said. He took a sip of his coffee, and the smell wafted through the kitchen. Mary had had a cup at the coffee hour after church and didn't need another, but it sure did smell good. "We knew that Abner Mast came back from the hospital this morning, so we went out to talk with him. But he wouldn't let us onto the property."

"What?" Elizabeth wrinkled her brow. "Why not?"

"That was what I was hoping you might be able to tell me," John said. "It was confusing. I would have thought he would want to talk to us, given that we're trying to find the person who did this to his family. And he was very nice. Perfectly pleasant. But he wouldn't let us come onto the property, which, again, seemed really odd."

"The Amish typically try to avoid involvement with the police," Mary said. "I'm sure it was just that."

"Even when we're trying to help them?" John broke off a piece of his cookie. "It doesn't make any sense."

"I can't think of any other reason he would be hesitant," Martha said. But even as her sister said the words, Mary wondered. *Did* Abner Mast have something to hide? Immediately, she felt awful. This poor man had just survived a traumatic accident. His wife and young child were still in the hospital. Surely no one could blame him for feeling a bit reticent at the moment. Mary decided to bring up the idea that had come to her while she was gardening.

"What about the car itself?" she asked.

"What about it?" John said.

"Do you know where it is? Can we see it?" Mary asked.

"It's impounded at the moment," John said. "And I'm afraid I can't let you in to see it. But believe me, we are searching it very thoroughly and following up on every lead."

Mary believed they were. But she also wanted to keep try-ing. They would just have to find another way to get to that impounded car.

Martha and Elizabeth chatted with John for a while after Mary went back out to wrestle the garden into submission, but John said he had to get back to the station, and a little while later, Elizabeth and Martha were headed down Route 340 toward Lancaster. Elizabeth was driving, so Martha was enjoying the drive, taking in the beautiful old wooden barns and the rolling hills. Historic homes, with the clean, simple lines of colonial construction, and Victorians, dripping with elaborate gingerbread trim, sat back on wide yards sur-rounded by mature oak and elm trees. Along the roads, in front of stone fences and wooden gates and in gardens, daf-fodils were just starting to bud. By this time next week, the cheery yellow flowers would be in full bloom, Martha guessed.

They made a stop at a print shop Elizabeth knew of, and Martha printed out a couple hundred flyers she'd designed early that morning to advertise the bake sale. They would hang them up around town and also give them out at the shop. If they wanted people to show up, they needed to get the word out.

Then, with the flyers tucked safely into the trunk, they continued on to Lancaster and found the coffee shop easily, in a small storefront in a shopping center not far from the vet's office. When they stepped inside, they saw it had been done up very nicely, with old wooden boards, probably reclaimed from some barn in the area, hung on the walls, and mismatched tables and chairs. It had the air of a cozy, homespun space, and it smelled like coffee. Martha inhaled deeply.

"Welcome to Joanna's," the young woman behind the counter said. She had clear skin and wide brown eyes and a head of curly red hair. "What can I get you?"

"I'd like a decaf latte, please," Elizabeth said. The woman nodded and looked at Martha.

"Do you have tea?" Martha scanned the menu board, but there were so many things she'd never heard of that she didn't know where to start.

"Absolutely. Green, jasmine green, oolong, mint, white, or black?"

"Just tea. Do you have Earl Grey?"

"Coming right up." She smiled and rang up their order.

"Is there anyone who works here named Felicity?" Martha asked as she handed over her credit card.

"Not that I know of," the woman said. "I mean, I guess I don't know everyone who works here, but I've seen the schedule, and that name doesn't sound familiar."

"How long have you worked here?" Elizabeth asked.

"A few months," she said. She ran the card through a reader and then turned the screen. "Just use your finger," she said, and Martha signed the screen.

"Is there anyone here who has worked here for longer? A few years?"

"Hmm." She handed back the card and thought. "I think Jeremy might have been here that long. He's the manager. Do you want me to check?"

"That would be great," Martha said.

"Hang on. I'll go ask." She turned and vanished through a door that led to the back. Martha looked around the shop as they waited. Most of the tables were occupied by people hunched over laptops. A few were scrolling through their phones. In the corner, two women were chatting quietly. It seemed most people came here to get away from people, not to connect with people, Martha surmised.

"Hi there."

Martha turned around at a man's voice.

"Here's Jeremy," the cashier said.

"Teegan said you wanted to talk to someone who's been here a while?" Jeremy asked.

"That's right," Martha said. She tried to figure out the best way to phrase this.

"We were hoping to talk to someone named Felicity. We're told she worked here a couple of years ago," Elizabeth said.

"Oh yeah. I know Felicity." Jeremy nodded. "Cool girl."

Teegan went back to the counter and started to make their drinks, but Martha thought she was still listening.

"Does she work here now?" Elizabeth asked.

"Nah. She left about a year ago, when she finished her social work degree."

"Do you know how we might be able to get in touch with her?" Martha asked.

Jeremy started to speak, but then he paused. "Why?"

Martha tried to figure out what to say, but Elizabeth jumped in. "We're asking on behalf of a friend of ours named Adam Fischer. He's Amish, and he used to come in here sometimes a few years back. He said he got to know Felicity."

"Oh, wow. You know that Amish kid?" He laughed. "That's crazy."

"So you know who he is?"

"Yeah. I mean, we don't get a lot of Amish kids coming in here, you know?" He scratched his beard, which could use a good trim, Martha thought. "He was a nice kid. What's he up to now?"

"He's married and has a baby on the way," Elizabeth said.

"Did he stay Amish?"

"Yes, he joined the church," Martha said.

"Huh." Jeremy was wearing some kind of leather cuff on his wrist, and the snap caught the light. "That's too bad."

"What do you mean?" Martha asked.

"I mean, he was so smart. I know it's hard for them to leave, but he seemed like he really could get out. I'm sorry he didn't make it in the end."

Martha tried to respond as diplomatically as possible. "He did decide to join the church," she said. "And he seems very happy with his decision so far."

"Well, that's good," Jeremy said. "I'm glad he's happy. He was a nice kid."

"I have a decaf latte and an Earl Grey at the bar," Teegan called. Martha moved to the bar and took the drinks, and she handed the latte to Elizabeth as Jeremy kept talking.

"He had such a crush on Felicity. It was really sweet."

"What makes you say he had a crush on her?" Elizabeth asked.

"Oh, he would come in here with these puppy dog eyes and just stare at her. It was clear he didn't have a lot of experience with love. But I think Felicity was into him, actually. I don't know. She used to talk with him all the time."

"Would you know how we could get in touch with her?" Martha asked again. Now that he knew why they were asking, he seemed more willing.

"Sure." He pulled his phone out from a pocket of his jeans. "Here's her number."

Martha quickly dug a pen and scrap of paper from out of her purse, and she wrote down the number.

"We were also wondering," Elizabeth started. "Adam lost his driver's license—the actual card—around this time. Is there any chance anyone here found it?"

"Huh." Jeremy tucked his phone back into his pocket. "Not that I know of."

"Do you have a Lost and Found?" Elizabeth asked.

"Sure. But it's mostly just sweatshirts and water bottles. That kind of thing. I don't remember ever finding a driver's license. I kind of think that if we ever found anything like that, we'd just mail it back to the address on the front."

That was what Martha would do with it too. But no one had done this.

"Is there any way to check and see if anyone might have found it?" Martha realized she was starting to sound kind of desperate, but there were only a few places Adam could have lost the thing, and so far they'd struck out at both places.

"I can ask around," Jeremy said. "I doubt I'll find much, but I can try."

"We'd appreciate that," Elizabeth said. She reached into her purse and pulled out a business card from the shop. "You can get in touch with us here."

"Oh, wow." Jeremy looked up from the card. "You guys run Secondhand Blessings? My mom loves this place."

"That's so nice to hear," Martha said. "Thank you."

"And please let us know if you hear anything about the license," Elizabeth said and turned to go.

"What do you think?" Martha asked as soon as they were back in the car.

"I think this is a terrible latte," Elizabeth said. She turned on the engine, and heat started to pour out through the vents, but she didn't put the car into gear.

"I'm sorry to hear that, but I meant what do you think about what Jeremy said?"

"He seemed honest enough," Elizabeth said. "I got the sense that he really didn't know anything about the missing license."

"I got that sense too," Martha said. "Maybe we'll have better luck with Felicity."

"Let's give her a call now."

"I like the way you think." Martha pulled the scrap of paper from her purse, and Elizabeth got her phone and entered the number. Martha listened as it rang.

"Voice mail," Elizabeth whispered, and then she left a message explaining who she was and asking Felicity to call her back about Adam Fischer. "We'll see if we get a response," she said. Then she buckled herself into the seat and turned to Martha. "So. Where to now?"

"How about McGee's?"

"How about what?" Elizabeth narrowed her eyes.

"McGee's. It's a pub not far from here." Martha gave her an innocent smile.

"Wow. This is turning into a whole different kind of day than I was expecting."

"Not for a drink." Martha laughed. "That's one of the places where the credit card taken out in Adam's name was used. I thought we could see if anyone there remembers him."

"Ah. Got it. That makes more sense." Elizabeth put the car into gear. "For a second there, I thought my sister had been kidnapped and replaced with an impostor."

"No such luck." Martha pulled up the bar on her phone and found directions. "It's only a short way from here."

A few minutes later, Elizabeth was parking outside a short, squat building covered in white stucco. There were neon signs in the small windows, and when they opened the door, an overly sweet smell, mixed with the tang of disinfectant, greeted them. The space was dim, but there were half a dozen people hunched over the bar, most of them nursing drinks and watching sports on one of the screens.

Martha looked at Elizabeth, who sucked in a breath, pressed her lips together, and then stepped in. As the door fell closed behind them, the room got even darker. Martha followed Elizabeth to the bar and waited while the bartender finished pouring a drink for a man at the end. Then he turned and smiled as he walked toward them.

"Good afternoon." His hair was flecked with gray, but he was lean and muscular. He wiped his hands on a white towel as he walked toward them. "What can I get you ladies?"

"Oh, we're not—" Martha started to say, but Elizabeth interrupted.

"Seltzer with lime, please," she said, giving Martha a significant look. "Two of them."

"Coming right up." He smiled, and Martha noticed that one of his front teeth was crooked. Elizabeth sat down on one the stools, and Martha's mind reeled. They couldn't sit down here. They weren't staying. They didn't belong here. What if someone saw them here? They would think—

But as the bartender slid the drinks in front of them, Elizabeth said, "We were wondering if we could ask you a question."

"You mean you didn't just come in for the atmosphere?" He flashed a smile. Elizabeth laughed, and Martha realized that they probably weren't typical customers. Martha was wearing a long tan skirt and a button-up top. Most of the men around her were wearing jerseys or T-shirts with NASCAR drivers on them.

"Not this time." Elizabeth put her feet up on the stool's footrest. "We were actually wondering if you might remember a customer who came in here around Christmastime. He was a young kid, probably around twenty-one, and issued an ID with the name Adam Fischer."

The man blew out a breath. "Can you tell me anything more about him?"

"I'm afraid we don't know more about him," Elizabeth said. "He was using a stolen ID, and we're trying to find out more about him."

"Ah." The man set the towel down on the bar. "Well, I'm afraid I'm not going to be much help in that case."

"You check IDs, right?" Martha asked.

"Naturally," he said, but there was something in his voice that made Martha doubt his words.

She took a sip of her drink, the ice rattling around in the glass as she lifted it. It was refreshing, she had to admit.

"So you wouldn't have seen the name on his ID," Elizabeth said.

He shrugged. "It doesn't ring a bell."

"He used a credit card with that name," Martha said.

"I'm sorry to say I don't memorize the names on the credit cards that are handed to me."

Martha had to admit she understood. She almost never checked the names on the cards that were handed to her in the shop. She just ran them, anxious to make sure customers got in and out quickly.

"And without more information, I'm afraid I don't know how much help I can be." He said it kindly, but the message was clear.

Martha tried to think of another angle to jog his memory, but Elizabeth drained her glass and then thanked him. "We appreciate your help." She started to push herself up. "How much do we owe you for the drinks?"

"They're on the house." The man flashed his smile again, and both Elizabeth and Martha thanked him and then turned to go. The floor was sticky in spots, and Martha was very grateful to step outside. She took in deep lungfuls of clean, fresh air.

"It wasn't that bad," Elizabeth said. She pushed the fob on her key ring to unlock the car.

"It wasn't good," Martha said.

"Well, it wasn't helpful. That's the main problem," Elizabeth said. She climbed into the car, and Martha sat down in the passenger seat. "Where to next?"

"The credit card taken out in Adam's name was also used at a gas station and a couple of clothing stores at the mall," Martha said. "And we could stop by the racetrack to see if he might have lost it there."

"You really want to brave the mall on a Sunday afternoon?"

It was the most crowded time of the week, Martha knew. But she nodded. "We'll be taking our lives in our hands, but I say we try it."

"Okay." Elizabeth put the car in gear, and they drove to the Park City Center, the local shopping center, and drove around for a while before she found a spot at the far edge of the parking lot. Martha knew some women loved to shop, but she had never understood the impulse. And as she stepped into the mall, she remembered why she didn't like coming to places like these. It was too bright, crowded, and full of competing smells—cinnamon, perfume, rubber—that gave her sensory overload. Plus, it was full of stores selling things that surely no one really needed. A whole store full of candles? She consulted the highlighted credit card bills and directed Elizabeth to an Abercrombie and Fitch store at the far end of the main level. After talking to the clerks at that store and three others, they headed back out to the car.

"We struck out there," Martha said. No one remembered anyone using a credit card with the name Adam Fischer, which wasn't that surprising, Martha thought.

"What are you talking about?" Elizabeth set a brown paper shopping bag on the back seat before sitting down in the driver's seat. "I got some good deals."

"I suppose you did."

Elizabeth had never cared much about fashion, likely because she'd spent so much of her life on the farm caring for Mama and Daddy. But since she'd met John, she'd taken a bit more care with her appearance, and Martha was glad for her. She deserved to feel good about herself. But that didn't mean Martha wanted to spend Sunday afternoon in that mall ever again.

They stopped at the gas station where "Adam" had used the card, but no one there had any information about him. Finally they stopped at the racetrack, but it was mostly deserted, and the lone grounds worker they found had no idea about a lost license. The whole trip had been a frustrating waste of time. And yet the farther they got from town, the more Martha's shoulders unhitched. The green hills rolled by, and the trees, just starting to bud, gave her hope that warmer days were ahead.

"Do you want to make one more stop before we head back home?" Elizabeth asked.

"Where?" If it was another shopping center, Martha was out.

"I was thinking about what John said earlier, about Abner Mast not wanting to talk to the police. I thought that was odd, even considering their usual hesitation to get involved with the police."

"I thought it was odd too. But I was at the Mast house yesterday. There wasn't anything secretive or shady about it. My guess is that it was just typical Amish reticence."

"Maybe." Elizabeth wasn't sure, Martha could tell. "John has been around plenty of Amish people, though. He's used to their ways. If he thought it was strange, I think there might be something more going on."

Martha glanced at Elizabeth. Her lips were pressed together.

"Are you thinking we should check with Rachel?"

"I was."

"Okay." Martha nodded slowly. "I guess it's worth a shot. She'll probably say it was nothing, but at least we'll get to see her."

Elizabeth drove past their own driveway, and Martha saw that Mary was still out in the garden, but she was holding what looked with a tape measure. Good for her. Martha was thrilled Mary had taken the garden on as a project. She couldn't wait to see the garden back in bloom. Mama had always taken such pride in it.

They pulled into the driveway of the Fischer farm. Thomas and Matthew were playing with a puppy by the barn, and Dorcas was skipping rope by the side of the house. They all looked up when the car drove up.

"Hello," Elizabeth called as she stepped out of the car.

"Hallo," Thomas and Matthew answered in unison. Shy little Dorcas bobbed her head.

"Maam is inside," one of the twins said. Matthew, Martha thought. Or was it Thomas? She could never tell them apart.

"Thank you, Thomas," Elizabeth called, and she headed toward the house. It was but one small reminder that Elizabeth had been here longer than Martha and Mary. She had seen these children grow up from the time they were babies. She had a shared history with this family in a way that Martha, having spent so many years in Kansas, didn't have.

Elizabeth walked right into the house—something Martha could never bring herself to do—and Martha was reminded again how Elizabeth and Rachel had been neighbors and close friends for years. They found Rachel rolling out piecrust in the kitchen. Fourteen-year-old Hannah was chopping vegetables on a cutting board on the far end of the counter, and the kitchen smelled like onions and roasting beef. There was a large stockpot bubbling away on the stove.

"Hallo!" Rachel called as they walked in. "How are you?"

"We're good. And you?"

"We are well." Rachel set the rolling pin down and turned to a bowl that sat next to her. "I am making a peach pie for Silas's birthday." There was an empty jar on the counter with a handwritten label that said PEACHES. She'd canned them herself last summer, Martha saw. "Peach is his favorite."

"That will be delicious, especially at this time of year," Elizabeth said. "When summer is so close, yet so far."

"We will all enjoy it," Rachel said with a smile. "So. What is going on? Do you have news?"

"I'm afraid we don't have any real news yet," Martha said. "But we're trying." She explained the stops they'd made that day, and Rachel laughed when Elizabeth told them about going into the pub.

"I cannot picture you in a place like that," Rachel said.

"It did reassure me that we'd made good life choices," Elizabeth said. "But we came here because John stopped by the house earlier and told us that he'd gone to see Abner Mast, and Abner behaved...oddly."

"Oddly how?" Rachel carefully transferred the piecrust to the dish and set it into place.

"John said he wouldn't let him come very far onto the property," Elizabeth said. "John thought it was strange, considering he was there trying to help find the person who did this to his family."

"We tried to tell him about how the Amish are reticent to talk to the police, but John seemed to think this was odd, even with that." Martha watched Rachel's face as she listened. A look she couldn't understand passed over her features.

"We wondered... Well, we thought we would check to see..." Elizabeth let her voice trail off.

Rachel was now rolling out a second piece of dough, for the top of the pie, Martha guessed. Her hands kept moving, deftly stretching and smoothing the dough, but she didn't say anything for a moment. Even though Hannah's back was turned, she had stopped chopping and Martha was sure she was listening in. Martha had been dubious about this errand, but as the silence stretched out, she started to think that Elizabeth might have been right.

"He should not have been difficult to the police, especially when they are trying to help him," Rachel finally said. "But I think I might know the reason why." She hoisted the mixing bowl and carefully scooped the peaches, glistening and flecked with cinnamon, into the pie tin. "You know that many Amish around here breed dogs."

Martha nodded, but her stomach sank. Amish puppy mills had become a national headline in recent years. Most of the Amish she knew who bred animals were caring and responsible about how they treated the animals, but there had been a few cases, unfortunately profiled on national news, of farms where hundreds of dogs had been kept in tiny, dirty cages and fed little. Puppies had been separated from their mothers and sold well before they were ready.

"Most of the people who breed dogs do a wonderful job caring for the animals," Rachel said. "But as you know, the few that care more about profits than the animals give all of them a bad name." She used a wooden spoon to smooth out the fruit and get it to lie level in the crust. Martha couldn't believe she hadn't set the rolled dough in the refrigerator to chill or at least prebaked it. How did her piecrusts turn out so beautifully? "Abner Mast raises dogs," Rachel continued. "He is one of the responsible ones. He treats the animals well and truly cares for them. Our new puppy came from his farm, and the boys are loving it."

"Wait." Martha didn't understand. "I was there at his house, and I didn't see any dog cages." She also hadn't smelled any dogs, and she doubted dogs would keep quiet as strangers drove up and went into the house. She had heard dogs barking, but surely if he'd been breeding the animals, there would have been enough of them that she would have noticed.

"That is because he does not keep the animals in cages," Rachel said. "That is inhumane. He, like most of the breeders around here, keeps them in large pens, where they are free to move around and play. He treats the animals well. But because of the stories that have hit the headlines in recent years, people are very quick to call anything an Amish puppy mill. There was a man in our church who was reported to the authorities after a woman bought a dog from him and the dog got sick. She did not know how to care for a dog, that became clear, but she claimed it was the fault of the breeder and reported it to the police as a puppy mill. It is nothing of the sort, but he was fined a large amount of money and, after the nasty reviews this woman posted on the internet, he lost many customers." Satisfied that the fruit was level, she carefully folded the top crust and laid it out on top of the pie.

"People are very quick to make assumptions about things they know very little about," Rachel continued. "And many of the people who breed dogs in this area became afraid. So my guess is that Abner was nervous to let John onto the property for fear that he would discover the dogs and accuse him of things that were not true."

Elizabeth was nodding, but Martha was still not convinced as Rachel explained further.

"I think it is a very valid fear, unfortunately. We have seen what has happened to other breeders. People do not understand, and they stretch things out of proportion. But it would be a big blow to the Mast family if he were to lose the income he gets from breeding the dogs. So, I do not think he will talk to the police."

Martha tried to understand. "But John wants to help him catch the person who did this to his family. Doesn't Abner want to find the person?"

"Of course." Rachel was fluting the edges of the piecrust beautifully. She did it so effortlessly.

"Isn't making sure justice is done more important than worrying about whether John will misunderstand what he's doing with the dogs?" Elizabeth asked.

"The dogs are his livelihood," Rachel said.

"But if he's not doing anything wrong, why wouldn't he be more interested in justice?"

Again, Rachel didn't answer for a moment. Instead, she kept pinching the edges of the piecrust together, no doubt thinking carefully about what to say. Finally, she spoke. "I do not know that it is more important. That is a very Englisch way of thinking about it, I think. We are not so concerned with justice, at least not in the way you are probably thinking."

"But don't you want to see whoever did this caught and punished?" Again, Martha struggled to understand. Hadn't Rachel specifically asked them to help find the man who had stolen Adam's identity? If she didn't care about justice for Adam, what were they even doing trying to catch the guy?

"I do want to see the man stop using Adam's name to do bad things," Rachel said. "Very much. But your question was about justice. And while I do hope we catch the man who stole Adam's identity, it is not my place to think about justice. It is the Lord's place to dole out justice."

Martha thought about this. It was true, of course. But it wasn't the whole truth. Was it?

"The American legal system is also pretty good at doling out justice," she said, but Rachel just continued fluting her pie-crust. Martha could see that Elizabeth was turning this over in her mind too, and she could see Elizabeth also didn't know how to feel about Rachel's words, but that she was considering them.

"So you will go talk to him?"

Martha looked up. Rachel was looking at her, expecting an answer.

"Who?" Elizabeth looked as confused as Martha felt.

"Abner. If he will not let the police onto his property to help him, you must go instead."

"Oh." It took Martha a moment to catch up, but then she nodded. "Right. Okay."

"We were planning on it anyway," Elizabeth said.

They were?

"Oh good. I am so glad." Rachel finished fluting the pie, and then she scooped it up and opened the oven door and slid it inside. "I am sure he will be able to tell you about the car and the man who was driving it. That will help a lot."

"I'm sure it will," Elizabeth said.

Martha thought she was probably right. But she also hoped that Abner would change his mind and talk to the police, if not at his home, then somewhere else. And there was no guarantee that Abner would talk to them, either.

"Have you heard anything more about when his wife and son will be home?" Martha asked.

"They are hoping Miriam will be able to come home soon," Rachel said. "Miriam apparently has a concussion and a few broken bones, and they want to keep an eye on her, while Abel is still recovering from the surgery."

"I'm sure it will be good for them to be home," Elizabeth said.

"I am certain it will," Rachel said.

Elizabeth turned to go, but before they left, there was something else Martha wanted to ask Rachel about.

"I was thinking about decorations for the bake sale," Martha said. "I was thinking about color schemes, to make sure everything has a cohesive look."

"Color schemes?" Rachel asked.

"Right. You don't want people just bringing random table-cloths and whatnot, otherwise it could look garish."

The look on Rachel's face made Martha realize she might have said that too harshly. "It will help to give people an idea of what you're looking for, so the whole event is coordinated."

"Do you have a color scheme in mind?" Rachel asked.

"No, not really," Martha admitted. "I always like pinks and reds to give an event a pop of color, but…"

"We do not use red too often," Rachel said.

Martha nodded. It wasn't unheard of, but the color was rare among the Amish. "Maybe a more subtle blue?"

"I will do my best," Rachel said.

"What about tables? Do we need to rent them?"

"I can get tables," Rachel said. "You do not need to worry about that."

"And tablecloths? We'll want matching ones, probably white."

"I will make sure we have them."

Martha hesitated. It wasn't that she didn't trust Rachel. It was just that... Well, a more sophisticated look would lead to more sales. Martha was afraid that if she wasn't involved, the whole thing would look chintzy.

"I will take care of it," Rachel said again. She said the words kindly enough, but there was a note of finality in her voice that made Martha know better than to argue.

Rachel would handle the decorations then too. They would be done the Amish way, whatever that turned out to be. Martha had no idea how this event was going to turn out.

Elizabeth always felt a sense of peace whenever she was on the Fischer farm, and a small part of her wanted to stay here longer, but she knew they had to get home. They'd been away long enough, and she knew Martha was anxious to get started on dinner.

When they got home, Mary was curled up on the couch under a blanket reading a book. A mug of tea sat on the side table next to her, tiny wisps of steam curling up. She smiled and lowered the book as they walked in. "Productive day?"

Elizabeth wasn't sure how to answer. "Kind of?"

"What does that mean?"

Elizabeth lowered herself down into the chair across from the couch. Martha had already disappeared into the kitchen to get to work. Elizabeth would go help her in a moment.

"We struck out checking out the places where the Adam impersonator used the credit card. No one remembered him.

And I realized that if I ever set foot in McGee's again it will be too soon."

"That place on Horseshoe Road?"

"That's right."

"I could have told you that, and I've never been inside." Mary made a gagging noise at the back of her throat.

"Yes, well, now we know for sure." Elizabeth sighed. "We did talk to Rachel to find out why Abner Mast wouldn't talk to the police."

"Oh yeah? What was that?" Mary picked up her mug.

"Rachel says he raises dogs, and he was afraid John would think he ran a puppy mill."

"Does he?"

"Rachel insists he doesn't. I would assume she knows." Elizabeth shrugged. "But she thinks that's why he wouldn't let John come onto his property."

"So he's just not going to talk to the police?" Mary took a sip of her tea. A whiff of peppermint drifted toward Elizabeth.

"I guess not. Rachel asked us to talk to him."

"Well then." Mary set her tea down on the table. "What are we doing sitting here?"

"What?" Elizabeth looked around. "It's almost dinnertime."

Mary laughed. "You sound like Martha."

"Abner will probably be about to eat dinner too," Elizabeth said.

"Perfect. Then we know he'll be home."

"I was thinking we would go tomorrow."

"Tomorrow we have to work, and most likely so does he. On Sunday evening he's likely to be home."

Elizabeth thought for a minute. There wasn't really any reason they couldn't stop by and see if he was willing to talk now, she supposed.

"Okay." She pushed herself up. "Let's go see if Martha wants to come."

Mary followed a few steps behind her as she walked into the kitchen. Martha was chopping chicken breasts into thin strips.

"We want to go talk to Abner Mast now," Mary announced as she walked in.

"Now?" Martha's face scrunched up. "It's almost dinnertime."

Mary went through her logic for why it was a good time to visit, and finally, Martha sighed, set her knife down, and turned off the oven.

"Give me five minutes to wash up," she said.

"You don't have to come," Mary said. "We can talk to him and report back."

"If you think I'm missing this, you're out of your minds." Martha ran the hot water and washed her hands in the sink.

A few minutes later, they were in Mary's car, and Martha was in the passenger seat giving directions. As they pulled out of the driveway, Elizabeth saw the freshly turned soil of the garden plot.

"Mary?" Elizabeth asked. "Were you in the garden with a tape measure earlier?"

"Yep. Sure was." Mary pulled out onto Ronks Road. Elizabeth waited for her to go on, but she didn't.

"Were you measuring your rows?"

Mary shook her head. "Not yet. Bill is going to build raised garden beds for me."

Bill Richmond was a contractor and a good friend of the family, and Mary went out with him sometimes. "Why do you want raised beds?" Elizabeth asked.

"Raised beds are so much easier on your back. And this way, I can add new soil. Plus, they just look so cool, don't they?"

"And you were able to get Bill to agree to this?"

"He was happy to. He's coming over Tuesday to get started."

Mary asked them to tell her about their visit to McGees's earlier, and she was howling with laughter by the time they parked in the Mast driveway. Elizabeth noticed that there were several buggies parked by the barn. Abner must have visitors. Elizabeth felt a twinge of doubt. Maybe this wasn't the best time after all. But Mary was already striding confidently toward the house, and Martha was a few steps behind her, hurrying to catch up.

Elizabeth picked up the loaf of lemon poppy seed bread they'd brought, and she followed her sisters toward the house. The front door was just opening as Elizabeth stepped onto the porch.

"Hallo." A large woman with brown hair threaded with silver was looking at them curiously.

"Hi. I'm Mary Classen Baxter, and these are my sisters Elizabeth and Martha," she said. "We're friends of Rachel Fischer."

"Ah." That seemed to set her at ease a bit. "Are you the Englischers she said would be coming to talk to Abner?"

"That's right." Elizabeth nodded. How in the world had Rachel told them this already without cell phones?

"Come in." She stepped back and gestured for them to come inside. "I am Gertie Mast, Abner's mother. Leora Raber is married to my eldest son, Joseph."

Elizabeth knew that Leora was Rachel's sister who often came to the quilting circle that met in the shop. So this was Leora's mother-in-law, then.

"It's nice to meet you," Elizabeth said. "And we're sorry to interrupt."

"It is all right. We have finished dinner, and the men were just about to go out to the barn to do chores. Now is a *goot* time." They stepped into the house behind her. "Rachel tells us you will help find out who did this horrible thing."

"We're certainly going to try," Mary said.

They followed her into the kitchen. Fresh loaves of bread rested on the counter next to containers and baskets of every shape.

"Look at all this!" Martha said, looking around. "This wasn't here when I picked Rachel up yesterday."

"There is more in the fridge. And the freezer is packed too," Gertie said. "Our community has been very generous." Just beyond the kitchen was the small dining nook, where four people were crowded around a wooden table.

Gertie said something to them in Pennsylvania Dutch, and a young man stood up from the table. His arm was in a sling, and there was a bruise on his cheek.

"This is my son Abner," Gertie said, gesturing at him. "And this is my husband, Enoch, and our older son, Eli, and his wife, Rebecca, is there on the end."

"Hello. It's nice to meet you," Elizabeth said, and introduced her sisters.

"These are the Englisch ladies who have come to talk to you, Abner," she said. "They are going to figure out who did this to you."

Abner and his mom went back and forth in Pennsylvania Dutch for a moment. Elizabeth had picked up enough of the language over the years to understand that Abner was expressing hesitation, and his mother was encouraging him to trust them.

Finally, he nodded, and said, "I must tend to the animals. Will you come with me?"

That brought instant argument from his father and brother, and Elizabeth pieced together that they wanted him to stay inside and talk to her instead of heading out to the barn. Elizabeth had to admit she hadn't been sure how he would milk a cow with only one arm. Finally, Abner sighed, turned to them, and said, "They will handle the chores. We will go into the living room and talk."

Gertie nodded and smiled, and watched as they followed him into the living room. The three sisters sat down next to each other on the couch that had been piled with laundry just the day before. There was a table with a built-in propane lamp and a small side table. The windows were bare, and of course there were no family photos to make the space feel more personal.

"We're so sorry about what happened," Mary said when they were all seated. "How are your wife and son doing?"

"Abel is doing better," Abner said. "I was at the hospital earlier, and they say the surgery was successful, and he should be okay. And Miriam is eager to get out of the hospital. She says she feels fine and does not like being there. But the doctors want to keep her one more night, and I would rather she stay there until the doctors are sure she will be all right."

"That's wise," Martha said. "Better to be safe than sorry."

Elizabeth agreed, but she also knew that the medical bills piled up the longer they were there. She hoped the fundraiser Martha was working on would raise enough to help make a dent in the bills.

"I am hopeful they will both come home tomorrow." Abner shifted in his seat. "Rachel Fischer tells my mother that you have solved many mysteries." His voice was halting and his mannerisms awkward, and Elizabeth wondered if it was being alone with three Englisch women that was making him uncomfortable or if he was always a bit awkward.

"We do have a good track record," Martha said. "And we really want to help figure out who did this to you and your family."

"I am told that the car he was driving was registered to Adam Fischer," Abner said.

"That's right," Mary said. "And obviously we know that isn't true. Someone took his identity and opened up credit cards and bought a car in his name, and even showed his identification as his own when he got in legal trouble. We are trying to find him so we can put a stop to this and make sure he's punished for his crimes."

Adam didn't say anything. Elizabeth thought about what Rachel had said about justice. Was this really a "very Englisch way of thinking about it"?

"Did you see the man who caused the crash?" Elizabeth asked.

"A bit. I—"

"Hang on," Martha said. "Maybe we should start at the beginning. When did you first see the car?"

Elizabeth hated to admit to herself that Martha was probably right. Her mind was so logical, and that was often a much better way to approach a thorny problem. Still, it rankled just a teensy bit.

"We were returning from a visit to family," Abner said. "It is not far from here, and it is a journey we have made many times. But this time, as we were about halfway up that long hill on Cherry Hill Road, we saw cars come up over the hill. There was one in the correct lane and one in our lane coming right toward us."

"That's not a passing zone," Martha said, shaking her head.

"I do not know that he was passing the other car. They were going so quickly that I actually got the impression they were racing."

Elizabeth groaned. Of all the stupid, selfish, pointless things that could have led to this accident...

"Drag racing down the back roads of Amish country." Martha was shaking her head. She was obviously as put out by it as Elizabeth was.

"That must have been scary," Mary said softly.

"I believe the phrase is 'my heart stopped,'" he said with the hint of a smile. "I tried to pull off the road, but Self-Control would not budge."

"Self-Control?" Mary's eyebrow was raised.

"My father likes to name our horses after the fruits of the Spirit," Abner said with a shrug. "He had already gone through all of the more poetic ones."

"I love it," Martha said. "We could all use a bit more self-control. What a good reminder."

"It is too bad he is a very stubborn horse. He could use a bit more gentleness, if you ask me."

Elizabeth laughed, and then Martha gestured for him to go on.

"I could not get off the road in time," Abner said. "The driver did not see us until just before he hit us. He tried to brake, but he was going too quickly, and he hit the side of the buggy, toward the back."

"What happened when the car hit the buggy?" Mary asked gently. "Do you remember any of it?"

"I just remember a loud boom, like something had exploded. I do not remember much after that." He took a deep breath, and Elizabeth felt bad asking him to relive what had to be one of the most horrible moments of his life.

"Of course, my first thought was for Miriam and Abel. Miriam was thrown clear out of the buggy, and Abel was crying from somewhere behind me. But while I was trying to find them, I did see the driver step out of the car."

"What did the car look like?" asked Mary.

"It was silver," said Abner. "It was a small car, but I do not know anything about cars, so I did not know what kind of car it was."

"Did you see what the driver looked like?" Elizabeth asked.

"It all happened very quickly," Abner said. "I think he had brown hair, but I cannot be sure. He was Englisch, obviously. I do not think I could tell you any more than that."

"What did he do when he stepped out of the car?" Martha asked.

"He seemed quite stunned. Then the other car, the one he had been racing, backed up. It must have stopped when his friend hit us. The driver of the first car saw his friend appear, and then he jumped into the other car, and they sped away."

"They just drove off?" Martha had known that it was a hit-and-run accident, but it still seemed shocking to think about someone hitting a buggy and simply hopping in another car and leaving the mess behind.

"I suppose he knew he was going to be in big trouble," Abner said. "And if you are correct that the car was not registered in his own name, I suppose he thought he had nothing to lose."

They needed to find a way to see that car, Elizabeth thought. She had to find a way to get John to let them see it.

"Do you remember anything else about the man?" Martha's voice betrayed a tiny hint of desperation, and Elizabeth understood. So far they hadn't learned anything from talking to Abner that they hadn't already known. "What he was wearing, or anything that like?"

"There is one thing," Abner said slowly. "As he was getting out of his car, I thought I saw a word on the front of his T-shirt. It was the name Charles."

"Charles?" Elizabeth looked at Martha and Mary, who looked as confused as she felt. "Why would he have the name Charles on his shirt?"

"I do not know," Abner said. "I do not suppose that is some new Englisch trend, wearing your name on your shirt?"

"If it is a trend, it hasn't hit the middle-aged ladies of Bird-in-Hand yet," Mary said with a laugh. "It's not something I've ever heard of."

"Sports jerseys often have names on them," Elizabeth said. "But on the back."

"This was definitely on the front," Abner said. "And I know what sports jerseys look like. This was definitely not one of those."

"But why would he be wearing it on his shirt if it wasn't his name, and it wasn't a jersey?" Martha asked. "Isn't it even weirder to wear someone else's name on your shirt?"

"It's strange no matter how you look at it," Elizabeth said. "You're sure that's what it said?"

"I am not sure, no. This all happened in just a few seconds, and I was very shaken up and distracted. But that is what I think I saw. The name Charles."

"It could be a last name," Elizabeth said. "We should look into Charles as both a first name and last name."

"Okay. We'll see if we can make anything out of that," Mary said. "Anything else? Glasses? Hats? Distinguishing marks?"

"Nothing else I remember," he said. "I am sorry."

"That's just fine," Martha said. "Thank you for telling us what you do remember."

"I know the police are examining the remains of the car," Elizabeth said. "We hope there will be something in the car that will help identify the man who was driving."

"Yes, let us hope so." There was a look on Abner's face that she couldn't read.

"The police want to help, you know," Mary said softly. "They're not here to poke around into anything else. You can talk to them."

Abner was quiet for a minute, pressing his lips together. He seemed to be fighting the urge to say something.

"There is nothing bad going on here," he finally said. "The dogs are well taken care of. They have plenty of room to roam, and they are raised humanely."

"That's what Rachel told us," Elizabeth said. "And we believe her."

"Not everyone does," Abner said. "People want to assume that bad things are always going on right under the surface for the Amish. They read one story about an Amish man who raises dogs and does not treat them well, and suddenly they think every Amish person who breeds dog is running a puppy mill."

"We know." Mary was using her most soothing voice, the one she used to calm Martha down when she started getting worked up. "We understand. Maybe you could talk to the police in town? That way you wouldn't have to worry about them coming here."

"But you will be trying to find this man, this Charles, right?" Abner asked.

"We will," Mary promised. "We absolutely will. But the police have more resources than we do, and access to all kinds of tools that we don't have. And they want to catch the man who did it. Whether or not he's named Charles."

Abner nodded, but he didn't say anything.

"Think about it, anyway," Elizabeth said. "And here." She pulled one of the store's business cards out of her purse. "Please give us a call if you remember any other details."

"I will."

Elizabeth sure hoped he would, because right now, she wasn't at all convinced they had anything to go on. They would look into the name Charles. Beyond that, she wasn't sure where to look.

CHAPTER SEVEN

Mary arrived at the Lancaster Public Library a few minutes before it opened Monday morning. The red brick building was tall and grand, flanked with columns and topped with the words LANCASTER FREE PUBLIC LIBRARY. Mary had spent so many happy hours in this building as a child, before the smaller local branch had opened in Bird-in-Hand. As soon as the doors were unlocked at ten, she stepped inside and breathed deeply. She loved the way libraries smelled. Then she headed toward the reference desk, the place she thought she was most likely to find Kathleen, the head librarian she'd become friendly with.

Kathleen was squinting at her computer screen but looked up and smiled when she saw Mary approaching.

"Well hello, stranger." Kathleen took off the glasses that were perched on her nose. "How is everything going?"

"It's going fine, especially now that spring is just around the corner." They chatted about life on the farm and Kathleen's college-aged son's plans to move home for the summer, and then Kathleen asked, "So what can I help you with today?"

"Well…" Mary wasn't sure how to start this exactly. "Arrest records are public information, right?"

"Oh, this already sounds fun." Kathleen laughed. "Yes. They are public record, and you can find the original records at the courthouse, but we have access to the database through a portal on our computers here."

"Would you be able to show me how it works?"

"Naturally." Kathleen pushed her chair back and stood. "I hope this means you're working on another mystery."

"Yes." Mary laughed. "It's not for personal reasons, I promise."

"Hey, I don't judge," Kathleen said as she led Mary across the main floor and up a flight of stairs to a bank of computers labeled RESEARCH TERMINALS. Mary sat down in front of one of the computers, and Kathleen dragged a chair from a neighboring terminal and sat down next to her.

"You would use this database." Kathleen clicked on an icon, and a screen popped up with a lot of links. Kathleen clicked on a link labeled LANCASTER COUNTY COURTHOUSE and then a series of links to get to a search field.

"I never would have found that on my own," Mary said.

"You would have, with enough time," Kathleen said. "But I'm happy to provide the shortcut."

"Thank you." Mary looked at the screen. "What if I want to look into an arrest that happened outside Lancaster County?"

"Then you would go back"—Kathleen took the mouse and clicked on the browser's back arrow a few times—"and select the county you want to search."

"Thank you."

"You're very welcome. I need to head back downstairs, but let me know if you need any help."

"I certainly will." Mary thought for a moment. She knew "Adam" had been arrested for a DUI in State College, which was in Centre County. She decided to start there, and she found the right county tab and found the right search field. She then typed the name ADAM FISCHER into the search field and held her breath until the results popped up.

There they were. An arrest for Driving Under the Influence, in October of the previous year. She clicked on that link and found a PDF of the original paperwork that was filed when he was brought in. No mugshot, though. That would have been useful. Mary scanned the document carefully, looking for any clue that would give away his real identity. His hair and eye color were both listed as brown. Mary pulled a little notebook from her bag and recorded that. It wasn't all that surprising, since the real Adam met those specifications too, but now they knew for sure. His height was recorded as five feet and eleven inches. So, relatively tall, but so far, he seemed like a fairly average guy. Which wouldn't make it easy to identify him based on looks, unfortunately. She kept looking. The document listed the name of the arresting officers and the location where he'd been stopped, which had been a street in State College. Apparently he'd blown through a stop sign, and when he was stopped by the police, he had failed a field sobriety test. He had told the officers that he hadn't been drinking, but they recorded that they could smell alcohol on his breath. The arrest had taken place on a Saturday, in the late afternoon. Mary suspected that if she checked it out, she'd find that there had been a home football game that day—Penn State's football games were famously rowdy. But she didn't need to get distracted by checking into that right now. She looked over the whole document, but she didn't find much that would be useful in determining who the man really was.

She went back and clicked on the next link, which led her to a citation for public intoxication a few weeks before the DUI arrest. The police had picked him up at a home football game after he'd been caught urinating on the opposing team's bus. Charming. This guy was a real class act, Mary thought. The officers hadn't charged him with anything, but they had held him for a few hours to "dry out." The information recorded was the same: brown hair, brown eyes, five foot eleven inches, the same driver's license number listed.

A picture of what this guy was like was emerging with each piece of information they learned about him. But then, the kind of person who would steal someone else's identity in the first place wasn't exactly going to be an upstanding citizen.

Mary clicked on another link for a public intoxication arrest, but she didn't learn anything new. None of the entries contained information about what had happened after he'd been arrested, so she didn't know whether he'd been punished for any of the crimes. She had to imagine the DUI, at least, would have carried some kind of punishment, but apparently it wasn't enough to keep him off the road. But, again, the kind of person who would steal someone's identity wasn't likely to worry about things like suspended licenses.

Mary looked through all the arrest records and didn't find anything useful, but when she clicked back, she found links for other sorts of records. Hadn't John said something about a restraining order? She clicked on a few links before she found the right field, and then she typed Adam's name in. Bingo. She pulled up the document and scanned it.

"Adam" had been named on a restraining order that had been filed by a woman named Brianna Hartman in the fall of the previous year. Brianna said "Adam" had attacked her and then returned to her dorm room several times, and she was afraid to go out.

This guy just got better and better, she thought. But at least, with this new information, they had someone who had actually met the man pretending to be Adam. She printed out a copy of the report, and then, after searching through the files a while longer, she closed out of that database.

But there was another database she'd used before, she realized. This one contained vital records—birth, marriage, death. She opened it and typed in the name Susannah. Her sisters had told her about the letter Elizabeth found, and she wanted to know more about the mystery woman. Her fingers hovered over the keyboard. She didn't have any real information about Susannah. No last name. She decided Susannah was probably around the same age as Daddy, since the note said they'd grown up together. She entered a birth year range of five years before and after 1929, when he had been born. She hit RETURN, and hundreds of results filled the screen. She scanned them quickly but realized that she was going to need more information to narrow down her search before this would turn back anything useful. Any one of these could be her, and there was no way to tell.

She tucked the printout into her purse and headed downstairs. The shop would be open by now, and her sisters were no doubt wondering when she'd be back. But as Mary walked past the rows and rows of beautiful books, she had a thought.

It wouldn't take that long, she decided. Just a quick detour. She turned and walked to the bank of computer terminals lined up along the wall and pulled up the library's catalog. GARDENING, she typed into the search field. With the press of a button, she had the Dewey decimal number for the gardening books, and two minutes later, she was crouched down on the floor, scanning the three shelves full of books. *Beautiful Year-Round Blooms. Gardening for Dummies. The Week-by-Week Vegetable Gardener's Handbook. The Vegetable Gardener's Bible. Easy Container Gardening.* She would just take two or three, she decided, but five minutes later she walked to the checkout desk with ten volumes on gardening.

"Getting excited about spring?" the young man at the checkout desk asked with a chuckle. He scanned the barcodes, one at a time.

"Just a bit," she admitted.

"It'll be here before you know it." He pushed the stack of books across the desk toward her. "These are due back in three weeks."

"Wonderful. Thank you."

Mary hoisted the armful of books and carried them to the car, where they sprawled across her back seat. Libraries were the greatest invention ever, she thought as she started the car. They just let you take as many books as you wanted! For free!

Mary started the drive back but made an impulsive stop at a garden center outside of town. She knew she shouldn't indulge too much, but the potted rosebushes and the bright annuals were too much to resist. She wandered the aisles, eyeing the various seedlings, imagining them in her garden, and finally selected a few green bean seedlings. She'd start with these, and then later in the spring, once the garden bed was built and the soil prepped, she'd come back for more. For now, she needed to get back.

She continued home, and after she carried the books into the house, she went over to the shop. Elizabeth was helping a customer sort through the linens, and Martha was behind the counter, looking at something on the computer screen.

"Hi there."

Martha looked up. She had that dazed, confused look in her eyes that said she had been completely engrossed.

"What are you working on?" Mary asked, sliding behind the counter next to her.

"I'm trying to find a man named Charles," Martha said, wrinkling her brow.

"How's that going?"

"About how you'd expect." Martha let out a sigh. "It's one of the most popular names in the country. It means 'man,' but I knew that already because of Chuck."

That was right, Mary realized. Martha's husband had also been named Charles, though Mary had always known him as Chuck.

"There are more than two hundred students named Charles at Penn State currently," Martha continued. "And those are just the ones I could find who publicly list their affiliation with the university on social media."

"That doesn't narrow it down very much does it?"

"Nope, even if his name really is Charles, which, again, seems kind of unlikely. Most people don't exactly go walking around in T-shirts with their names on them."

"Maybe we should, though. It would certainly make things easier, especially at large gatherings. You'd never have to introduce yourself again."

"I suppose it would." Martha smiled and shook her head. "But unless our young man is ahead of the curve, I don't know how fruitful this line of inquiry is going to prove."

Mary stifled a smile at Martha's formal turn of phrase. It would only anger her sister if she laughed about it now.

"I was thinking I might run over to the Bird-in-Hand library at some point to see if they have yearbooks from Conestoga Valley High School," Martha said.

"That's an idea," Mary said. It sounded like something of a far-fetched plan to her, but she didn't want to discourage her sister. How would she know what to look for?

"I was thinking that if our Adam impersonator is from the area and attends Penn State, he most likely graduated from the local high school in the past few years," Martha continued.

"And you'll be looking for...students named Charles?" Mary asked.

"I'll look for students named Charles, and, well...students not named Charles too." Martha shrugged.

"Can I come with you?" Elizabeth asked.

Mary hadn't noticed that Elizabeth had come up beside them.

"Of course." Martha nodded. "Research?"

"You're looking for a Charles. I'm looking for a Susannah. I'm hoping they have really old yearbooks there."

"I hope you both find what you're looking for," Mary said. "I'll hold down the fort here." She lowered herself onto the stool behind the counter. "If it helps at all, I've discovered that our man has brown eyes and brown hair."

"Well then. That only narrows it down to *most* of the male population around here."

"I also found the name of the woman who took out a restraining order on him. It's Brianna Hartman, and she's a student at Penn State."

"Well, that is useful," Martha said. "She must know him. We need to talk to her."

"That's what I was thinking too," Mary said. "I'm hoping to find out more about her and hopefully talk to her."

"There's just one issue," Martha said.

"What's that?"

"The restraining order was filed against Adam Fischer?"

Mary nodded.

"In that case, Brianna couldn't have known him all that well, since she apparently didn't even know that wasn't his real name. But she would at least recognize his face."

Mary thought about this, and realized that was only one of the problems the restraining order raised. "Adam" and Brianna were both probably students at Penn State. But Penn State wouldn't have any records for an Adam Fischer...or at least *this* Adam Fischer. Was it possible "Adam" wasn't even actually a student? That he just lived in State College? Or did he have any real connection to State College at all?

"We need to talk to Brianna," Martha said.

"How about you make that trip to the library to find yearbooks," Mary said, though she was doubtful how much it would help, "and I'll see if I can find a way to get in touch with Brianna?"

Martha pushed herself up. "That sounds like a good plan."

Elizabeth and Martha's trip to the Bird-in-Hand library was fruitless, as it turned out. Martha had flipped through the yearbooks of Conestoga Valley High for the last five years and the only kid named Charles was African American, which meant he did not match the description Abner Mast had given. Either their man's name was not Charles or he went to some other high school, maybe one of the prep schools in the area. But the library didn't carry those yearbooks. Well, it had been a long shot anyway.

And Elizabeth hadn't had any more luck. The library did not have yearbooks going back to the forties, when Daddy would have been enrolled in East Lampeter High, the precursor to Conestoga Valley. And the only birth records she found after an online search on which Daddy was listed as the father were their own three. That didn't necessarily mean he hadn't had another child, though, Elizabeth knew. Susannah might not have necessarily listed him as the father on the birth certificate.

They'd returned to the house to close up the shop and eat dinner, and now she and Martha were gathered at the table while Mary fed the animals. Martha was staring at her laptop, while Elizabeth was working on her own computer, staring at a genealogy site, slowly entering their family tree into the website. She'd read many stories of long-lost family members being reunited because of those mail-in DNA kits that were so popular these days. She didn't really understand how it worked—something to do with how the computer alerted you when it located people who had DNA similar to yours, she thought. Maybe she should get one of the kits so she could see if there was anyone they were closely related to searching for matches too.

"How's it going?" Mary asked as she stepped inside and kicked off her boots. She closed the door before the cold air could come in.

Martha let out a sigh, and Elizabeth slumped in her chair.

"That good, huh?"

She took off her coat and sat down next to Martha, looking at her computer screen. "What are you doing?"

"I'm looking up Brianna Hartman," Martha said. "This is her Instagram profile."

"Wow. She really likes that pouty lips pose, doesn't she?"

Elizabeth scooted closer so she could take a look, and she saw what Mary meant. Nearly every photo was a selfie that showed Brianna making some kind of weird fish face. Still, she was a pretty girl, with long, honey-colored hair and striking green eyes.

"This is her moving into her dorm in the fall," Martha said, scrolling down the page. There was a picture of her in front of a tall brick building. "Hastings Hall, here I come!" was the caption. The next photo was Brianna with her arm around a girl with long black hair and the caption "Roomies!" A girl named Lynn Min was tagged in the photo.

"It's strange how much of their lives young people put online, isn't it?" Elizabeth said. "I don't even know her, and I know where she lives and who her roommate is and what kind of lipstick she prefers."

"As well as what she sleeps in"—Mary pointed to a photo of Brianna sitting on a bed in a T-shirt and flannel pajama bottoms—"and what she likes to eat." There were plenty of pictures of meals in the feed.

"I guess it's just normal for kids these days," Martha said.

"I guess," Elizabeth said.

"Were you able to get in touch with her?" Mary asked.

"I figured out the Penn State e-mail format and sent her a message, but she hasn't responded." Martha kept scrolling through the photos. They were moving so fast it was making Elizabeth a little bit sick. "But I'm thinking it might make sense to just go and find her and talk with her in person."

"I guess you know where to find her," Mary said wryly.

"Indeed. And I could also stop in at some more of the places 'Adam' used the credit card to see if anyone remembers seeing him."

"It's probably a good idea," Elizabeth said. "I'd go with you, if you want to take a day trip."

"Bill's coming to build the garden beds, so I need to stay here," Mary said. "But with the store closing early on Tuesdays, it seems like a good day for you guys to go."

They agreed Martha and Elizabeth would go tomorrow, and then Mary turned to Elizabeth.

"And how about you? Any luck?"

"Not so far. I'm building the family tree, but I think we need to get some DNA into the system to see if there are any close matches. If anyone who is a close match to the DNA joins, it will alert me, and hopefully I can make a connection."

Martha let out a sigh. Elizabeth knew she didn't truly trust these systems. Elizabeth had similar fears herself. But wasn't it worth the risk if it would allow them to find a half sibling they hadn't known about?

"I was thinking about Susannah," Martha said. "Trying to figure out who she might be. The note says they grew up together, right?"

Elizabeth nodded. She'd read that note so many times by now that she practically had it memorized.

"I was thinking, maybe she was someone from church."

"That's pretty likely, I guess," Elizabeth had to admit. They all went to the same Mennonite church that their families had attended for generations. Why hadn't she thought of that?

"If she was from church, there may be someone at church who might know who she is."

"Huh." Elizabeth thought for a minute. Louise Birdsall had to be in her eighties, and she'd been around a while. Would she have known a Susannah who'd grown up with their father? "I guess we can ask Louise if she might know."

"It's worth checking, anyway," Martha said.

Mary had picked up the letter and was reading it again. "Do either of you know what a dogwood looks like?"

Martha's eyes narrowed. "Don't they flower?"

That sounded right to Elizabeth. "They have pink blossoms, right? Or white?"

"I don't know what they look like when they're not flowering though," Martha said. "Just green, I guess."

"Are you thinking we might be able to figure out what tree they carved their initials into?" Elizabeth saw where she was going with this now. It was a good idea, but, how would they ever find the right tree?

Mary walked over to the stack of gardening books she'd brought home from the library and checked the index of one, and then she flipped to a set of photos of trees.

"You're right." She held out the book and they saw a picture of a thin, spindly tree covered with gorgeous fluffy pink buds. "This is what they look like when they're in bloom."

"And they look like regular trees when they're not," Martha said.

"Yes. But there is a dogwood nearby," Mary said.

"There is?" Elizabeth thought for a moment and then sucked in a breath. "There is."

"Where?" Martha was looking from one sister to the other.

"I noticed it last spring. There's a gorgeous pink flowering dogwood near the end of the driveway at the Fischer place, by the fence," Elizabeth said. "I didn't know what kind of tree it was, but I noticed those beautiful blooms."

"You don't think…," Mary started.

"It would be quite a coincidence," Elizabeth said, "that the first tree we think of would be the one mentioned in the letter…."

"But not really that much of a coincidence. The letter says they grew up together," Martha said. "Daddy grew up here, on this farm. So it doesn't seem crazy to think that Susannah might have lived next door."

"It doesn't seem crazy, except…" Elizabeth let her voice trail off. That farm had been in the Fischer family for as long as she could remember, just as this farm had belonged to the Classens. Which would mean—

"Was Susannah *Amish*?" Mary asked.

It made no sense. But then, none of this made sense. Daddy having another love before Mama. There being a…a baby. Daddy was such a strong, upstanding man. It didn't mesh with anything she knew about him. But how else were they supposed to interpret what was written in the letter? And if he'd loved an Amish girl…

"Forbidden love." Martha laughed a little. "It's the oldest story in the world, isn't it?"

"Now hold on," Elizabeth said. It was true that if Susannah had been Amish, they wouldn't have been allowed to marry. If an Amish person married an Englischer, they would lose their community and have to live in the Englisch world—and potentially be shunned. "We don't know that she was Amish. That's just a guess."

"Susannah *is* a common Amish name," Mary said.

"It's also a common Englisch name, especially at that time," Elizabeth said. "She may very well have been Amish. But let's not jump to any conclusions."

"Let's go see," Mary said.

"What? Right now?" It was almost dark.

"No time like the present, right?" Mary was already heading toward the back door.

"I guess we might as well." Martha shrugged and stood, and then she walked toward the door and pulled her jacket on.

"Grab the flashlight, Elizabeth, would you?" Mary was already stepping outside.

Elizabeth didn't know what else to do. She pushed herself up, grabbed her coat and the flashlight from the pantry, and followed her sisters out of the house. They were already in Martha's car with the engine running, so Elizabeth slid into the back seat. The headlights illuminated the gathering dark as they drove down the driveway, turned left onto Ronks Road, and pulled in at the Fischer driveway a quarter of a mile down the road. Martha stopped the car at the end of the driveway, and they all climbed out.

"Should we go to the house and tell them what we're doing?" Elizabeth asked, but Martha and Mary were already ducking through the wooden rails of the fence and moving toward the tree. Its spindly limbs were bare against the silvery sky.

Elizabeth used the big sturdy flashlight, while Mary and Martha used the flashlight apps from their cell phones to search the tree. They didn't even know what they were looking for, Elizabeth thought. Even if it was this tree, they didn't know where Daddy and Susannah had carved their initials, and that would have been more than sixty years ago. Would the initials still be there? Was this tree even that old? Was there any way to tell without chopping the tree down to count the rings?

Elizabeth was about to give up when Mary let out a cry. "It's here."

"What?" Martha was already scrambling over to where Mary was, on the side of the tree closest to the road.

"It's here." Elizabeth looked up and saw that Mary was pointing to a tiny mark in the bark about six feet from the ground. You could barely make out the letters, but when she shone the light directly on it, Elizabeth could just see it, even though the bark had twisted and become distorted.

HC + SF

"Susannah Fischer," Mary whispered. Elizabeth didn't want to admit it, but she had to agree that Mary was probably right.

CHAPTER EIGHT

Martha and Elizabeth set off early Tuesday morning. Martha was worried about leaving Mary alone at the shop for so long, but Mary seemed unfazed. The shop was only open until two today anyway, she insisted.

Martha took a sip from the travel mug full of strong coffee, while Elizabeth was sipping tea in the passenger seat. A cold front had moved in overnight, and the clouds hung low and heavy in the sky, with a brisk wind that made it feel especially chilly after a few warmer days. Temperatures in the forties could feel downright tropical in the middle of January, but after you'd started dreaming of spring, it just felt cruel to have to put on a heavy coat again.

"You're quiet," Martha said as they cruised down the highway.

"I'm just thinking," Elizabeth said.

"About Daddy?" It hadn't been hard to guess. Martha hadn't stopped thinking about him either.

"Daddy and Susannah. And Daddy and Mama. It's just so crazy, you know?"

"Well, we don't know anything for sure yet," Martha said.

"We do know that Daddy loved someone before Mama."

"It sure seems like that's true."

"And it's not even all that surprising, when you think about it. He was in his late twenties when they married." Elizabeth took a sip from her travel mug. "It would be strange if he hadn't loved anyone before then."

"I guess you're right," Martha said.

"But it's just this whole other piece of our father's life that we had no idea about."

"I suppose there are probably plenty of things I've never told my children about." Martha didn't have any real skeletons in the closet or any big secrets, certainly nothing of this order. But she hadn't told her kids about all of her youthful mistakes.

"He must have continued to love her, in some way, if he kept the letter all those years," Elizabeth said. "It's sweet and sad at the same time."

"He loved Mama too," Martha said. From the stories Mama had told her, they fell hard for each other and were married only months after they met. "I have no doubt about that."

"You're absolutely right," Elizabeth said. "They were deeply in love, even decades into marriage. But it's possible to hold on to feelings for a lost love while falling head over heels for a new one, isn't it?"

"Of course," Martha said. "You're right."

They were both quiet for a minute, and then Elizabeth said, "I like knowing more about him."

"I do too," Martha said, and the car went quiet, as if Elizabeth was also lost in her own thoughts.

Martha knew they were getting close to State College when Nittany Lions flags and bumper stickers started appearing on cars, houses, and just about every other surface. They had decided to start by looking into the businesses where "Adam" had used the credit card, knowing the likelihood that Brianna was in class—or, if Martha's own children were any indication, still asleep—was very high. As they got closer to campus, there were more students walking around and riding bikes. Surely they couldn't all be heading to the gym, Martha thought. So why were all the girls wearing workout pants?

Soon, they were driving through the streets of the campus, curving between imposing academic buildings and glass towers that had to be dorms.

"The bookstore is just ahead," Elizabeth said, gesturing toward the stone building in front of them. It seemed to be some sort of student union building, and the official Penn State bookstore was inside, from what Martha could tell. They found a parking space in front of the building—Martha wasn't totally sure it was a legal spot, since you seemed to need some kind of permit, but she decided she wouldn't be here long enough for it to matter. They walked into the building, threading past sleepy-eyed students in sweats and more workout clothes, clutching cups of coffee and hauling heavy backpacks. Was one of them the man they were looking for? There was no way to tell, but the idea that they could be walking right past him and not even know it ate at Martha. They found the bookstore at the far end of the building.

"Where are the books?" All Martha could see were sweatshirts and bumper stickers and mugs and any other kind of Penn State paraphernalia you could possibly want.

"I think they must be upstairs." Elizabeth was pointing to the second floor, visible over the edge of an open atrium, where you could just barely make out the tops of bookshelves. "Did the credit card statement say what he bought?"

"No, just that he shopped here a lot." Martha pulled the highlighted bills out of her bag. "There was one large purchase back in September. I'm betting that was books for the semester. And then there were about a dozen smaller purchases throughout the year."

"I would guess many of them came from that section," Elizabeth said, pointing to an area to the side that sold snack foods of all kinds, as well as coffee and sodas.

"You're probably right," Martha said. Now that they were here, she was starting to understand that this wasn't going to be as easy as she'd hoped. The chances that any of the clerks here would remember a particular student seemed laughably small. This place was crawling with students. "Where should we start?"

"How about there?" Elizabeth pointed at the registers in the snack area. She held her head up confidently, but Martha could see that she was as dubious about this as Martha was.

Martha started toward the snack area. Elizabeth followed and grabbed a bag of nuts and a package of pretzels.

"Sustenance," Elizabeth said. "Plus, this way we don't look quite so suspicious. I mean, we still seem out of place, but maybe not quite so much?"

"Good thinking." Martha followed Elizabeth.

"Hello," Elizabeth said brightly to the woman behind the register. She stared back but didn't smile. She simply took the purchases and scanned the barcodes. She looked to be in her forties, her hair scraped back into a tight ponytail. "We were wondering if you might be able to help us."

"Yeah?" Her face betrayed no emotion.

"We're trying to find a student who shops here pretty regularly."

The woman stared at them. She didn't say anything, but her face said she thought they were nuts.

"He uses a credit card in the name of Adam Fischer," Elizabeth continued, her voice unnaturally bright.

"There are forty thousand students at this school, and they pretty much all shop here." She hit a button on the register and said, "That's seven fifty-two."

Okay then. They weren't going to get very far here, that was clear. Martha handed her a twenty, and the clerk made change, a scowl on her face the whole time.

"Thank you," Elizabeth said, her voice again unusually bright.

"You have to teach me how to do that," Martha said as they walked away.

"What? Be nice to people even when they're not nice back?"

"Act cheerful even when you don't want to."

"You can do it. I've seen you," Elizabeth said. She looked around the store and her gaze traveled up to the second floor. "I think we should try again on the books level."

Martha wasn't sure it would do any good, but they were here, so she figured they might as well. The second floor was calmer—at this point in the semester, most students probably had the books they would need—and they approached the register. The woman who worked here, most likely a student, Martha guessed, was more polite, but no more helpful in the end. So many thousands of students had bought books here, she insisted, and she had no way of knowing who the man who had used Adam's credit card was.

They emerged back onto the campus, decided that they would try to track down Brianna before they left, and tried the other local stores where the credit card had been used.

"She lives in a dorm called Hastings Hall," Martha said, consulting her notes. They located a map of the campus on a giant placard and found a small square labeled Hastings, part of a collection of dormitories called East Housing Area. "Did you bring your hiking boots?" This campus was huge.

"Let's drive," Elizabeth said.

"You don't have to ask me twice."

Hastings turned out to be a tall brick building surrounded by similar tall brick buildings. Martha recognized it from the moving-in-day pictures Brianna had posted online.

"This is it."

The bare trees that surrounded them did little to break up the expanse of brick. They parked nearby and waited outside the door until a student came out. Then they caught the door and went inside. The lobby was dimly lit with fluorescent overhead lights that popped and hissed.

A girl with long brown hair was coming through the lobby.

"Excuse me, do you know Brianna Hartman?" Elizabeth asked.

The girl shook her head and kept going. They asked a few more students before one girl, hoisting her backpack on her way to class, directed them to room 204.

Martha thanked her and nodded toward the stairs at the far side of the lobby. They found the room at the end of a long hallway covered in stained industrial carpet. Martha could hear music playing inside, and after Elizabeth knocked, it only took a few moments before the door was pulled open.

"Hello?"

It was her. Martha had seen her face all over Instagram, and now here she was. The same long, honey-colored hair, big green eyes, and sprinkling of freckles across her nose.

"Hi. My name is Martha Watts, and this is my sister Elizabeth Classen."

She didn't say anything, just looked confused. Martha noticed that she was wearing tight black pants and a fitted T-shirt.

"You're Brianna Hartman, right?"

She nodded. "You left me a voice mail."

"That's right." So she *had* gotten the message. "We're sorry to barge in like this, but we were hoping you might be able to help us with something."

"You wanted to know about Adam Fischer."

"That's right." Martha gave her what she hoped was an encouraging smile. "Do you have a moment? We'd love to ask you a few questions."

She hovered in the doorway. "My dad told me not to talk to the police without a lawyer present."

"Oh, we're not with the police. We're just trying to help our friend Rachel Fischer."

Brianna still looked unconvinced, so Martha added, "She's Amish."

For whatever reason, that bit of information seemed to be enough to get Brianna to open the door.

"Okay. I have to leave for class in a few minutes." She looked from Martha to Elizabeth and back again, and then she seemed to make some kind of decision. "Why don't you come in? I don't really want to talk about this in the hallway."

She moved aside, and Martha saw that it was a narrow double room with beds against two walls. Two dressers and two desks were the only other furniture. Brightly colored bedspreads and rugs and photographs taped to the walls did little to alleviate the gloomy feeling in the space.

Brianna gestured for them to sit and then lowered herself into the chair at the desk and set her phone, in a pink sparkly case, on the desk next to her. Her roommate's chair was piled with laundry. Martha looked around and saw that the only other place to sit was the two beds, one made neatly with a magenta comforter stretched over it, and the other a messy tangle of sheets. She and Elizabeth both took a seat on the magenta bed.

"So...who are you exactly?" Brianna had pulled her knees up and wrapped her arms around them.

"We're friends of Rachel Fischer. Her son is Adam Fischer. He's an Amish man, and someone has been using his identity. We're trying to help her figure out who it is."

Brianna nodded. "I know Adam Fischer."

"Except the guy you know is not really Adam Fischer," Elizabeth said.

Brianna shook her head. "I don't understand."

"We're trying to figure it out ourselves," Martha said. "Maybe it would help if you could tell us how you know the man who called himself Adam."

"I met him…" She let her voice trail off. "Wait. You promise you're not with the police?"

"We promise," Elizabeth said. "We run a secondhand shop on our family farm in Bird-in-Hand. We're only here trying to help our Amish neighbors."

Brianna hesitated a moment and then nodded. "Okay." She took in a breath and let it out slowly. "Well, I met Adam at a bar in town last fall."

Martha tried not to let the surprise show on her face. This girl was a freshman. She had to be, what, eighteen? Nineteen at most? But Martha just smiled and gestured for her to go on.

"I noticed him as soon as I walked in. He was really cute, and I was with a group of friends, and they noticed me staring and encouraged me to go talk to him. So I went over, and I saw that he was just taking his ID back from the bartender. They always check, you know, because the police are really strict about it around here."

Adam Fischer was twenty-two, Martha realized. Which meant that anyone using his ID would appear old enough to drink. How convenient.

"I walked up to him and saw on his ID that his name was Adam, so I said, 'Hi, Adam. I'm Brianna, and I think you're hot.'"

"How did he respond to that?" Martha asked, trying to keep her face neutral. Things worked so very differently now than when she was younger.

"He smiled, and we started talking. He got me a drink, and we hung out for a while. We ended up leaving together an hour or two later."

Martha did not like where this story was going. She could sense Elizabeth stiffen next to her.

"I thought he was just being a gentleman and walking me home," Brianna said. "But it turns out that's not what he had in mind."

Could she really be that naive? Martha couldn't imagine it, but she seemed to be genuine.

"What happened?" Elizabeth asked.

"He started kissing me. We kissed for a bit, but then he started getting more forceful. Well, anyway, he wanted to come upstairs, and I said no, and he got really mad and started yelling about wasting his night with me and all sorts of horrible things."

"Charming." Martha couldn't help it.

"Yeah. He turned out not to be such a great guy."

Who could have ever seen that coming? Martha wanted to say. But she bit her tongue.

"Did he eventually leave?" Elizabeth asked. She was much better at being gentle than Martha was.

"Yes, when he started yelling, a couple of girls from the dorm came out and chased him away. We all kind of look out for each other."

"That's nice," Martha said. "I'm glad they were there for you."

"Me too." Brianna started picking at the glittery silver polish on her toenails. "Maybe it seems silly. I can see now that I made all kinds of assumptions. But I'd only been in college a few weeks. I thought he was going to ask for my number, and he'd take me out on real dates. But that's not what he was interested in. That's not really how it works around here, I've discovered. I just thought… Well, I thought now that we were in college, people would start acting like adults. But that's not what it's like."

Martha had heard enough news stories to have an idea that dating on college campuses was a far cry from when Chuck had taken her out to dinner and given her a chaste kiss at the front door of her dorm. But she didn't want to get bogged down in that now. She needed to get Brianna back on track.

"Was that the last time you saw 'Adam'?"

"No." She shook her head. "He came back the next morning, saying his phone was gone. He wanted to know what I'd done with it."

"His phone?" Elizabeth's eyes narrowed.

"Yeah. He must have lost it at some point. I have no idea where. But for some reason he was convinced I took it."

"Why would he think that?"

"My therapist has been helping me unpack that for months now." She sighed. "She thinks it's because he needed someone to blame, and I was the best target. But I don't really know."

"So did he just come that once?"

"No. He came back a couple of times demanding I give back his phone. He was scary, honestly, threatening to tell everyone all kinds of awful things about me. Finally, my parents insisted I tell the police and file for a restraining order. That made him stop."

"Did you tell the authorities on campus?" Martha asked. That seemed like it would have been the natural first step. It also would have flagged the fact that there wasn't a student at the university registered under the name Adam Fischer.

"My parents thought they wouldn't really do anything. They thought it would be better to go straight to the police." She continued to pick at the nail polish. "My dad's a lawyer."

Martha was sure her parents must have been frantic, worried about their daughter who was far from home. She could understand the impulse to go straight to the people with the most power to protect her. And if her father was a lawyer, that was no doubt the route he was most familiar with and the one he trusted. But it would have been so much easier now for Martha and Elizabeth if they had started with the campus police.

"What did it entail?"

"Dad called one of his college buddies, Trent, who is a lawyer here in town, and he met me at the courthouse. We filed the paperwork, and then Trent served Adam the papers."

"How did you know where he lived?" Martha asked.

"Trent figured it out somehow. I didn't ask too many questions."

So Trent had figured out where "Adam" lived but not that his name wasn't really Adam. Which must mean that whatever sources Trent had used had Adam Fischer's name listed. Whoever this guy was, he had really gone deep with this. On the upside, Trent knew where to find him. They needed to get in touch with Trent.

"Did you have to go to court?" Martha wasn't sure how restraining orders worked.

"Yes. He showed up and acted contrite, and he's so charming that he managed to not get in too much trouble. He's not allowed to come within a hundred feet of this building, and he has to stay away from me, but that's about it."

"And he managed to go through this whole process without anyone realizing that Adam Fischer wasn't really his name?" Elizabeth asked. She sounded as incredulous as Martha felt.

"I guess." Brianna shrugged. "I don't know. This is the first I'm hearing of it."

It seemed incredible, completely unbelievable. But it was apparently true.

Martha tried to think about what they really needed to know from Brianna. She was the only one they knew so far who had actually seen this young man up close. "What did he look like?"

"Like KJ Apa."

"What?" Was she speaking another language?

"Do you ever watch *Riverdale*?" Brianna asked.

"Do I watch what?"

"We don't watch much television," Elizabeth explained. "Is he an actor?"

"Only, like, the hottest guy in the world. Here." She picked up her phone and touched the screen, and a moment later she held up a picture of a young man. Chiseled cheekbones, dark hair and eyes. Handsome in a conventionally Hollywood sort of way.

"And the guy you knew as Adam looked like this?"

"Not exactly, of course, but yeah, he reminded me of him."

So they were looking for a handsome young man. That might be some help, she supposed. Martha didn't remember seeing anyone who looked like a Hollywood star in the yearbooks she'd looked through, but she could check again.

"Is there anything else you can tell us about him? Any distinguishing characteristics? Any details at all that might give a clue as to who he really is?"

Brianna set her phone down and shook her head. "I don't know. I can't think of anything."

"Do you have the address Trent used to serve him the papers about the restraining order?" Martha asked.

"No, I don't have it."

"Can we talk to Trent?" Elizabeth asked.

"Sure. I can give you his number."

A few minutes later, they walked out of the dorm with a phone number for Trent and a promise from Brianna to let them know if she thought of anything more that could help.

"She's young," Elizabeth said gently as they walked away from the dorm.

Martha hadn't even said anything, but somehow Elizabeth knew what she'd been thinking.

"I know." Martha sighed. "Were we that naive when we were young?"

"I hope not."

Elizabeth had already pulled her phone from her purse and was dialing the lawyer's number. The wind whipped through the courtyard, shaking the bare tree branches. Martha waited as the phone rang, and then, finally, Elizabeth got an answer. Martha listened while Elizabeth explained that they wanted to talk to Trent and left a phone number with the receptionist. Then she ended the call and turned to Martha.

"He's on vacation in Iceland this week and most of next."

"Iceland?"

"I guess he wanted to photograph the aurora borealis."

"Huh." Martha didn't know how to respond to that. "To each his own."

"She said something about glaciers too."

"So what you're saying is he's out of the office."

"I left a message, but she said he's not checking in."

"Did you tell her this is important?"

"I tried. But apparently, cell phone reception isn't great out on the glacier." She shrugged.

Martha felt frustration rise. Trent was the only one who knew how to get ahold of this guy. Could they try to figure out where in Iceland he was staying and call the hotel? There had to be a way to get the information from him.

"She promised to give him the message when he comes back next week," Elizabeth said.

Martha tried to keep her frustration from overtaking her. They were so close...and yet they couldn't quite get there.

"We'll tell John," Elizabeth said. "Maybe the police will be able to get the information from Trent's office."

Martha supposed that was true. Just because Brianna hadn't wanted to talk to the police didn't mean a lawyer would duck them. It was an option. Martha didn't know what else to do, so she just nodded.

"Let's try visiting some of the other spots in town where the credit card was used," Elizabeth added.

Martha nodded again, but this whole trip was starting to feel more and more hopeless. None of the clerks they'd encountered so far had any recollection of the guy who'd used Adam's credit card. And why should they? But they'd come this far, and she didn't know what else to do, so they headed back to the car.

"We're going to find something," Elizabeth said cheerfully. "At this next stop, we're going to find a clue. I can just feel it."

Martha could only hope she was right.

CHAPTER NINE

Mary had just finished setting up the cash register when Bill Richmond stepped in through the door of Second-hand Blessings.

"You made it!" Mary waved, watching him cross the shop in long strides. Years of construction work had made his arms strong, and the gray flecks that were just starting to tint his hair gave him a distinguished air. "Thank you so much for doing this."

Bill had quickly agreed when she'd asked him to build raised garden beds for her. As a contractor, this was smaller than the jobs he normally took on, but he had done favors for the sisters before.

"I'm happy to help. And I only have one request in return."

"What's that?" Mary had already decided that he would get a share of whatever produce she managed to grow.

"That you come to dinner with me."

Mary laughed. "Why do I feel like I'm getting the better end of the bargain here?"

"So that's a yes?"

"Of course. When?"

"How's Friday?"

"Hmm. I'll have to clear my packed social calendar, but I think I can swing that."

"Then it's all worth it." Bill flashed her a smile. When he smiled like that, he really did look like a young Harrison Ford. "Can you show me where you want me to build it?"

Mary looked around the shop. She wasn't supposed to leave it unattended, but there was no one here, and she wasn't really leaving, just going out into the yard for a minute.

"Sure thing. Hang on one second." She quickly scrawled a note that said she'd be back in five minutes, in case anyone came in, and then she followed Bill out into the yard.

The day had dawned cold and gray, with a bitter wind. It was one of those cruel days that reminded you that spring was fickle, and she was even more grateful that Bill was willing to help her even on a day like this.

"I was thinking one box could go here," Mary said, pointing to a patch of the tilled dirt. "And the other just a few feet to the right."

"That seems good. I'll go ahead and get started then."

"Do you need anything?"

"Nope. I've got my tools and the lumber in my truck. I'll just get that set up."

"Thank you. I don't know how to repay you."

"Dinner Friday. I'll hold you to that."

"I'll be there."

Mary laughed and headed back inside, grateful for the heater vents that were pumping hot air into the space.

"Hi there, Mary."

"Linda." Linda Martin was standing by the counter, holding a brown sweatshirt. She must have come in while Mary was outside. "How are you?" Linda was part of the crew that came by the shop most Saturdays to sell their estate sale finds, and it felt odd to see her here on her own.

"I'm doing fine." She pointed to the sweatshirt. "My granddaughter is a squirrel in the class play this weekend, and she needed something brown to wear."

"A squirrel?" Mary knew Linda took care of her grandchildren after school while their mom worked, and ever since her husband died a few years ago, she'd been very involved in their lives.

"A talking squirrel, apparently. She has one line, and she's been practicing it incessantly."

"What play is it?"

"I don't know. One that involves a lot of woodland creatures, I guess." She shrugged. "But at least I knew a good place to get a costume for not too much money."

"I'm glad you found what you need." Mary picked up the sweatshirt and found the price tag. She rang up the purchase and took the twenty-dollar bill Linda handed her.

"Was that Bill Richmond out there?" Linda asked.

Mary was ashamed that her first response was a flash of jealousy. She must have recognized Bill's truck. Why was Linda so familiar with Bill? But then Mary realized she was being ridiculous and mean. Linda had been married to Denny for decades, and even if she hadn't been, it was no business of hers if other women were interested in Bill. He was a good-looking guy, after all. Of course they were.

"Yes. He's building me raised-bed gardens." Mary kept a smile on her face to mask the flood of emotions that was coursing through her. She counted out Linda's change carefully.

"Mama had such a beautiful garden, and I'm going to get it going again this year."

"He fixed up our bathroom for us last year. He does good work."

"I'm glad to hear that." She handed Linda her change. "I can't wait to start planting."

"Oh yes. Deciding what to plant is always one of the most exciting parts of my year."

"I'm loving it. I'm about to place an order from the seed company, but I've got some green bean seedlings I picked up at the garden store that I'm eager to get in the ground."

Linda tilted her head. "Are you doing a hoop house?"

Mary recognized the term from her research. A hoop house was basically a makeshift greenhouse built from sheets of plastic. It seemed like a lot of work and overly fussy to Mary.

"I wasn't planning on it."

Linda didn't say anything for a moment.

"Why?" There was something she wasn't saying.

"It's a bit early to be planting green beans, isn't it?"

"It's almost April. I figured that was late enough." She slid the sweatshirt into a plastic bag.

"I don't want to tell you what to do," Linda said. "But I've never planted this early in the year. The last frost date for our area isn't until April twenty-third."

Mary had read something about frost dates in one of the gardening books she'd checked out yesterday, so she knew that was the date the Old Farmer's Almanac predicted would be the last frost of the year in a given location. Mary hadn't taken it too seriously.

"That's only thirty percent accurate, right?" She'd read that too, that it was just an average. Little better than a guess, really.

"Yes, technically." Linda took in a breath. "You do what you want, obviously. But I'd wait on the beans if it were me."

"Thanks, I'll keep that in mind." Mary appreciated that she was trying to be helpful. But Mary was pretty sure it would be fine. Spring was here. She handed Linda the bag and grabbed one of the flyers from the stack they'd placed on the counter. "Here, take one of these. There's a bake sale Saturday night to raise money for that Amish family that was hit by a car. Come on by."

"Isn't it terrible?" Linda looked down at the flyer. "This is a good thing you're doing. I'll try to stop by."

Linda waved, and then when she left, Mary looked around the shop. There was plenty to do in here. There always was. She could straighten up or dust, or she could inventory and price some of the new things that had come in in the past few days, but instead, Mary decided to sit down at the computer and do a little research. How hard could it be to find one little car?

The sisters pulled up at the gas station listed on the credit card statement, where the clerk was friendly but had no memory of a guy with chiseled cheekbones and brown hair. Most likely he had simply swiped his card at the gas pump like she always did, Martha thought. They asked about security camera footage and were told the footage was erased after three days.

"Adam" had used the card here several times, including just before the card was cut off, but that was long enough ago that the footage was long gone.

They went next to a convenience store a few blocks from campus. The card had been used at this store every few days for many months.

"There's a good chance he lives near here." Martha looked at the cracked asphalt street lined with run-down homes. What had once almost certainly been grand single family homes appeared to have all been chopped up and converted into student rentals. Sagging porches and overgrown lawns characterized most of the houses on the block. The barren tree limbs that stretched across the steel-gray sky made the view all the more depressing.

"But where?" Elizabeth gazed up the street. "There have to be hundreds of houses in the blocks around here."

"And most of them no doubt contain several apartments," Martha agreed.

"Do we just start knocking on doors asking if a guy with strong cheekbones lives around here?"

Martha let out a sigh. "Let's just go into the convenience store. If he comes in here regularly, maybe they'll know him."

The cracked linoleum floor and dim overhead lighting gave the place a run-down feel, but the shelves were stocked with items like organic protein bars and kombucha. This was definitely an area that catered to students.

The clerk, who gave off a distinct skunky smell as they approached, didn't seem to have any recollection of the man they were looking for.

"He came in here almost every day in the fall," Martha said.

"I don't know. Lots of people come in here." The guy shrugged.

Martha got the distinct impression that even if he did know something about "Adam," he wouldn't have said so.

They turned and headed back to the car and drove to the shopping center nearby.

"He really likes a store called Bonobos," Martha said, reading the lines she'd highlighted on the credit card statement.

"Like the monkey?" Elizabeth asked.

"I don't know. I guess." Martha scanned the names of the stores above the glass fronts. "It's at the far end."

Elizabeth drove through the parking lot and found a space near the store, and they went inside. The walls and racks were lined with shirts and jackets and pants in tasteful muted shades. They went to the register, and Martha prepared herself for frustration again.

"Can I help you find something?" A young man with a smooth head smiled at them from behind the register. Martha guessed he shaved his head, but it was hard to tell these days. In her day men had wanted a full head of hair, but these days they seemed just as likely to get rid of it all.

"We have a strange question," Elizabeth said.

"Hit me."

"We're trying to track down a customer who shopped here a few times," Martha said. "Have you worked here for a while?"

"Since I graduated last May." He shrugged. "English major."

"Well, that's wonderful. What was your favorite period of literature?" Elizabeth asked.

Martha only half listened as they chatted about Hemingway. Martha hadn't loved English classes like her sisters both had. She'd never been able to see the point of spending so much time studying the works of long-dead authors when there were real-world problems to solve.

"So, you're looking for a customer," the clerk said after he'd finished expounding on symbolism in *The Sun Also Rises*. "Can you tell me anything about him?"

"We think he's got brown hair and eyes," Martha said.

"And strong cheekbones," Elizabeth added.

"Okay..." He let his voice trail off. "Anything else?"

"He used a credit card with the name Adam Fischer," Martha said.

His eyes narrowed. "Adam Fischer?"

"But that's not his real name," Elizabeth said. "We're trying to figure out what his name is."

The clerk didn't say anything more for a moment. Something was going on with him. He recognized that name. For a brief moment, Martha wondered if *he* was the man they were looking for. He did have brown eyes and...well, who knew what color his hair was. He didn't look much like a movie star, but—

"I think I remember this guy," the clerk said. "I remember the name Adam Fischer."

"You do?" Elizabeth was watching him carefully.

"Yes. I do." He was nodding, as if things were falling into place in his mind. "I totally remember this guy."

"Can you tell us anything about him?" Martha asked. She tried not to let herself get too excited, but it was hard. Here, finally, was the first person aside from Brianna they'd come across who remembered him.

"I noticed the name first," he said. "I like to check the credit cards, just to see if they match up. My first week, we caught a guy using a stolen credit card with the name Marjory on it. My manager at the time spotted it, and when he asked him about it, it was clear he had no idea who Marjory was. Corporate has been all over us to reduce shrinkage, and they've really cracked down on stuff like that, so he was paying attention."

This was the first they'd heard of a store really trying to monitor theft, and Martha was glad to hear of it. Maybe they needed to start paying more attention at their own shop.

"What made you notice the name Adam Fischer?" Elizabeth asked.

"It sounds Amish," he said.

Martha hadn't expected him to nail it right off the bat.

"Ben King," he said, pointing to himself. "My parents were both born Amish. They left the church before I was born, but I have tons of relatives who are still Amish."

"Oh, wow."

"So you're very familiar with the Amish world," Elizabeth said.

"Yep. And when I noticed the name Adam Fischer, I made a joke about how we're the two most Amish guys in State College. I was just messing around. I didn't really think he was Amish. I mean, this stuff isn't exactly Amish style, right?"

Martha wanted to laugh at the idea of Silas Fischer, with his long gray beard and suspenders, shopping at a place like this.

"But instead of laughing, this guy just went off about the Amish, talking about how ignorant they are and how they don't know anything about the world. He talked about how dumb it is that they don't go to school past eighth grade. I tried to make a joke about how I'd just wasted four years of college racking up debt so I could study a book about bullfighting, but he didn't think it was funny. He was just...I don't know. *Nasty* is the word that comes to mind. He was just nasty about it. It was weird. I mean, I get that the Amish do some weird stuff, but there's no need to be awful about it, and he just was. I mean, that's my family he was talking about."

"What happened after that?"

"I rang him up and didn't really say a whole lot after that. I half suspected that the charge wouldn't go through, but it did. I thought about my boss's request that we ask for ID whenever we had suspicions, so I asked him, and he gave me attitude but he pulled out his license. It had his picture and the name Adam Fischer, so I had to let it go through."

"But?" Martha could see that he wanted to say something more.

"But I noticed the address on the license. It was in Bird-in-Hand. And I thought that was strange, because that area has such a big population of Amish. I thought it was really strange that he would have that name and be living right there and not be Amish."

"Turns out your suspicions were spot on," Elizabeth said. "We believe the guy you saw was using an ID stolen from an Amish man, and that he'd opened a credit card taken out in his name."

"Crazy." Ben's eyes widened. "Really?"

"Really." Martha nodded. "We're trying to help the real Adam Fischer find out who stole his identity."

"Huh." Ben had tilted his head and was biting the inside of his lip.

"Did you notice any distinguishing characteristics about him?" Elizabeth asked. "If there's anything at all you can remember, that would help us tremendously."

"I don't remember anything in particular," Ben said. "But I think I did save the security footage, just in case."

"You did?" Again, Martha didn't want to get her hopes up. But if he really had gotten a shot of this guy on camera, it could be exactly the piece of evidence they needed.

"I'm pretty sure I did." He nodded. "Our system only stores the footage for a week, so we're supposed to flag anything that seems odd and save it to the server, just in case. They go through this all in training, but this was the first time I'd actually had to do it, so I hope it worked."

"Would you be able to check?"

"Sure thing. Hang on." He held up one finger, and then he turned and walked through a door at the back of the store.

While he was gone, Martha turned and started browsing through the racks of clothes. Her son-in-law, Jared, might like that jacket, she thought. It was made of a nice houndstooth, and it was fitted in the style he liked. She walked over and glanced at the tag.

What in the world? That couldn't be right. But she looked again, and saw that she hadn't seen it wrong. She dropped the tag.

"The prices here are high," Elizabeth said, nodding.

"No wonder our guy had to have someone else pay for his clothes," Martha said.

A few minutes later, Ben came back onto the sales floor holding a thumb drive.

"Bingo," he said. "It's on here. I just rewatched it, and it's definitely the guy I remember."

He handed the thumb drive to Elizabeth, who thanked him.

"It's no problem," Ben said. "In fact, I'm glad to know that my sense wasn't totally off and that there was something shady about this guy."

"There was definitely something shady about him," Martha said. "We really appreciate your help."

"Glad to be of service."

They left a business card in case he thought of anything else he wanted to pass along. Elizabeth tucked the thumb drive into her purse, and they headed back out.

"Too bad we didn't bring a laptop," Martha said. "I'm dying to see what's on that footage."

"I am too," Elizabeth said, putting the car in gear. "I guess we'll have to wait until we get home, though."

"Well, is there anything else we need to do in town? Or shall we start heading that way?"

"I think let's head home."

They stopped for a quick sandwich at a local sub place, and then they started back toward home. They were halfway there, cruising down the highway, when Martha's cell phone rang. She dug it out of her purse. Mary.

"Hi there. Is everything okay?"

"Martha. Where are you guys?"

"We're on 22. We should be back in town in an hour or so."

"Well, hurry up. We've got to get going."

"Going where?" Martha asked. "What are you talking about?"

"You're never going to believe what I found out."

CHAPTER TEN

When they pulled up in front of the house, Bill Richmond was cutting two-by-fours on a sawhorse at the side of the barn. He wore a heavy flannel jacket and a beanie and thick gloves.

"She's got him hard at work," Elizabeth said, unbuckling her seat belt. "Poor guy, he must be freezing out here."

"He must really like her," Martha said. "To be willing to build garden beds for her on a day like this."

"I wish I knew how she did that."

"John is in the same boat, you know," Martha said. "If you snapped your fingers, he'd come running."

Elizabeth's cheeks turned pink, but she didn't respond. Martha climbed out and walked toward the shop, waving at Bill as she passed. Bill waved back and turned back to the wood. Elizabeth followed a step behind.

There were a few people browsing the racks of spring clothes, and Mary was helping an Amish woman sort through the bin of mismatched cutlery, looking for a spoon of a particular pattern.

Martha waved and headed to the register while Elizabeth went to see if the other customers needed help. A few minutes later, she'd rung up three pieces of tableware and two paperback novels that had been big a few years back. Then, after ushering the customers out the door, she flipped the sign to read CLOSED.

"So. Do you want to hear my news?"

"Of course." Elizabeth settled onto the stool while Mary leaned against the counter. "What did you find out?"

"I've been in here trying to figure out where the police might be keeping the car that 'Adam' was driving when he crashed into the Mast family's buggy. I understand why John can't tell us, but I just can't help thinking it would help me make sense of this whole thing if we could just see it. There has got to be some clue or something there. So I started out calling the East Lampeter Township office to ask where the impound yard was, but they wouldn't tell me. Then I tried googling it, but I didn't find anything."

"I don't imagine they'd put that sort of thing online," Martha said.

"I suppose not." Mary sighed. "Well, anyway, in the middle of all this, Bill came in, and he asked what I was up to."

"He probably needed to warm up." Elizabeth smiled. "He's out there working in the cold while you're in here under a heater." She gestured up at the heater vent that was blowing warm air down at them.

Mary wrinkled her nose at Elizabeth. "Actually, he wanted to ask what I thought of how he was joining the corners," Mary said. "But anyway, he asked what I was up to, and when I mentioned I was trying to figure out where the impound lot was, he said he knew."

"Really?"

"Hang on. Let me go get him, and he can tell you."

Mary turned and hurried out the door. A minute later, she came in, with Bill trailing a few steps behind.

"How's it going out there?" Martha asked.

Bill gave her a big smile. "It's good. I'm getting close to finishing the first box." He took the beanie off his head and ran his fingers through his hair to smooth it down. His gloves were hanging out of his pocket. "That heat feels good."

Martha gave Mary a triumphant smile, which she seemed to pretend not to see.

"It's so nice of you to do that," Elizabeth said.

"I'm glad to help." Bill had a day's worth of stubble on his face. He was handsome in an outdoorsy kind of way. "Plus, Mary promised me she'd share the bounty come summer."

"You have definitely earned yourself a zucchini or two," Mary said, nodding.

"And maybe a tomato?" Bill was smiling at Mary.

"One or two." Mary laughed. "Anyway, I was telling my sisters about the impound lot, and I thought you could tell them how you know about it."

"It's not really that great of a story," Bill said. "It's a fenced-in lot at the back of the East Lampeter Township offices, over on Route 340. Do you remember when they had a flood a few winters back? A pipe froze and burst over the weekend, and Monday morning they all walked into a big mess?"

Martha hadn't been living here then, and Mary was shaking her head, but Elizabeth nodded.

"I did a lot of the cleanup and repair work," Bill said. "So I was there a lot for the next few months. I asked about the lot at the back, because I was hoping to park there, but I was told the lot was for cars detained for evidence only."

"Now that you say that, I feel a little silly that we didn't think of that ourselves," Martha said. "The township office was probably the first place we should have checked."

Bill shrugged. "How would you know? You can't tell what it is from the outside."

"So wait. You're saying that the car used in the accident should be right there in the lot behind the town building?" Martha repeated, just to make sure.

"I can't say for sure one way or another, obviously," Bill said. He moved so he was standing just under the hot air vent. "But that's my guess."

"That's great news," Elizabeth said.

"So." Mary smiled at her sisters. "Are we headed to the township building?"

Like before, Martha tried to keep her hopes from getting raised. They would just go take a look and see. There might be a clue on the car, and there might not be. But it was certainly worth checking.

"Should we take a look at the thumb drive first?" Elizabeth asked.

"The what?" Mary looked from one to the other and back again. Martha realized that in all the excitement over the location of the impound lot, they hadn't told Mary what they'd learned in State College.

"Wait till you hear this," Elizabeth said, and she reached into her purse and pulled the small metal stick out.

"I'm going to head back out and finish that box," Bill said. "Let me know if you need anything else."

"Thank you, Bill." Mary gave him a big smile, and the look in his eyes made it clear that Bill thought it was all worth it.

While he walked toward the door, Elizabeth inserted the thumb drive into the slot on the side of the computer on the counter.

"We talked to a bunch of people in State College, and most of them didn't know anything about our guy, but the clerk at a clothing store remembered him," Martha said. She told Mary what they'd found out from the clerk, and a few moments later, a grainy black-and-white image appeared on the screen.

"This is inside the store?" Mary asked.

"Yes." Martha recognized the wooden shelves in front of the register, which had been piled with scarves and hats when this footage had been taken. "It looks like the camera is on the ceiling behind the registers."

"This was early January," Elizabeth said, pointing to the time stamp in the top corner of the screen. Martha checked the credit card statement and saw that the date on the footage matched the date of the purchase at the store. "At three o'clock in the afternoon."

A person was straightening a stack of sweaters to the side of the register, and though it was hard to tell from this angle, Martha thought it must be Ben, the salesman they'd met earlier. Ben looked up as a man approached the counter, his arms loaded with clothing. Ben turned and stepped behind the counter.

"That's got to be him," Mary said. "That's our guy."

A baseball cap covered much of his face, but they could see, even under his coat, that he was well-built, and judging by how he towered over Ben, he was quite tall.

"Can you pause it?" Elizabeth asked, narrowing her eyes.

Mary hit the space bar on the computer, and the image froze.

"Is there any way to zoom in?" Elizabeth leaned forward.

"Let's see." Mary used the mouse to tap the arrows at the bottom of the screen, and the man on the screen got larger. Martha leaned forward too, but even when he got bigger, he didn't come into any more focus. The angle of the camera meant that they couldn't see much of his face under the brim of his hat.

"What good is a security camera if you can't see the people who are on it?" Elizabeth sounded as frustrated as Martha felt.

"If he hadn't had the hat on, we'd be able to see more," Mary said. "But he also seems to be keeping his head down. Maybe he knows the camera is there and is trying to keep his face out of the shot."

He had been very tricky so far, so Martha wouldn't put it past him.

"He's hiding those legendary cheekbones," Martha said. Elizabeth snorted.

"Cheekbones?" Mary looked up.

"We'll fill you in later," Elizabeth said. She let out a sigh.

"You can tell that it's a Penn State hat. So that's something," Martha said. But even as she said it, she realized how useless that was. They already knew they were looking for a Penn State student.

"Let's play more," Elizabeth said. "Maybe he'll move or look up."

Mary hit the space bar again, and the images on the screen started to move again. They watched as Ben started to ring up the clothes and fold them neatly in a stack. Martha wished there was sound on the footage, but there was nothing, so they had to guess what was being said.

When he'd finishing ringing up the clothes, their suspect handed over his credit card, and Ben said something to him. Though they couldn't see his face, he shifted his weight from one foot to the other and leaned back.

"Ben said he asked our guy about the Amish-sounding name," Elizabeth explained to Mary. "And our suspect didn't have nice things to say about the Amish. I guess that's what going on here."

The two continued to talk, and it was clear that Ben wasn't pleased by what he heard the suspect saying. His shoulders tensed up, and his movements became jerkier. He said something, and the suspect dug another card out of his wallet—the driver's license, Martha guessed—and Ben consulted it before he handed back the credit card and then the receipt. The suspect slipped the card back into his wallet and tucked it into his pocket before reaching out to take the bag Ben was holding out.

Martha held her breath as he turned, hoping that they would be able to catch a glimpse of his face, cheekbones or no, but he kept his head down, and a moment later he vanished out of the shot. The footage played for a moment longer, and then the screen went black.

"Well, that was not nearly as helpful as I was hoping for," Martha said.

"No, it wasn't especially enlightening." Elizabeth sounded defeated. "After that drive, I was hoping we would have gotten something, but it looks like it was all a big waste of time."

"We can follow up with Trent," Martha said. "He knows where the guy lives. Hopefully we'll hear from him sooner rather than later."

"Who?" Mary asked.

Elizabeth pushed herself up as Martha explained.

"That's a real lead." Mary's voice brightened. "That's something we can work with."

"Yes, but he's in Iceland for the next week and a half."

"Iceland?" Mary's brow wrinkled. "What's the deal with Iceland? And why would anyone go there in March?"

"They like ice?" Elizabeth shrugged.

"Something about the aurora borealis," Martha said.

"Doesn't it get, like, two hours of sunlight this time of year?"

"I think it's a bit more than that." Martha shrugged. "But I suppose if you're going to see the Northern Lights, you don't mind a little bit of darkness."

"And glaciers." Elizabeth nodded. "Like I said, ice."

"Forget it. Sign me up for Hawaii." Mary pulled the thumb drive out of the computer and set it down on the counter. "Well, should we head out to the impound lot and see if there's anything there?"

"I think I'll stick around here," Elizabeth said. "I'm worn out from the drive."

She was more than a little frustrated too, Martha could tell. It would be good for her to have some time to sit and relax.

"Ready?" Mary was already slipping her coat on.

"Do you really want to leave while Bill is working out in the yard?" Martha asked.

"Oh, yeah. He'll be fine." Mary waved her hand. "Let's go." She held her purse and was ready to go.

"Okay. Thank you for holding down the fort." Martha looked at Elizabeth, who nodded.

They hopped in Martha's car, and it only took about ten minutes to get to the East Lampeter Township Building. It was a newer building made of brick, with a gabled roof and a covered entryway. It was surrounded by grass and, well, parking lots.

"So where is the impound lot?" Martha asked. There was no fenced-in lot that she could see.

"Bill said it was behind the building." But Mary sounded uncertain. Martha followed the road around to the back of the building.

"Is that it?" There was a small section of the lot surrounded by a fence just behind the dumpsters, near a back entrance. There was some sort of dark green plastic around the fence that shielded whatever was inside.

"That's got to be it," Mary said.

Martha pulled into a spot nearby, and they climbed out and approached the fence. The green plastic blocked most of what was inside from view, but there was a gap surrounding the opening of a gate. That must be what opened to let the cars through, she supposed. Now it was locked securely with a hefty padlock, but the gap in the plastic around the gate allowed her to peek in.

"There it is."

Mary was using her finger to point to a silver sports car parked near the building. The front end was crushed, and most of the windows were shattered. It was too far away to see much more than that, but it was the only silver car in the lot.

Martha pulled out her phone and started taking pictures.

"Make sure to get the license plate," Mary said, and Martha made sure she got a good shot.

"Let's see if we can get closer," Martha said. Mary started walking around to the side. There wasn't another break in the plastic until the very end, where the chain-link fence met the brick wall of the building. Martha peeked in, and Mary crouched down and looked below her.

"Wow." From this angle, you could really see the front-end damage. The metal had folded in like it was made of paper. The glass of the windshield had shattered and most of it was gone. Jagged edges clung to the metal frame, glinting in the light. Martha took more photos.

"He must have been going really fast," Mary said.

"It's amazing he walked away from this," Martha added. "I guess he's lucky the car had airbags." You could just see the white fabric of the exploded airbag resting on the dashboard.

"Too bad the buggy didn't," Mary said, shaking her head.

Martha had to force herself not to get angry. There was nothing fair about the fact that the man who'd been driving too fast in a vehicle registered under a stolen name had caused this horrific crash and walked away, while Miriam Mast had just come home from the hospital. But Martha needed to focus on studying the car and not let her emotions get in the way.

"Let's see if we can get a peek from the other side." Mary walked around the fence to the far side, and Martha followed. From this angle, they could see more of the crushed wheel well and the hood, which had folded in on itself, but if there was a clue here, Martha wasn't seeing it.

"It's too bad we can't get closer," Mary said.

"Maybe we should ask," Martha said. "The worst they can do is say no."

"Let's go around and look at the back one more time," Mary said, and started walking to the break in the fence again. Martha peered in.

"What's that?" Mary was squinting, pointing at something on the back of the car.

"What's what?"

"There's a sticker of some kind, just at the bottom of the back windshield."

Martha saw that she was right. But what did it say?

"Can you use your phone to zoom in?"

"Maybe." Martha aimed her phone at the back of the car and used the camera to zoom in. She took a photo and then pulled the phone back and took a look.

"Ves…Vespoli?"

"Ves-what?"

"I think that's what it says. It's hard to tell for sure." The sticker itself was clear, and the word was written in blue. There was a design next to it—it looked like some kind of curved *V.*

"Excuse me."

Martha snapped her head up, and she saw a man striding toward them. He wore khakis and a button-down, and though he didn't look like he was part of a security team, he looked like he meant business.

"I'm afraid I'm going to have to ask you to leave," he said.

"We were on our way out now," Mary said with an easy smile.

He watched them as they walked back to their car, and he didn't go back inside until they had left the lot.

"Would you mind if we made a few stops on the way back?" Martha asked. "To hang up posters for the bake sale?"

"That's fine with me," Mary said. "Where to?"

They stopped at the Village Bakery, the Bird-in-Hand Restaurant and Smorgasbord, the Old Amish Store, the Log Cabin Quilt Shop, and Greta's Coffeehouse, and the owners in each location were happy to let them hang the posters and promised to attend the bake sale. Hopefully they would get enough people to make it successful. Then they turned toward home. Martha let her mind wander, thinking through logistics for the bake sale prep—they would need to gather tables and tablecloths, a cash box, maybe a credit card reader—when Mary spoke.

"It's a boat."

"What?"

Mary was looking down at her phone.

"Vespoli. It's a kind of boat."

Martha thought about this.

"So he's a boater?"

"I guess." Mary shrugged. "I don't know."

"He would have to be. Why else would he have a bumper sticker for a boat on his car?" The police had probably already looked into this, but it wouldn't hurt for them to do some research.

"Turn left here."

"Here?" There was in intersection fifty feet ahead, but Martha didn't have a stop sign, so she hadn't started braking.

"Yes. Trust me."

Martha slowed the car quickly and flipped on her blinker. Thankfully, no one was behind them, or that move could have been dangerous.

"Why exactly am I driving like a maniac?" It was a good thing Martha trusted her sister.

Mary gave her a knowing smile. "I have an idea."

CHAPTER ELEVEN

Elizabeth was sitting at the kitchen table reviewing the footage from the security camera they'd gotten earlier. *There has to be a clue here,* she thought. Rationally, she knew there might not be a thing she'd missed, but she still had to look. It was the only real lead they had at this point.

She played the video again, pausing it every few seconds to study the details. There was the suspect piling an armload of clothes on the counter. There was Ben King starting to ring them up. There was the suspect handing over the credit card. There was Ben King asking about the Amish name. There was—

Wait. Elizabeth zoomed in on the image on the screen. What was that? She looked at the spot on the man's arm and then zoomed back out. She wasn't imagining it. Elizabeth took a screen shot of the image and saved it to the computer.

She may have just found a clue.

Martha pulled into the driveway and studied the sign on the old barn.

RANDY FERRIN, SHIPWRIGHT

"It doesn't look like he's here." Mary pointed to the barn doors, which were closed tightly. There were no cars in the driveway, and there was no movement in the house.

"Let's check it out." Martha climbed out of the car and walked toward the sign. "How do you know this guy?"

"I met him at that artisan fair I went to in the fall."

Martha vaguely remembered it. Something about booths and Mary selling some of her paintings. She'd had to be out of the shop on a Saturday at one of the busiest times of the year.

"His booth was next to mine. It was great, because he had a full-out wooden boat on display, so people kept coming over to check it out, and then they'd notice my paintings. I sold a few of them to people who came to check out his boat." Mary followed Martha, just a step behind. "We chatted during the slow periods. He's a nice guy."

Now that Martha was in front of the sign, she could see the smaller writing.

RANDY FERRIN, SHIPWRIGHT
BESPOKE WOODEN WATERCRAFT
OPEN SPORADICALLY

Beneath that was a phone number. Mary was already pulling out her phone. She dialed and held the phone to her ear while Martha looked around. The yard was neat, the barn and the house well-kept. But it was quiet. No one was here, that was clear.

"Voice mail," Mary said, and then she left a message for Randy, reminding him who she was and asking him to call her back.

"He'll get back to us," Mary said as she climbed into the car.

Martha nodded, but she didn't feel much enthusiasm.

When Martha and Mary got back to the house, Martha went in to start dinner while Elizabeth fed the goats and chickens and Mary went out to look over the garden beds Bill had finished. It wasn't until after dinner, when Martha was starting to work on the next day's baking, that they had time to catch Elizabeth up on what they'd learned at the impound lot.

"If the car looks like that, I can't imagine what the buggy looked like," Elizabeth said, looking down at the photos on Martha's phone.

"I assume it's not good," Martha said, then she looked down at her bowl. Had she added one cup of flour or two? She didn't remember. She sighed and dumped the flour from the bowl back into the canister and started measuring it out again. Martha loved baking and usually looked forward to this part of the evening, but she was worn out. It had been a long day, and she was having a hard time keeping her eyes open.

"The only real clue we picked up was the bumper sticker on the rear windshield," Mary said. She touched the screen to scroll to the picture that showed the small blue letters.

"And that's a brand of boat?" Elizabeth wrinkled her brow.

"From what we can tell, yes," Mary said. "We tried to find out more from my friend Randy, who builds boats, but he wasn't around. I left a message, so hopefully he'll call us back soon. I'm hoping he might be able to tell us more."

"And hopefully we'll get a call back from Trent," Martha said. She scooped up a cup of flour and leveled it off. She should be sifting the flour first, but she didn't have the energy right now.

"I also discovered something while you were gone," Elizabeth said.

"What's that? Did you find out about Susannah?"

"I'm afraid not. But I did watch that security camera footage again."

"You must have been hard up for entertainment." Martha dumped the flour into the bowl.

"I couldn't stop thinking there must some clue there that we were missing."

Martha wanted her to be right, but they had watched it pretty carefully. There was nothing there.

"Did you find anything?" The tea kettle whistled, and Mary hoisted it up and poured the water over a bag of chamomile tea in a delicate china mug.

"Maybe." Elizabeth set the phone down and turned to her laptop, which was resting on the table. "Come look."

Mary set the teapot back on the burner before she came around to stand next to Elizabeth. Martha dumped the second cup of flour in the bowl before she joined them.

"Look here." Elizabeth had frozen the video on an image that showed the man in the hat reaching for the bag of clothes. "See this?"

She pointed at the screen, where his sleeve had ridden up a few inches. And there, on the inside of his wrist, was a tattoo.

"How did you see that?" Mary asked.

"And what *is* it?" Martha thought it looked like a couple of lines joined at an awkward angle. It almost looked like a lower-case *h*, but with a tail.

"It's only there for a split second," Elizabeth said. "But I was watching really carefully. As for what it's supposed to represent, I have no idea. It looks like an abstract symbol of some kind."

"Huh." Martha leaned back and thought about what this meant. "So our guy has a tattoo on the inside of his wrist."

There was something niggling at the back of her mind.

"Unfortunately, I'm not sure how much that helps us, really," Elizabeth said. "Because I don't know how to figure out which of the 40,000-plus students at Penn State have tattoos."

"But it's better than nothing," Mary added. "It's something we didn't know before."

"Hang on."

Both Mary and Elizabeth turned to look at Martha.

Could she be remembering this right? It couldn't be....

"What is it?" Mary asked.

"I want to check something." Martha turned and walked out of the kitchen, down the hallway, and grabbed her purse, which was sitting on the table by the door. She dug out the credit card statements and scanned them. She could have sworn she'd seen...

There it was. She hurried back into the kitchen. Both Mary and Elizabeth were looking at her, waiting for her to say something.

"Get Inked," Martha said.

"What?" Mary wrinkled her brow.

"Can you look that name up?"

Elizabeth shrugged and typed the name into the computer. "It's a tattoo shop." Elizabeth looked up. "In Lancaster."

"He used the credit card there back in November," Martha said. She hadn't recognized the name, so she hadn't realized what kind of business it was until now.

"Wow." Elizabeth was trying to process this information, Martha knew. "We should tell John about this."

"But we were given strict instructions to stay out of it," Mary said.

Martha hated to admit that Mary was right. "Let's hold off talking to him until we have solid evidence."

Elizabeth looked hesitant, but she didn't argue.

"It doesn't necessarily mean that Get Inked is where this guy got the tattoo," Mary said slowly.

"But it's worth checking out, isn't it?" Elizabeth asked.

"Yes," said Martha. "I think it probably is."

CHAPTER TWELVE

It was a little warmer today, thank goodness. The sun was peeking through the morning clouds, and the forecast promised a nice day ahead, though it wasn't supposed to get up above the low fifties. Still, Mary was encouraged enough to start the morning on her hands and knees in the garden, planting the green bean seedlings in neat rows in the rich, dark soil. Bill had spread the bags of earth he'd brought from the garden center before he'd left yesterday, and now, the smell of the fresh dirt and the feel of it between her fingers felt so wholesome, so right. Mary could see now why Mama had loved this so much. It felt like she was joining generations before her stretching centuries back in time, coaxing food from the earth.

Once Mary had all the plants in the ground, she pushed herself up slowly. She might have to get those gardening pads for her knees, she realized. Being crouched down close to the ground felt good, but it also hurt her joints.

Still, it looked great to see those little green seedlings planted in neat rows. Soon, they'd start producing buds, and then the tiny start of the vegetables would follow. They'd have fresh produce all summer long. They'd save so much money, and tomatoes, picked fresh from the garden, tasted so much better than the kind you bought at the store.

And later, maybe this afternoon, she'd plant the seeds in the other garden bed, and soon this place would be a riot of color, peonies and zinnias and impatiens and dahlias. There would be fresh flowers inside the house and around the shop all summer long. It would be so beautiful. She couldn't wait.

With a sigh, Mary realized her time was up. For now, she had to get breakfast and get ready to open up the shop. She gathered her tools and her gardening gloves, and she carted them to the shed. Then she rubbed her hands together to brush the dirt off and headed into the house.

"It looks great," Elizabeth said, handing Mary a fresh cup of coffee.

"Bless you." Mary took the coffee and took a long drink before setting the mug down on the counter to wash her hands.

"I'm going to head on over to the shop to get things started," Elizabeth said.

"That sounds good," Mary said. "I'll be over in a minute."

Mary carried the cup of coffee upstairs with her and drank it in sips while she got dressed. She needed to remember to call Bill today to thank him again for the garden beds. Soon they would have plenty of fresh produce. She couldn't wait.

There were a few customers as soon as the shop opened, so Martha waited until the rush had passed before she drove over to the Fischer place. Luke waved as she pulled into the yard. Silas was hitching one of the draft horses to a plow. Martha could never understand why the Amish still dug their fields the old-fashioned way. Some things the Amish did—shunning technology, raising their own food, organizing their lives around God and the community—seemed like a dream to Martha, but plowing a field with a horse was so inefficient. A tractor could knock the task out in a day or two, instead of the weeks Silas and his sons would be out here this spring.

But it wasn't her business. The Amish could do as they pleased when it came to their farms. This fundraiser, though— Martha knew Rachel thought her way would be best, but Martha had done this many times before. She'd organized dozens of events at her church back in Kansas, not to mention Trish's wedding. They'd had more than three hundred people, and the whole event had gone off without a hitch thanks to Martha's careful planning.

Martha found Rachel hanging the wash on the clothesline at the back of the house. Phoebe was crouched down in the family's garden plot nearby, pulling out weeds. Rachel waved, and Martha walked toward her. This was one thing where the Amish had it right, she thought. The dryer was more efficient, but there was nothing like clothes dried in the breeze.

"I wanted to tell you about the online ads I have running," Martha said. Jared had showed her how to do this a few months back. "They're geo-located, which means that they're targeted toward people in the area."

"That is wonderful."

There was something in Rachel's voice she couldn't read.

"What is it?"

"Nothing. This is good."

"You're thinking something," Martha insisted.

Rachel paused, and then she said, "I am not worried that people will come. But you are trying to get the word out, and that is good. It is just different from how we do things. But that is all right."

But Martha could see that she was a bit bewildered.

"This is getting the word out to so many people," Martha insisted. "How will people come if they don't know about it?"

"They will come." Rachel smiled. "Trust me. They will come."

Yeah, because I'm getting the word out, she thought. But she bit her tongue.

"I have good news," Rachel said brightly. "Abel is home from the hospital."

"That *is* good news."

"He is still in pain, and it will be some time before he is running around like a little boy again, but the doctors say he will make a full recovery."

"I am so glad." And then Martha added, "And it means it's more important than ever that we make a lot of money for the family on Saturday night."

Rachel nodded, but then she changed the subject. "How did your trip to State College go yesterday?"

"Oh. I haven't told you." Martha updated her on everything they'd learned yesterday, from talking with Brianna to the video footage to the tattoo to the sticker on the back of the crashed car.

"Vespoli is the name of a boat maker?" Rachel's eyebrows rose.

"That's what the internet tells us."

"Well, the internet is never wrong," Rachel said with a smile. "And you can always trust Siri. That is one thing I have heard many times."

Martha laughed. "I'm not sure that's quite accurate." How did Rachel know about Siri?

"Mary is trying to find out more from a boat maker she knows in the area. Hopefully he'll be able to tell us more."

"I wish I was able to help you there. I do not know too many Amish who are into boating."

"No, I suppose not."

"So where is this tattoo parlor?"

"It's in Lancaster. We're planning to swing by there today to see if they remember this tattoo or this guy."

"Are they open now?"

Martha looked at her watch. It was almost eleven. "I'd have to call to find out."

"If it is open, I would like to go with you to ask them about this man."

"Really?"

"Why should you and your sisters get to have all the fun?" Rachel was smiling, and Martha let out a laugh.

"Let me check." Martha pulled out her phone and found the phone number for the shop. She called and got a recording that said they opened at eleven.

"But the time we get there, they'll be open."

"Then we will go."

"Okay." Martha wasn't going to argue.

Soon they were driving down the road, the naked tree branches flying past. For the first few miles, Martha enjoyed the peaceful hum of the motor. But then she thought of something. Would Rachel know anything about the mysterious Susannah Daddy had loved? Rachel hadn't grown up on the Fischer farm. She'd moved there when she married Silas. But if Susannah had been a part of the Fischer family, it was possible Rachel knew of her or had met her.

"Do you know of someone named Susannah Fischer?" Martha asked.

"I knew three Susannah Fischers." Rachel smiled. "Which one are you asking about?"

Martha laughed. "I'm looking for the one who was probably in her late teens or early twenties in 1950."

"Oh. In that case, I do not know. I am sorry." Rachel adjusted in her seat. "Is she related to Silas's family?"

"I'm guessing so, but I don't know for sure," Martha said. "Elizabeth found a note in one of Daddy's coat pockets." Martha went on to explain what they discovered, including finding the initials carved into the tree.

Rachel chuckled. "You three were out there with flashlights two nights ago?"

"Yes, we were. I'm sorry, we should have come to the house to ask, but we didn't think it would disturb anyone."

"It is all right," Rachel said. "I do not mind. It is just that Thomas told me there were strange lights at the end of the road, and I told him to go back to bed. I thought he was just trying to get out of going to sleep."

"Whoops." Martha slowed as they came up to a STOP sign. "I guess we owe poor Thomas an apology in that case."

Rachel shrugged. "It is all right. I guess I should have checked. It is possible he does tell the truth occasionally."

Martha remembered the struggle of getting little ones to bed, especially after the time had recently changed. This Amish community observed Daylight Savings, though Martha knew some communities did not.

"So you think that your father might have been in love with someone named Susannah Fischer who lived on our farm?"

"That's our current theory," Martha said. "And there's more. From the letter we found, it sounds like there might have been a baby."

Martha wasn't sure what kind of response she'd been expecting from Rachel, but it wasn't the knowing nod Rachel was giving now.

"You're not surprised by that?" Martha asked.

"I do not know." Rachel let out a long breath. "On the one hand, I would be surprised that your father would keep a brother or sister from you for so long. He was a good, upstanding man, and that seems completely out of character for him."

"And on the other hand?" The traffic was getting heavier as they got to the outskirts of Lancaster, and the fields and trees gave way to warehouse buildings and stoplights.

"These things happen more than anyone likes to admit. That is not to say that I approve, just that we need to be realistic that this kind of thing is actually quite common, and it does not do anyone any good to pretend otherwise."

Martha wasn't sure what to say. Rachel was right, of course. Babies were born out of wedlock all the time. But she hadn't expected this answer from her Amish neighbor.

"You are surprised," Rachel said.

Martha nodded.

"Our community has many of the same problems that the Englisch world does," she said. "It may not be obvious from the outside, but unexpected babies are something we have dealt with as well."

"What happens in your community when someone turns up pregnant when they aren't supposed to be?" Martha asked.

"It is the same as with any other sin. They confess and repent, and they are welcomed back into the community."

"They aren't married quickly to prevent scandal?"

"Oh yes. Certainly that happens more times than not. But still, when the baby shows up before nine months of marriage, the community welcomes the child as it would any other."

"So if a baby had been born to Susannah…"

"Someone would know about it, certainly," Rachel said. She paused for a moment and then said, "We could ask Anke."

"That's an idea." Anke, Silas's mother, lived in the dawdy haus on the Fischer property. She had come to live at the farm when she had married Silas's father, Paul, many years before. "Would she have known Susannah?"

"I do not know. But she is the most likely of anyone I can think of to be able to tell us who she was and what happened to her. Would you like me to ask her to talk with you?"

"That would be wonderful," Martha said.

"I will talk to her when we get home."

They were only a few blocks from the tattoo parlor, which was in a part of town that Martha knew was considered up-and-coming. There were cute shops and cafés mixed in with industrial warehouses and tire shops. Get Inked was housed in a storefront on the first floor of a residential building, squashed in between a vegan bakery and an auto repair shop.

"That is convenient. You can eat vegan cupcakes while you get your car fixed," Rachel joked.

"I will never understand baking without butter and eggs," Martha said. "What's the point?"

"Even people who cannot have eggs or butter like to have a treat sometimes."

Martha supposed she was right.

"Shall we?" Rachel pointed toward the door of the tattoo parlor.

"I'll follow you."

Martha had never been inside a tattoo shop before, and she felt certain Rachel hadn't either, but Rachel pushed the door open and strode in like she owned the place. When Martha stepped in behind her, she found a neat shop with lots of exposed brick and polished wood, and a man with a handlebar mustache and a ponytail sitting behind the counter. He was looking at Rachel with wide eyes.

"Hallo," Rachel said with a smile. "How are you this fine morning?"

"I'm—I'm good." The man sat up straight as he stumbled over his words.

To be fair, he probably didn't get too many Amish in here. "I'm Martha Classen Watts," Martha said, holding out her hand. He looked from Rachel to Martha and back again. Then again, he probably didn't get too many women in their fifties either.

"And I am Rachel Fischer."

"Stu." He shook each of their hands, and then, recovering himself, asked, "And what I can help you with today?"

Martha noticed that there were framed posters with different designs on the walls, as well as thick binders that she assumed were full of suggested designs.

"We are hoping you might be able to help us with something," Rachel said.

Stu nodded. "We have some great new designs, if you want to check them out." Martha couldn't tell if he was joking or not.

"Now that is tempting," Rachel said. "But I am afraid that is not exactly what we had in mind."

"We were actually wondering if you might recognize a tattoo," Martha said. She had pulled her phone out and was opening her photo app. She'd saved the still from the video as a photo, and she held it out now. "We know this man used a credit card here back in November, and we're trying to find anyone who remembers anything about him."

"Are you guys police or something?" Stu asked.

Rachel looked at Martha and laughed. "Now that would be a good idea. The Amish police force."

"I'm afraid it's nothing as exciting as that," Martha said. "The man in this photo stole her son's identity"—she pointed to Rachel—"and we're just doing some detective work on our own."

"Stole his identity?" Stu seemed at a loss. "Isn't your son…"

"Amish." Rachel nodded. "And someone has stolen his driver's license and his social security number, and used a credit card in his name here."

"Right." It was clear that Stu didn't understand, but he must have decided not to pursue it. "So, you're looking for this guy?" He looked down at the image on Martha's phone.

"That's right," Martha said. "You can't really see his face, but we thought you might be able to recognize the tattoo."

"Huh." Stu took the phone and used two fingers to enlarge the image. "Well, I think I recognize the tattoo. Unfortunately, it's a very common design." He pressed his lips together. "Let me see if my coworker can help." He pushed himself up and walked to a door that led to the back of the shop—where the tattoos were actually done, she assumed—and ducked his head inside. Martha couldn't imagine that random group of lines was actually a popular tattoo, but then she didn't understand a lot about tattoos, apparently. A moment later, Stu came back, followed by a girl in a black T-shirt with the sleeves cut off. She had tattoos all the way up both arms, and a stud in her chin, just below her lip.

"Mel, Rachel and Martha. Rachel and Martha, my coworker, Mel."

Mel did a double take when she saw Rachel's long blue dress and apron, but she recovered quickly. Stu explained the situation, and Mel nodded.

"Stu is right that this is a common design," Mel said. "It's the Chinese symbol for strength, which, as you would imagine, is pretty appealing."

Martha just kept smiling. "Have you done many of these?"

"Yeah, probably a half dozen or so in the last year," Mel said.

"Any on the inside of the wrist?" Martha asked. It seemed a memorable spot to give a tattoo. She couldn't even imagine how much it must have hurt.

"I haven't done any there," Mel said.

"We don't know for sure that this is the tattoo he received here at this store," Martha said. "But we do know that he used a credit card here."

"So it could have been another design?" Mel asked.

"It could," Martha admitted. "We don't really know much beyond the fact that he used the card here. We just thought…"

"It makes sense," Mel said. "Well, I can tell you that I didn't do that symbol on an inside wrist any time in the last year."

"And I just work the front desk," Stu said before Martha could ask. "But there are three other people who do designs. We could ask them."

"Jase has only been working here since January," Mel said.

"Right. So we'd have to track down Will, who he replaced. And Billy and Irving."

"Would that be possible?" Martha smiled as sweetly as she could. "We'd really love to find this man."

"You don't keep records of tattoos done, do you?" Rachel asked.

"I'm afraid not." Stu shook his head.

"And you don't recognize him?" Martha asked.

Stu looked back down at the image on the phone. "I don't."

Mel was looking at it, narrowing her eyes. "He goes to Penn State?"

"That's what we assume," Martha said. "And there's a chance his name is Charles."

"Huh."

Martha waited, hoping Mel would elaborate on that.

"What?" Stu was looking at her, waiting for more.

"I was just thinking. He looks like this guy I went to high school with. His name was Charlie Mathis."

"What do you mean he looks like him? You can't even see his face in this photo." Stu shook his head.

"He just, I don't know, has the same kind of presence as Charlie."

"The same presence?" Martha repeated it, trying to make sense of it.

Stud shifted on his stool.

"Where did you go to high school?" Martha asked.

"A private school on the north side of town."

That could explain why he hadn't appeared in the local public high school's yearbook.

"Does Charlie have a tattoo like this?" Rachel asked.

"I don't know." Mel let out a breath. "Look, maybe it's not him. But you asked, and said the name Charles, and he kind of reminds me of a guy I know named Charlie who goes to Penn State. So I thought it was worth mentioning."

"Thank you," Martha said. "We appreciate it, and we'll look into it." It seemed a bit tenuous to her, but at this point, she wasn't going to turn down any kind of clue.

"Thank you for your help," Rachel said.

"And if you can ask those other people whether they remember doing this particular tattoo, we really would appreciate it,"

Martha added. She left a business card from the store, and Stu promised to be in touch.

By the time Martha dropped Rachel off at home, she had a plan for how to find out more about this Charlie Mathis. If he had anything to do with this, she would find him.

Mary had taken advantage of Martha's absence to do some baking. She knew Martha loved Mama's German chocolate cake, but she wasn't as quick as Martha was, and it took longer than she'd planned to get the cake in the oven. She hoped it would be finished baking by the time Martha got back. For now, though, the cake was in the oven, and after she cleaned up the kitchen, she picked up her phone.

The first number she called was Trent's, but the receptionist at his law office informed her that he was still unreachable and that she would pass along the message when he got back. Then she called Felicity again, with no answer, and Randy Ferrin, her boat maker friend again, but he didn't answer either. Why wasn't anyone picking up their phones?

Mary set her phone down and sighed. It seemed that with every new piece of information they found, they got further away from answers.

The house smelled different when Martha walked inside. Sweet, like someone had been baking. But the oven was off, and there was nothing in the oven or cooling on the counter. It must be left over from the baking she'd done the night before.

She knew she should head over to the shop and relieve Elizabeth and Mary, but it would only take a moment to do a quick search and see what she could find out about Charlie Mathis. She sat down in front of her computer and opened a browser window. A reminder popped up on her calendar, alerting her that tomorrow was her birthday. As if she might forget.

She typed the name Charlie Mathis into the browser window. The first thing that popped up was a link to a profile for a Charles Mathis on some kind of corporate site. Martha clicked on it and saw that it was a profile of a man in his fifties who was a partner at a law firm in Lancaster. This might be the father of the guy she was looking for, she thought.

She clicked back to the search page and sorted through more results—posts of Charles Jr.'s golf scores in local competitions, newspaper articles about cases he was cited in—before she added the search term "III" and found an Instagram page for Charlie Mathis, who was, according to his profile, a senior at Penn State.

Martha scrolled through the photos he'd posted. Charlie appeared in a few of the pictures, and Martha noted that he was tall and had brown hair. His cheekbones weren't especially notable, but she supposed it could be the same guy who had appeared in the security camera footage. It was hard to say whether he had the same, well, "presence" as the guy they were looking for. Martha wasn't even sure what that meant. But scrolling through the photos he'd posted, she did learn about him.

Charles Mathis III seemed to be interested in art and had posted photos of different art galleries he'd visited, as well as shots showing what he was working on in his own studio. Martha didn't necessarily love the art itself—lots of splatters that looked accidental, if you asked her—but she did like to see a young man interested in the arts. He had also taken pictures of interesting shadows and sunsets, and she was starting to think that she must have made too many assumptions about college kids. Well, there it was. Mixed in with his artfully shot images, there was a shirtless selfie. Why did young people feel the need to show off so much skin?

Still, there was little left to the imagination, which made it easy to see that Charlie did not have a tattoo on his inner wrist. It was not him.

Martha let out a long breath and closed the laptop. The connection had been dubious, at best. She was grasping at straws. But she hadn't realized how much she'd been hoping that this, finally, would be the clue that would point them in the right direction. They were running out of leads. She didn't have any idea where to turn next.

CHAPTER THIRTEEN

When Martha came downstairs Thursday morning, she was surprised to see both of her sisters already up and moving around in the kitchen. The sun was barely up, but Martha had woken up and hadn't been able to go back to sleep, so she had come downstairs to start the coffee. But she could smell that the coffee was already brewing as she got to the bottom step.

"Wait, you're not supposed to be awake yet," Mary called as she stepped into the living room.

"We're bringing you breakfast in bed." Elizabeth was loading a jug of cream and a bowl of sugar on a wooden tray.

"Oh, you guys. That's sweet. But it's totally not necessary."

"Well, now that you're downstairs it's not," Mary said. "But we were hoping to surprise you."

"Since you're already down here anyway, you might as well come over here and eat at the table." Elizabeth set the tray down at Martha's place, and Martha saw that there were packages wrapped in pretty pink paper and topped with bows. "Happy birthday!"

"You didn't have to do this." But even as she said the words, Martha felt pleasure wash over her.

"Of course we did. How often do you have a birthday?" Mary said. She gestured for Martha to sit down.

"It happens every year, actually," Martha said.

Mary set a cup of coffee down next to the tray. "That's rare enough that we can celebrate you. Come. Sit. Eat."

"This is really sweet." Martha obediently lowered herself into her chair. They'd made cornmeal pancakes and scrambled eggs, and they'd even cut up fruit to go with it. "Thank you for remembering."

"Of course we remembered." Elizabeth sat down with a mug of steaming coffee. "Now eat. And open your presents."

"She can't do both at the same time," Mary said.

"Oh yes I can." Martha poured real maple syrup from the jug on the table and then cut off a piece of pancake and popped it in her mouth. It was warm and sweet and buttery.

"These are so good," she said after she'd swallowed.

"Presents." Mary gestured at the pink boxes.

Martha unwrapped a soft wool sweater from Mary and a new set of baking trays from Elizabeth. There was a card from Craig and Molly that had a gift card inside. Practical and useful.

"That one's from Kyle," Mary said, pointing to the square, flat box wrapped in light blue paper. Martha tore the paper off and saw that it was a plaster cast handprint from her grandson Mick.

"Isn't that precious?" Martha held it up and pictured the sweet two-year-old. He had brown hair in gorgeous curls that Laura couldn't bring herself to cut, and he had the shyest little smile.

"One more." Elizabeth held out a padded mailing envelope. Inside were handmade cards from Martha's daughter

Trish's kids, Elliot and Celeste, as well as a box of stationery monogrammed with her initials.

"That's really nice," Elizabeth said, and Martha nodded, biting her lip. They were all such thoughtful gifts, and made her feel so loved.

"Thank you," she said. "What a nice way to start the day."

"Now finish your breakfast," Mary said, looking down at Martha's plate. "The pancakes are no good when they're cold."

Martha took another bite. "Wrong. They're still delicious."

Mary and Elizabeth insisted she couldn't help with cleaning up the kitchen or barn chores, and Martha used a few quiet moments to use her new stationery to write thank-you notes.

Soon enough, it was time to open the shop, but just as Martha was pulling on her coat to head across the yard, Mary appeared.

"Guess what?"

"I can't even begin to guess." With Mary, it really could be anything. The day was cold, and the wind had a raw edge to it. The weather forecast had said there was a storm moving in tonight.

"I got a call from Randy Ferrin."

"The boat maker?"

"That's right. He was out of town visiting his son and grandchildren, but he's back, and he said he'd be around this morning."

"Did you ask him about Vespoli?"

"I started to, but he had another call come in that he said he needed to get, and suggested I stop by to talk to him. I'm going over there now. Want to come with me?"

"You better believe it." Martha hesitated. "But it's Thursday. The quilt circle is happening, which means the store will be busy. Is it fair to leave Elizabeth alone?"

"I already talked to her about it. She's fine with it."

"Okay then. I'm right behind you."

Martha followed Mary out to her car, and a few minutes later they were pulling up in front of the boat maker's shop. This time, there was a maroon CR-V in the driveway, and the door of the shop was wide open.

Martha stepped inside and looked around. The old barn had beautiful post-and-beam construction, and the exposed wood had aged to a gorgeous shade of gray. The interior walls had been plastered over and painted white, and framed nautical charts hung on the walls. Several wooden shells in various stages of construction were placed on supports throughout the open workshop space. The whole place smelled of sawdust and varnish. It was wonderful.

"Hi there!" A man in a checked flannel shirt and saggy jeans walked toward them from the back. "Mary. It's so great to see you."

He was wiping his hands on a rag as he approached.

"Randy. This is beautiful."

Randy leaned in and gave Mary a kiss on each cheek, like he was European, though his accent marked him as native to New England.

"Thank you. I have fun." He had a neatly trimmed beard that was more gray than brown and startlingly blue eyes. "Thanks for coming to see it. I'm sorry I missed you the other day."

"No problem."

Mary turned and gestured toward Martha. "This is my sister Martha."

"Martha. Great to meet you. Randy." He held out his hand.

"It's very nice to meet you." His hand was rough and calloused, which made sense, given the work he did.

"Was your visit with your family nice?" Mary asked.

"It was wonderful. I always love seeing the grandkids."

"I hear that. I miss mine. My family stayed back in Indiana when I moved home."

"And mine stayed in Maine, where they were raised, even after we moved here. My wife was from the area and wanted to move home, as her health was failing. Now that she's gone, I think about moving back, but I like it here. It's quieter, the cost of living is lower, the people are nice, and the winters are certainly better. They still had a foot of snow on the ground up there." He shook his head. "If it weren't for the grandkids, I'd never look back."

"Well, we're glad you're here," Mary said. She looked around the shop, taking in the half-finished boats. "This is really wonderful. Did you build all of these from scratch?"

"I do everything by hand. Mostly dinghies. Small sailboats, that kind of thing. I do some custom orders, and some I sell at boat shows or arts and crafts festivals, like where I met you."

"It's really incredible." Martha couldn't even imagine how much work went into shaping the curved wooden hull of the boats on the sawhorses.

"Not too many people left doing it the old-fashioned way. But that's the way I like to do things."

Looking around the shop now, Martha realized how little she knew about boating. Was there a difference between a dinghy and a sailboat? She wasn't even sure.

"So you said you had a question. How can I help?" Randy asked.

"We're trying to find the man who was driving a car that had crashed into an Amish buggy Friday night," Mary said.

"I heard about that. So terrible."

"We got a look at the car the other day," Mary said. "And we saw that it had a bumper sticker with the word *Vespoli* on it."

"We realized that was a kind of boat," Martha said. "We were hoping you could tell us a bit more."

"Vespoli?" His brow knit. "Those are racing shells."

"They're what?" Martha had no idea what that meant.

"Vespoli is a company that makes boats for crew."

"Crew?" Martha had a vague idea of what that was. She'd seen it on the Olympics. "The sport where all those people sit in those skinny little boats with those long oars?"

"And the short dude at the front shouts at them to row?" Mary added.

Randy laughed. "That's not quite how it works, but you've got the gist. Those racing shells are made of very light fiberglass, so I don't make anything like that, sadly."

"So if someone were to have, say, a bumper sticker that said Vespoli on their car..." Mary let her voice trail off.

"I would guess they rowed crew," Randy said.

"Huh." Martha thought this through. "And if the person who had that car went to Penn State..."

Randy shrugged. "I couldn't say for sure, of course. But you might check if he rowed for Penn State."

Martha wasn't sure how to do that, but that was going to be the first thing she did when they left here.

"Simple," Mary said. "How many people named Charles who row for Penn State can there be?"

"Charles?" Randy tilted his head. "His name is Charles?"

"We don't know that for sure," Martha explained. "But we think there's a chance, because when he stepped out of the car, he was wearing a shirt that had the name Charles on it."

Randy pursed his lips and thought for a minute, and then he laughed.

"The Head of the Charles."

"What?" Both Mary and Martha said it at the same time.

"I bet he was wearing a T-shirt from the Head of the Charles. It's the most famous collegiate crew race of the year. It takes place every fall on the Charles River, in Boston."

"Oh." Martha was slowly putting the pieces together. It wasn't his name after all. "So it sounds like a good bet that he really is a…crewer?"

"A rower." Randy smiled. "And yes, that seems pretty likely to me."

"Thank you. You may have just given us the clue that cracks this whole thing open," Mary said.

"I'm very glad of that," Randy said with a smile. "Now, while you're here, can I interest you in a hand-crafted boat?"

Martha tried to imagine herself rowing across one of the local ponds in a wooden boat. She loved the image, actually. That would be so relaxing, and such good exercise. Being on the water, surrounded by trees and the soft breeze, sounded like heaven. But she couldn't imagine when she'd find the time.

"They really are beautiful," Mary said, running her fingers across the hull of one of the boats. "But I'm afraid we're not in the market at the moment. If we ever are, we'll know who to call."

"Keep me in mind."

"We really appreciate your help," Mary said. "Thank you."

"Any time." He shook their hands, and then they walked out of the shop.

"Penn State crew team," Mary said as soon as Martha got into the car. Martha started to respond, but then she noticed that Mary was talking into her phone.

"Who are you calling?"

"Siri." Mary laughed and touched her screen, and then she held out her phone. "Here we go."

On the screen was a webpage about the crew team at Penn State. Mary looked at the screen for a moment, and then she touched a tab at the top of the page, and photos of the men's and women's crew teams appeared on the screen.

"It's one of these guys," Mary said. Martha took the phone and studied the page. There were actually several photos of different men's teams, labeled JV Heavyweight and JV Lightweight and Varsity Heavyweight and Varsity Lightweight.

"Do you think he's a lightweight or a heavyweight?" Martha asked.

"I have no idea." Mary shook her head. "Even those lightweight guys look pretty big to me." They all wore some kind of tank top and shorts combo with the school's mascot on the front, and, aside from a few tiny girls in the front—those must be the people who called out the commands, Martha guessed— they all looked like they spent way too much time at the gym. Aside from the coxswains, any of them could be the guy they'd seen in the security video.

"Brianna said he was older, so I'd guess he's Varsity," Martha said. But even that didn't help much. There had to be two to three dozen men on each varsity squad. How were they supposed to figure out which one was their guy?

"Look. Their names are at the bottom of each picture." Mary pointed, and Martha saw that she was right. In tiny print, there was a list of the names of the people featured in the pictures. One of them had to be the name of the guy who had stolen Adam's identity. But which one? "We can do research on them. We think our guy grew up in the Lancaster area. How hard can it be to find out which members of these teams are from around here?"

"Even if we just focus on the varsity men's teams, there still have to be forty or fifty names here. It will take us forever to research each one."

Mary flashed her a big smile.

"I guess we better get to work."

Elizabeth had hoped to sit in on the quilting circle, but with her sisters gone, she couldn't do much more than check in on the group between helping customers and ringing up purchases. It seemed as though they were having a good time, though, and there were nearly a dozen women here today— mostly Amish, but not all. There was Rachel and her daughter Phoebe, as well as Rachel's sisters Leora and Marietta, plus Leora's daughter Abigail. Anne Hostetler and Betty Yoder were also here, as well as a few other Englisch women. Elizabeth was able to tell the group about her new quilt project and get their advice on patterns to try. Leora suggested Hunter's Star, while Phoebe said she liked the Rail Fence pattern. Elizabeth promised to look into those, and the women chatted and laughed as they worked on their projects and shared information and gave advice, and Elizabeth was disappointed when it was time for them to go.

As the group of women was heading toward the door, Rachel gestured for Elizabeth to come over. Elizabeth held up a finger and finished ringing up a set of place mats and one of Martha's lemon poppy seed loaves before handing the customer the bag and waving goodbye.

"I am sorry to bother you, but I did not want to say this in front of everyone else." Rachel's voice was low, and Elizabeth had to lean in to hear her. Phoebe hovered near the door, waiting for her mother. "I was talking to Martha yesterday, and she was asking about someone named Susannah Fischer."

"Yes, she told Mary and me that she asked you about her."

"I did not know Susannah, as that was well before my time. But I did talk to Anke last night, and she knew the name. She said she would be willing to tell you what she knows about Susannah."

"That would be wonderful."

"I know that you cannot leave today, since your sisters are away, but she told me that she is free tomorrow morning around ten, if you would want to come by for a visit."

"Great. I'll plan to stop by then."

After dinner and cake, Martha had received calls from her kids, one after the other, almost like they had planned it, though she felt sure they hadn't. She'd gotten to talk to each of her grandkids, even tiny Mick, who sang her a song he'd learned at playgroup.

After she'd hung up, Martha had considered what to do. It was her birthday. She could get away with doing anything she chose. She could curl up with a book, or watch some mindless television, or take a hot bath and just relax. Clouds had rolled in, dark and heavy, and a hot bath sounded heavenly. But her eye kept being drawn to her laptop, where she'd pulled up the webpage that showed the photos of the Penn State crew team.

She would just do a bit of research, she decided. Just to see whether she really could figure out if any of them were from the Lancaster area.

But once she started, she couldn't stop. She'd begun with the students in the Varsity Heavyweight crew team, systematically looking up each man listed under the photo. She'd been able to learn a scary amount about each of the boys just from researching them online. Matt Able was a senior from Punxsutawney who liked to spend his weekends playing Dungeons and Dragons. Brian Bennett was a junior from

Allentown who seemed to spend too much time at parties, to Martha's eye, but he was majoring in chemical engineering, so he couldn't be as silly as his pictures made him seem. Hunter Phelan was a sophomore who'd excelled at crew in his hometown of Philadelphia, and he was into music. He'd posted pictures of himself at various rock concerts, as well as at classical performances. By the time she'd worked her way through the varsity squad, she'd found two that were from the Lancaster area, as well as one man from Harrisburg, which was close enough to keep him on the list. She also had a beautiful spreadsheet, which helped her keep track of each man's name, hometown, and interests. So far, none of the interests they listed online had included drag racing or shopping on stolen credit cards, but Martha held out hope.

"Still at it?" Mary was coming down the stairs in her pajamas. "You really know how to party, Birthday Girl."

"Ain't no party like a spreadsheet party, 'cause a spread-sheet party don't stop."

"Huh?" Mary was looking at her like she was nuts.

"It's something Craig used to say. Only when he said it, it wasn't usually about spreadsheets."

"Ooh—kay..." Mary shook her head. "When you're singing about spreadsheets, you know it's time to go to bed."

"I've got one here for the fundraiser Saturday night as well." Martha clicked on the other open spreadsheet and showed it to Mary.

Mary's only response was, "Bedtime."

"I know you're right." Martha saved her spreadsheet. "I just keeping thinking that if I look up one more name, I'll find him."

"The internet won't vanish by tomorrow. You'll be able to keep working on this then."

Martha took one more look at the spreadsheet on her screen. The lines were starting to blur. "What about you? Why are you up?"

"I'm just getting water." Mary reached up into the cabinet and pulled down a glass. "Then it's lights out for me." She filled the glass and came around the counter to look at the screen. "What kind of monster spreadsheet is that?"

"I've got some pivot tables going on."

"You've got what now?"

"It doesn't matter." Martha sighed. "You're right that I should get to bed."

"Did you have any luck?"

"A few leads. But there's a lot more still to do."

"And you will," Mary said. "You'll get it all done, because that's what you do. But right now, it's time for bed."

Martha closed her computer and followed her sister up the stairs.

CHAPTER FOURTEEN

Martha could tell before she even stepped out of bed Friday morning. The birdsong outside the window was muffled, and the sunlight had an ethereal, too-bright quality.

There was snow on the ground.

Martha moved toward the window, wrapping her flannel robe around herself, and peeked out. Sure enough, it had snowed last night. Not a lot—maybe an inch. But enough to ensure that the fundraiser tomorrow night would be messy and muddy and all-around too cold. Even the sunshine beaming down this morning wouldn't melt and dry everything out in time. Martha pressed her forehead against the glass. It was cold, and it helped her find clarity.

She would make one more, last-minute pitch to move the fundraiser, she decided. After breakfast, she would head over to the Fischer farm and try to convince Rachel to reconsider the location. She knew Ruth Yutzy wanted to host the event at the Fischer barn, but Martha had been to an Amish mud sale before, and that wasn't exactly the vibe she wanted for this fundraiser. At least the inside of their shop was dry and heated, and their parking lot was paved.

She came downstairs and found Elizabeth sipping coffee and staring out the back door.

"It snowed," Martha said, though obviously Elizabeth had noticed that herself.

"It sure did."

Martha poured herself a mug of coffee and came over to join Elizabeth by the door. Then she saw what Elizabeth was looking at. Mary was crouched down in her garden bed, bundled up in boots and her heavy parka, trying to brush the snow off the tender green plants.

"We should probably go help her," Martha said.

"I was thinking the same thing," Elizabeth said. "But I needed some caffeine before I could face any more snow. I thought we were done for the season."

"It sure did feel like spring was here for a few days there. But welcome to March in Pennsylvania." Martha remembered a snowfall in late April when she was a kid. Because so many of the trees already had their leaves, it had brought down many tree limbs and taken out power across the county. It had seemed like such a great adventure to eat by candlelight when she was a child. Now, snow in spring just felt like dashed hopes.

It was a wet, slushy snow, the kind that was no good for snowballs or snowmen or anything, really, except for slipping and sliding on icy pathways.

"It was too early for her to plant those beans." Elizabeth shook her head. "She knew that."

"But we can't remind her of it," Martha said. "Hope springs eternal."

"You're right." Elizabeth drained the last of her coffee and set her mug in the sink. "Okay. I'm going to get dressed, and then I'll go out to help her."

"I'll be just behind you."

An hour later, they'd scraped most of the snow off the plants. Martha didn't know enough about gardening to know whether the plants would make it or not, but she assured Mary that she could always plant more.

Martha cleaned herself up, and then while her sisters went out to open the shop, she climbed in her car and headed next door to talk to Rachel.

She found Silas, Luke, Ephraim, and Adam clearing the snow from the yard and carrying it to a pile behind the barn. She realized they were intending to clear the whole thing by hand. Silas waved as she went into the house, slipping on the slushy snow.

She found Rachel inside the house cooking down large pots of apples.

"Hallo, Martha." She wiped her hands on a kitchen towel and waved.

"Hallo," Phoebe called. She was slicing apples carefully, while Hannah was peeling them, one after another.

"You guys are hard at work here," Martha said, sizing up the situation. "It looks like we will have plenty of apple pies to sell at the bake sale."

"That is right." Rachel used a wooden spoon to stir the fruit. "There will so be much food there. We will make so much money for the Mast family."

Martha hesitated. But this was what she had come to say, after all.

"Do you still think it will be okay to have it here, after all that snow?" She gauged their reaction before continuing. "It's not too late to change the location if you wanted to have it at the shop instead."

"The inside of the barn is dry," Rachel said. "And that is where we will be setting up the tables. I think it will be all right."

"And Daed and the boys are clearing off the snow in hopes that the yard will dry out," Phoebe said. "So hopefully it does not turn into a mud sale." Phoebe smiled in such a charming, earnest way that it melted Martha's heart, just like it always did.

"I do thank you for your offer," Rachel said. "I appreciate it. But trust me. I have this under control."

It was exactly the same thing Martha wanted to say to Rachel. *Just trust me. I have this under control.* She bit her tongue. She wasn't great at giving up control. But Rachel wasn't going to change her mind, that was clear. And, well, it wasn't as if lives were at stake, Martha thought. Sure, it was disappointing to know how much more money they would have made if Rachel had simply listened to Martha. If she had trusted her to get the word out and trusted her organizational skills. But at the end of the day, she had to let it go. She had tried. At this point, she had to let Rachel do it her way, and maybe she'd learn a lesson for next time.

"Have you found the man who stole from Adam yet?" Hannah asked, looking up from the apple she was peeling.

"Hannah." Rachel then said something to her daughter in Pennsylvania Dutch. Hannah argued back, clearly not liking whatever it was her mother had said. Rachel responded, and then Hannah turned to Martha and said, "I am sorry."

"That's quite all right." Martha didn't think she'd been particularly sassy, but she appreciated that Rachel was trying to keep her daughter's tone respectful.

"Actually, I do have a few new developments," Martha said. She filled them in on the trip to Randy's studio, and the revelation that it was likely a member of the Penn State crew team they were looking for.

"That is good news," Rachel said. "But what is crew?"

Martha started to explain that she had certainly seen it on the Olympics, but then she realized that Rachel had most likely never seen any Olympic event.

"It's a sport where you row really skinny boats really fast with super-long oars," Martha explained, knowing what a bad description of the elegant sport it was.

"I am often amazed by the ways Englisch people come up with to get exercise," Rachel said.

Martha laughed. She knew Rachel and her family did so much hard labor just to survive that the idea of exercising for fun seemed odd. The boats and oars no doubt added another element of ridiculousness.

"Here. I'll show you." It only took a moment for Martha to find a YouTube video of a crew race.

And, she had to admit, it did seem ridiculous the way she'd described it. But it really was beautiful to watch.

"There cannot be too many people on the crew team, can there?"

"Actually, there are more than you'd think." Martha pulled up the webpage with the photos on her phone and held it out so Rachel could see. "I've started researching each of them to see how many of them are from the Lancaster area, but I still have many names to go."

Both Hannah and Phoebe had stopped what they were doing and had come over to look at the phone.

"One of these men is the one who stole from Adam?" Phoebe asked.

"We think there's a high likelihood of that." Martha handed her the phone so she could see it more clearly.

"Why don't you ask Adam if he recognizes any of them?" Phoebe suggested.

Once she'd said it, it seemed obvious. If it was someone Adam had encountered while he was on rumspringa, there was a decent chance he might recognize him.

"That's a good idea," Martha admitted.

"I will go get him." Hannah slipped out of the kitchen and went to the door to put her boots on.

"Put on your cloak!" Rachel shouted, but Hannah was already out the door. Rachel shook her head.

After she had disappeared, Rachel and Phoebe looked over the photos, searching for a face that looked familiar.

"The pictures are so small," Rachel said. "It is hard to tell much of anything."

"It's kind of a long shot," Martha admitted. "But it's worth checking to see."

A few minutes later, Hannah came inside, followed by Adam. They both took off their boots, and Adam took off his hat and coat, and walked into the kitchen.

"Hallo, Martha." Adam's cheeks were pink from the cold. "Hannah said you have some photographs for me to look at."

"Right." Martha nodded. "We think there's a good chance the man who stole your identity is one of these men." She held out the phone, and Adam took it. He used two fingers to enlarge the picture of the Heavyweight JV team, and studied each face carefully. Then he moved on to the Lightweight JV team. Rachel and Hannah were both looking over his shoulder, trying to see the screen.

Martha held her breath, and she was about to lose hope, when she saw something in Adam's face change. A muscle in his jaw flexed, and there was a look in his eyes that she couldn't read.

"What is it?" Rachel asked.

Adam didn't say anything for a moment, just continued looking down at the photo. Finally, though, he pointed at a face on the screen.

"I know who this is."

CHAPTER FIFTEEN

Elizabeth saw that Martha's car was parked in front of the Fischer house when she pulled into the driveway. She must be here making plans for the fundraiser. Hopefully neither of them would be gone too long, since Mary was alone in the shop, and Fridays could often be busy days. Elizabeth pulled around the side of the barn and followed the dirt drive around to the dawdy haus, which was set a few hundred feet back from the main house. The small wooden structure was painted a clean white, and the miniature yard was pristine.

Elizabeth carried the tray of brownie bites to the door and knocked gently, and a few moments later Anke answered the door.

"Hello there." Silas's mother was in her early seventies and had been having memory problems. She'd improved a lot lately, though, and was living back in the dawdy haus on the Fischer property. The Fischers were extra careful about checking in on her. Elizabeth hoped she would be relatively lucid today. "Come in." Her white hair was mostly covered by her kapp, and her long black dress brushed her feet as she took the plate and stepped back. "It has been too long. How are you, Elizabeth?"

"I'm doing well, thank you. How are you?" Elizabeth's mother, Elma, and Anke had been good friends, but Elizabeth hadn't spent much time in her presence on her own. "This place is lovely. You've had it redone, haven't you?"

"Just a coat of paint," Anke said, gesturing at the white walls. "And Silas put some new cabinets in the kitchen for me. He takes good care of me."

Elizabeth noticed there was a new electric stove as well— added, no doubt, after Anke had left her gas stove on and nearly burned down the house. "I'm so glad."

"Now, Rachel tells me you had questions about my husband's sister Susannah." She gestured for Elizabeth to have a seat at the scarred wooden table. Elizabeth sat and ran her hands over the dented surface. How many meals had been shared on this table?

"Is that who she was? I didn't know."

"If it's the same Susannah Fischer I know of, that was Albert's eldest sister."

Martha did some quick math in her head. "Would she have been born around 1930 or so?"

"I don't know. That sounds about right." Anke sighed. "My memory is not what it used to be, you know. But I do remember the old days more than more recent things. And I think Susannah was probably fifteen years older than Albert. He was the youngest, you know."

Elizabeth nodded. She had guessed as much, since he had inherited the farm.

"I didn't know her all that well, because she was married and had several children by the time Albert and I started courting. And she passed away many years back. But tell me what you want to know."

"Well..." Elizabeth wasn't sure exactly how to say this. "I found a letter in my father's things. It was...well, here." She handed the note to Anke and watched as she took out her glasses and adjusted them before looking down at the paper. She read it through once and then placed her hand over her heart and read the note again. When she finally looked up, there were tears in her eyes.

"You have just solved a great family mystery," Anke said, brushing at her eyes with a finger. "We knew there had been a man, but no one ever knew who it was. She wouldn't say."

"So it *was* Albert's sister Susannah, then, who wrote this?"

"I believe it was," Anke said. "And I suppose you want to know what happened to her after she wrote this?"

Elizabeth nodded. "And to...well, it seems that there was a baby."

"It does seem that way, doesn't it?" Anke looked down at the paper again. "That explains much of what I was told happened. Now, keep in mind that I heard all of this second-hand, but you know how women talk at family gatherings and such."

Elizabeth nodded.

"The story I heard was that Susannah was married to Lloyd rather quickly, and in June."

Elizabeth understood the significance of that immediately. Amish weddings were almost always held in November or early December, after the harvest was in. To have been married in June would have meant that there was a reason the wedding needed to be rushed. A reason like a baby.

"Was Lloyd…"

"I do not know what he was told. He was older, and had been married before. His wife had passed, and he had young children, so it made sense that he might be eager to find a bride. Especially a pretty young one like Susannah."

"She was pretty, then?" Elizabeth wanted to know as much as she could about this woman who had captured her father's heart.

"Very much so. Even when I met her, when she was much older than when all this went on, she was beautiful. She had long, thick hair, and there was just this grace about her."

"And…when was the baby born?"

Anke shook her head. "That was the question. Everyone expected there to be a baby, but no baby was born. Not until more than a year and a half after the marriage. People were not sure if something happened to the baby or if there never had been one, and there had been some other reason the marriage was rushed. With Lloyd needing help with the children, it is possible that the Bishop gave permission for a wedding at the odd time."

"Do you think that's what happened?"

Anke thought for moment before she said, "No."

"Why not?"

"Lloyd was a nice enough man, but it did not make sense for Susannah to rush into a marriage with him. She must have had many suitors. There had to be a reason. What I could never figure out was, if there was a baby on the way, why did she not marry the father?" She gestured at the letter. "But if it was Henry…"

She let her voice trail off. Elizabeth understood. If the father had been Daddy, their marriage would not have been allowed, not without Susannah being shunned. If she'd wanted to remain part of her community... Well, even if she had been willing to leave, these things were not always for a young girl to decide, even now. Elizabeth imagined it would have been even more impossible so many years ago.

"So what happened to the baby?" Elizabeth asked.

"I do not know." Anke ran her hand along one of the dents in the table. "I would guess that for whatever reason, she lost the baby shortly after the marriage. These things are not spoken of, but they are very common."

Elizabeth felt an inexplicable sense of loss at these words as she realized they were probably true. She hadn't realized that a small part of her had already grown to love the idea of another sibling.

"Which meant that all of it—the marriage to Lloyd—was unnecessary," Elizabeth said. If Susannah hadn't been married off hurriedly, would she and Daddy have found a way to end up together? It seemed impossible...and if they had, Elizabeth and her sisters wouldn't exist. But still, a part of her mourned for her father. He had clearly loved Susannah. It must have been devastating for him when she'd married another man. He and Mama had genuinely loved one another and had built a strong, happy marriage, but he must have lost his first love. And the fact that he'd kept her note all these years made Elizabeth think that he'd never forgotten her.

"Oh, I do not know if I would say it was all unnecessary," Anke said. "I believe that Gott knows what He is doing, even when we don't. Susannah and Lloyd enjoyed a long marriage and had many children together. Who is to say it would have been better if she had married someone different?"

She was right, of course. God's plans were always better than our own. And yet part of Elizabeth couldn't help but wonder what might have happened if things had been different. If Daddy and Susannah had been allowed to marry, to raise a family. But they couldn't change what had happened.

"And I, for one, am glad that Henry married Elma." Anke was smiling at Elizabeth knowingly.

"I am too, obviously." It had worked out for the best. There wasn't any reason to think otherwise. But still, a small part of her ached for her father, who had lost a great love and possibly a child. She'd never known that about him. There was so much she didn't know. But still, there was joy in knowing that she understood him a little better than she had before.

"Thank you for sharing," Elizabeth said.

"Your father was a good man." Anke said quietly. "A great man. Do not let this tarnish your memory of him. Young people make mistakes, but your father learned from this and went on to love and serve the Lord and his family all the days of his life."

Elizabeth nodded as she realized that this hadn't actually tarnished his memory. On the contrary, it had made her understand and love him even more. This letter, for all the shock and confusion it had brought, had taught her things she'd never known about Daddy, and for that, it had actually been an incredible gift.

CHAPTER SIXTEEN

W ho is it?" Martha asked.

"Which one is it?" Hannah was leaning in, trying to get a better view of the small phone screen.

Adam was still looking down at the photo of the Penn State crew team. Martha could see from here that he had narrowed in on one face—a good-looking young man with dark hair.

"His name is Evan Harper." Adam swallowed. "He worked at the vet's office."

"He did?" They'd asked at the vet's office, and they hadn't mentioned him.

"He only came in part time, off-hours mostly, I think. He cleaned the animal cages, took out the trash, mopped the floor, that kind of thing. I only ever crossed paths with him a few times. I believe he was not a true employee, exactly."

"What do you mean?" Martha wasn't following.

"I think he was doing some sort of community service by being there. I believe it was…well, I never got the full details, but I got the sense he had done something bad, and instead of sending him to jail, he had been sentenced to community service."

"Interesting." Martha didn't want to make too many assumptions, but it did seem somewhat likely that someone who had gotten into legal trouble as a teenager might have stolen Adam's identity. "What happened to him after that?"

"I do not know. I did not keep in touch with him. He stopped working there before I did, but I do not know why." Adam paused, and Martha wasn't sure if he was going to go on or not. Then he looked down before he said, "He was not very kind to me."

"What did he do?" Rachel asked gently.

Another pause. "He did not think very highly of the Amish, and he was not afraid to tell me so. He thinks we are slow, that we are not smart."

"He does not sound like a very nice guy," Phoebe said.

Martha wanted to laugh. Phoebe had summed it up nicely.

"The question is," Rachel began, "now that we know who he is, what do we do next?"

Martha had an idea.

Mary knew the bean plants were not going to make it. She appreciated that her sisters had tried to help her save them, but they were gone, and it was her fault. Mary had let her excitement about spring get the best of her. She should have listened to Linda.

Still, she thought as she stood outside the garden beds, it wasn't going to be the end of the garden. She would have to wait a few more weeks before she put any more seedlings in the ground, but there was plenty she could do in the meantime. She could order her seeds and prep the soil. She might start some more seedlings indoors. She would plan.

She closed her eyes and tried to picture what it would look like in three months. Flowers would be bursting forth, a riot of color. The first beans and peppers would be flowering. The whole plot would be lush and green.

Mary took in a deep breath and let it out slowly. The garden would be just like it had been when Mama was alive.

She couldn't wait.

The waiting room was empty when Martha pushed open the door of the vet clinic, and a woman with white hair sat behind the front desk. This must be Edna, Martha thought. Elizabeth was still visiting Anke, so Mary had stayed behind at the shop. But Mary had told her about Edna. She'd warned that she didn't seem to be the most on top of things.

"Hello. Welcome." Edna gave her a big smile. "What can I do for you?"

Wow. Mary had also told her that Edna wore thick glasses, but she hadn't expected them to be quite that thick.

"My name is Martha Watts. I believe you spoke with my sister Mary earlier this week. We're helping our neighbor Adam Fischer look into identity theft."

How could Edna work with all the piles of paper everywhere? How could she possibly find anything? Martha had the strongest urge to start filing.

"That's right. I remember her." She let out a laugh. "Hey, look at that! I remembered something!"

Martha smiled. It sounded like Edna was joking, but it was hard to tell.

"I've been so loopy on cold medicine this week that I'm not sure I could have remembered my own name a few days ago," she said, laughing. Martha wasn't sure it was something to laugh about, really, but she kept a smile on her face. "Anyway, did you find Adam's driver's license?" Edna asked. "I still can't get over the fact that an Amish kid was driving a car."

"Not yet," Martha said. "But we actually do have a lead. Do you remember a boy named Evan Harper?"

"Evan Harper?" Edna tilted her head. Martha noticed that she had a tissue tucked into the sleeve of her sweater. "Now that name is familiar. Why is that name familiar?" She tapped her chin.

"I believe he did some cleaning and taking out the trash."

"Huh. That does sound familiar, but…" She shook her head. "It's in there somewhere, but I just don't know."

"Is there anyone else here who might remember him? Maybe the vet?"

"Now that's an idea." Her face brightened. "Let me go see if he's available. It's my son-in-law, you know."

Martha nodded. Mary had told her.

Edna picked up the phone and made a call, and then she gestured toward the door that separated what Martha assumed was the examining rooms from the waiting room. "It turns out he's in with a patient, but my daughter Lisa is available. She's in the office. You can go on back and talk to her. Third door on the right."

"Thank you." Martha went through the door and walked down the hallway, which was decorated with artful black-and-white photos of dogs and cats. A very unhappy kitty was wailing in one of the exam rooms. Butterscotch made the same sound whenever he had to go to the vet.

The third door on the right was partially open, and she knocked on it gently.

"Come in."

Martha stepped into a small office that was impeccably neat. Reference books were lined up precisely on the book-shelves, and the desktop was empty except for a sleek computer screen and keyboard. A woman with brown hair lightened by highlights turned and smiled.

"Hi there. I'm Martha Watts."

"Lisa. You're helping Adam Fischer, right?"

"That's right."

"Have a seat." She gestured at the empty chair next to the desk. "Adam was such a good kid. Smart and motivated. He really had it together. I was almost sad to hear that he'd decided to join the Amish after all." She put her hand up to her mouth. "Oh dear. That's horrible, isn't it?"

"It's understandable," Martha said. She liked this woman's open demeanor. "It's a shame he couldn't become a vet and also join the church. But that's not how it works." She lowered herself into the chair. "I can tell you that he's very happily married and has a baby on the way."

"I'm glad to hear it." Lisa took off her reading glasses. Martha saw that there was some kind of spreadsheet on her screen. A woman after her own heart. "So, my mom said you were asking about Evan Harper?"

"That's right. Adam mentioned that he'd worked here, but your mom didn't seem sure."

Lisa let out a sigh. "Mom's memory isn't great these days. She's... Well, truthfully I'm not sure how much longer we can let her keep working the front desk. I end up redoing most of the paperwork she does. But the patients love her. And her doctor says it's good for her to stay active and engaged in tasks she enjoys, so we keep her on."

"It's nice that you let her do it."

"It's nice having her around. And she's getting more forgetful, sure, but so far, so good." She sighed again. "Anyway, Evan Harper. Now that kid was a handful."

"Do you remember him?"

"I don't think I could forget him if I tried." She grimaced. "That wasn't very kind, was it? I'm sorry. It's just... He was one of Barry's projects."

"Projects?"

"My husband, God bless him, is the most kindhearted person in the world."

"I guess that explains how he ended up working with animals for a living."

"You're totally right." Lisa shook her head. "Well, his friend from college—they both went to Penn State and were in the same fraternity—called one day. This was maybe two and a half years ago? I don't remember. Anyway, he asked for a favor. His son Evan had gotten into trouble. He'd been caught torturing an animal. I didn't ask for specifics."

Martha cringed. She didn't even want to imagine what might have happened.

"He was a minor, just barely, and his father could afford a very good lawyer. He's in some kind of banking or something like that. So Evan was sentenced to community service, and he was supposed to find something to do that would teach him to care for animals. I said at the time that being around animals probably wasn't the best idea, given what he'd gotten into trouble for, but Barry, bless him, wanted to give Evan a try."

"I take it things didn't go well?"

"It was okay at first. We mostly had him clean the cages and sweep the floor and things like that. I was actually glad for the help. No one likes cleaning out animal cages." She leaned back in her chair. "And he was mostly here at odd hours, when we were closing and just after, because of his summer job. Some cushy job that his father had set him up with, I don't remember what it was—interning at some law firm or something—in any case, it was certainly a few steps above lifeguarding at the Y, which was what I did to earn money the summer before college."

"I bagged groceries at the market," Martha said.

"It's a shame we weren't born rich, right?" She shrugged. "Anyway. It went fine, but then we started to notice things seemed a little off. Small things at first, like the filing cabinets looked like they'd been riffled through."

"What's kept in the filing cabinets?" But Martha already had a pretty good idea what Lisa was going to say.

"Well, there's one for patient records, but that's not the one that was disturbed. The one for our own financial records and personnel files was the one that had been opened."

"And you think it was Evan?"

"It had to be. Who else would do something like that? It certainly wasn't Adam." She shook her head. "And a few months later we found out a credit card had been taken out in the name of the practice, and someone had charged thousands of dollars' worth of clothes and electronics and whatnot."

"Really?" He'd done it before Adam, then, Martha realized. Adam wasn't his first victim.

"We called the credit card company when we figured it out, and we weren't responsible for the charges, thank goodness. But that was later, after he wasn't working here anymore. When he was still here, we started to notice other things. One day, Mom said there was money missing from her wallet. Maybe there was, I don't know, but this was back when she was first starting to show signs of dementia, so we just chalked it up to her being forgetful. But maybe he really was going through people's wallets. I was never sure."

"Adam's driver's license went missing right around the end of his tenure here."

Lisa let out a sigh. "Well, I suppose we might know how that happened." And then, a moment later, she said, "I'm so sorry."

"It's not your fault."

"No, but I saw signs that something wasn't right. I sure wish I had done something about it before it escalated. First we noticed that the cages were not being cleaned very well. Adam also cleaned cages for us, but the cages he cleaned were always impeccable. Better than I would have done, even. And the animals loved him. You know how there are some people animals just flock to? He was one of those people."

"I've always thought animals are a good judge of character," Martha said.

"I agree." Lisa nodded. "Which is why I got worried when I realized the animals did not like Evan."

"What do you mean?"

"Well, we noticed that certain animals would cower when he came near their cages."

"Oh dear."

"He wasn't supposed to be near the cages alone, and we never caught him doing anything, but as you can imagine, that caused concern. I told Barry we couldn't keep him on. He still had a few months left of his community service, but we decided he'd done enough."

"Did you tell anyone why you were letting him go?"

"I wanted to. I thought we needed to tell the judge what we suspected. But Barry wanted to protect his old friend, so he didn't. Which I think was probably a mistake, given that you're now here asking about him."

"I don't know that he's done anything involving animals," Martha said. "But we're pretty sure he stole Adam's identity. In addition to Adam's driver's license going missing, there were credit cards taken out in his name, and they were used to ring up thousands of dollars of debt."

"Same song, different verse." Lisa sighed again. "Now I really wish I'd said something back then. Adam doesn't deserve this. He's such a good kid."

"He's a good man now," Martha said. "And I know he's going to be grateful for your help in figuring this all out."

She knew how it had happened now. Evan must have gone through Adam's wallet at some point while they were both working here and taken the driver's license. Adam was only a year or so older than Evan, and they both had brown hair and brown eyes. He must have realized the potential of a license without a picture and taken it. And he could have gotten Adam's social security number from the personnel files.

But there was something that didn't add up. Evan seemed to have been using Adam's license for years, but he hadn't opened the credit card using Adam's social security number until this past fall. She wondered why there had been the delay, and then wondered if it was because there had been other credit cards he'd been using in the meantime. Maybe he'd only started using Adam's name and number once another card had been canceled. She hated to think that there had been more victims, but unfortunately, she thought it seemed likely.

"Thank you so much for your help," Martha said. "I think you just gave me what we needed to know."

"I'm so glad," Lisa said. "So what are you going to do now?"

Martha thought for a moment, and then she smiled. "We're going to put a stop to it."

CHAPTER SEVENTEEN

Martha and Elizabeth sat down across from John and Officer Hooper and laid out what they'd discovered. They went through all the evidence, showing them the still from the security camera footage, the photo of the wrecked car, and the photo of the crew team. Then they went through the conversation with Lisa at the vet's office. Once they'd finished making their case, Martha sat back. She glanced at Elizabeth, who returned her smile.

"We weren't able to find a current address for Evan Harper," Martha said. "So we don't know where to tell you to go to find him and arrest him. But I'm sure you have tools to help with that kind of thing."

The police officers didn't say anything for a moment.

"Well?" Martha hadn't expected them to jump for joy necessarily, but she had expected more of a reaction than that.

"It's really quite impressive detective work. Thank you," John said slowly. "We are investigating a number of leads, and this is very promising material."

Martha took that to mean the police hadn't yet narrowed in on Evan themselves, and she felt another jolt of excitement.

"We will follow up with each of these leads and look into Evan Harper," Officer Hooper said.

"Check out his Instagram account," Elizabeth said. "You can see photos of him with the things he bought with the credit card taken out in Adam's name." Mary had discovered that last night, and Martha had been sure the police would jump at that.

"And we know he got into trouble for abusing animals when he was younger. You know how people who abuse animals often graduate to larger crimes later," Martha said. In her mind, there wasn't a much worse crime than abusing animals, but she knew not everyone saw it that way. And she wasn't sure there were statistics backing up her statement, but she felt sure it was true nonetheless.

"We will review what you've presented and continue our investigation," John said.

"Though in the future, we'll have to ask you not to tamper with police evidence," Officer Hooper said, gesturing at the photos of the car.

"We didn't tamper with it. We just looked at it through the fence," Martha said. She didn't mean to sound snippy, but she felt more and more frustrated with each passing moment. They kept talking about investigating Evan Harper, but that's what the Classen sisters had already done. It was him. He was their guy. So why weren't they talking about going out to State College and arresting him?

"There's no doubt Evan is the one who stole Adam's identity," Elizabeth said.

"We know that you believe that," Officer Hooper said. Martha felt like she'd been slapped. She more than believed it; she knew it was true. Why didn't they?

"And we are grateful for the lead," John said. "We will conduct a thorough investigation, and we will take appropriate actions."

An appropriate action would be to leave the room, go out, and arrest him now, Martha thought. Before he caused more damage or caused another crash.

"You don't believe us," Elizabeth said.

"That's not it," John said. He reached out and touched Elizabeth's hand, and then seemed to remember that he was at work and pulled back. "It's just that we need to make sure we have solid evidence before we make an arrest. We need to make sure the case holds up in court. It won't do any good to rush out and arrest this guy if we can't make a strong enough case to keep him behind bars. The last thing we need is for him to get free on a technicality."

Martha could see his point, sort of. But still.

"How long will that take?" Elizabeth asked. Elizabeth was feeling the same way, then.

"We'll move as quickly as we can," John said. There was a note of frustration in his voice. Well, that made three of them.

"Every moment he's out there, he's endangering those around him," Elizabeth said.

"We understand. And once again, we thank you for your help on this matter." There was a note of finality in John's voice. That was it, then. They were being dismissed.

Martha looked at Elizabeth, unsure of what to do. But Elizabeth was already pushing herself up. Her shoulders were stiff, and she was biting her lip. Martha hoped this interaction wouldn't affect her budding relationship with John.

"Please let us know if there is anything we can do to help," Martha said with as much calm as she could muster, and then she followed her sister out of the room. She waited until they were back in the car before she vented her frustration.

"They didn't even seem that grateful," she said as she turned the key in the ignition.

"I think they were," Elizabeth said. She let out a sigh. "But I guess it doesn't look good for them to have us come in and solve the crime for them."

"It doesn't matter who solved it," Martha said. "The important thing is making sure he's behind bars."

Elizabeth buckled her seat belt and leaned back against the headrest. "I guess they have to go through the proper channels. And I can see the point about being certain they have enough evidence to make sure the arrest sticks. But it just seems like jumping through hoops, when they should be out there stopping him."

"I wish there was some way we could make them move faster."

"Sadly, I don't think there's much chance of that." Martha backed the car up and then pulled out of the parking lot. As she turned onto 340 and headed back toward home, she noticed that Elizabeth had pulled out her phone.

"I wonder what kind of evidence it would take for them to step in and make an arrest now," Elizabeth said as she typed something onto her phone screen.

"I don't know. At this point, it sounds like anything short of a confession wouldn't be enough."

"Huh." Out of the corner of her eye, she could see that Elizabeth was using two fingers to enlarge something on her phone screen.

"What does that mean?"

"It means, I wonder if we could get a confession ourselves."

"We don't know how to get ahold of him, remember?" There were still patches of white along the sides of the road, spaced between the green shoots of the earliest daffodils.

"What if we did know where to find him?" Elizabeth was grinning.

"What do you mean?"

"Want to take a trip to State College tomorrow?"

CHAPTER EIGHTEEN

Martha couldn't believe she was doing this. There was no way she could make a trip to State College the day of the fundraiser. There was too much to do, too many last-minute details that needed to be dealt with. But at the same time, she didn't want to miss this. And Rachel had insisted that she had the fundraiser under control. She promised everything would be fine, and well, Martha had already lost control of the event anyway. Might as well let Rachel do things her way at this point.

So here she was, in the passenger seat of Mary's car, heading down the highway once again. Adam Fischer was in the back seat, quietly watching the landscape go by. Martha knew it had been difficult for him to get away this morning, leaving a very pregnant Leah to handle the morning farm chores, but he had been certain that he wanted to come and see Evan himself.

Elizabeth had stayed behind to open the shop, though she'd been disappointed to, in her words, miss the fun. Martha wasn't so sure it would be fun, but here they were nonetheless. In twenty minutes, they would be at Bald Eagle State Park, where Penn State's crew team practiced. Today the team was also hosting a regatta. A half hour from the campus, the park was in a more rural area, so at least there was that.

"How do all those people get in the boat without it tipping over?" Mary asked as they drove down the highway.

"I don't know," Martha said.

"How do they steer the boat? Do they control it with the oars?"

"Merriam-Webster says the coxswain does that," Martha said. She'd had to look up the word when she read it on the college's website.

"That's such a weird word, isn't it? Coxswain. Cox-son. I wonder where that comes from, and why they decided it needed all those extra letters."

"I have no idea," Martha said. Mary had had an extra cup of coffee this morning and was excited about what they were planning to do, that was for sure.

"I read that they get up ridiculously early to practice. Like, they have to be at practice before 5:00 a.m. Isn't that crazy?"

"And then they have to exercise once they get there." Martha shook her head.

"It still makes more sense to me than football," Adam chimed in.

Martha laughed and wondered how much football Adam had ever seen. "I'm with you on that one."

Mary chattered as they drove, and soon they were pulling into the park entrance. They told the guard they were there for the regatta and followed signs toward the parking lot near the lake. Martha knew they were in the right place when she saw trailers loaded with racing shells parked along the edges of the lot. There were young men and women in sweat suits from various colleges wandering everywhere. Down by the shore, a team of eight women was hoisting a boat from the water and setting it on their shoulders, and then they began to carry it back toward the trailers. A few people gave the three of them curious glances as they climbed out of the car and looked around.

"Penn State's outfits are blue and white," Mary said, scanning the crowd. Down at the water, a group of boats was racing past, oars flying. It was louder than she had expected, with the seats sliding back and forth as the oars slipped in and out of the water, but elegant at the same time. They almost seemed to be gliding over the surface of the lake.

"That doesn't exactly help." There had to be dozens of men and women wearing blue and white here. "Adam, do you see him?"

"I do not see anyone I recognize as Evan," he said, shaking his head. "But it has been several years since I last saw him."

"You'll recognize him when you see him," Mary said, with more confidence than Martha felt. What if they'd come this whole way and they didn't even pick him out? "I'm going to find him."

Mary walked quickly and caught up with a group of girls wearing jackets with *Penn State* written in big blue letters on the back. Martha wished she had a quarter of Mary's confidence.

"Excuse me." The girls stopped and looked quizzically at Mary. "I'm trying to find Evan Harper. Do you know where I can find him?"

"He's a lightweight, right?" a girl with flaming red hair asked her friend, a tall brunette. "I think that race is next."

"Yep. He's third seat." The brunette turned to Mary. "They're out on the water right now. But if you stay here, you'll be able to watch them go by in a bit."

Mary scanned the shore. "The boats get out of the water here?" She pointed to a wooden dock at the waterfront.

"That's right. They launch and get out at the dock down there," the redhead said. "So if you don't care about seeing the end of the race, you can wait here."

"Where would I go if I wanted to see the end?"

"You can walk down that path for a ways, and you'll be able to watch the boats cross the finish line." The brunette shrugged. "You can't see a whole lot because it's pretty far away, but you can usually see who won. And it takes them a while to row back to the dock, so you can beat them back for sure."

Mary turned back to Martha and Adam. "Do we want to see the finish?"

Both the redhead and the brunette's eyes widened when they saw Adam.

"Might as well," Martha said. She'd never seen a crew race in person.

"Thanks for your help," Mary said to the girls, and they nodded, still staring at Adam, before they finally turned away. As they walked away, the brunette leaned in to the redhead and said something, and they both started giggling.

"I do not think they see many Amish people at these races," Adam said with a smile. Martha was glad he seemed to have a good attitude about what could have been an uncomfortable situation.

"I would imagine not," Mary said. "Well. Shall we?"

It wasn't hard to find the path through the trees the girls had mentioned, as dozens of people were walking toward the water's edge and back. They followed the path and saw a vast expanse of flat blue water, dappled with sunlight. The tree limbs along both sides of the shore were still bare, but Martha could imagine how this place would look in a month, when the tender green leaves would bring the shoreline back to life. It would be stunning.

At the far left side of her field of vision, Martha could see the boats from the race that had just finished rowing along the shoreline back toward the dock. The rowers were wearing the same kind of tank top and shorts combo she'd seen in the photos online, and they would have been freezing if they weren't all sweating. Once they'd vanished out of view, there wasn't anything disturbing the calm, smooth surface of the water.

"It seems to be a very silly sport, does it not?" Adam asked. "Why not just get a boat with an engine?"

Martha couldn't help it. She laughed out loud. "I was thinking the same thing."

"It's supposed to be very hard. A full-body workout," Mary said.

"I have no doubt you're right," Martha said. She decided to leave it at that, because she began to make out a low, rhythmic sound coming from the left.

"That will be the next race," Mary said. "See if you can spot him."

It was another minute or so before the boats came into view around the bend in the lake, and then Martha spotted the Penn State boat quickly. They were the closest to the shore, and the men were wearing blue and white. They were gliding back and forth on the seats, pulling the oars smoothly through the water. The coxswains were all shouting at the teams through headsets, and a motorized boat followed along behind them. Race officials, Martha assumed. Around them, people on the shore were yelling and cheering for their favorites. She'd had no idea what a loud sport this would be.

"That is him," Adam said. "The third from the front."

Martha wasn't sure how he could tell with how quickly they were moving, but he seemed certain.

They watched as the boats flew past them toward the buoys that marked the end of the race course. Just behind the finish line, the team wearing orange—Bucknell, Martha gathered from the cheering fans wearing Bucknell sweatshirts—pulled ahead, and the screaming on the shoreline increased. Bucknell's boat crossed the buoys first, and all the men in the boats seemed to collapse. They continued to row, but they moved slowly, and they were all gasping for air. From the shore, it hadn't looked like they were working very hard, but she supposed they were. It took a few minutes for them to catch their breath, and then they turned the boats around and started to row back toward the dock.

"Let's go back," Mary said. They walked back down the path and waited in the clearing by the parking lot. The boats came into view and pulled up along the dock and began to unload. At the signal from the coxswain, the men unscrewed their oars and slid them along the dock out of the way, and then, at another signal, they climbed out of the boat. Martha kept waiting for the boat to tip, but it never did. The rowers each picked up his oar and carried it toward the trucks. Martha, Mary, and Adam moved closer. They hadn't decided what they would do when they saw Evan or exactly how this would unfold. But to Martha's surprise, Adam walked directly toward him.

Now that he was close, Martha could see that Evan was tall and muscular, and had the sharp cheekbones Brianna had talked so much about. She could see how a college girl would have found him attractive, but there was a swagger in his walk, even when he must have been exhausted from the race, that Martha found off-putting.

Evan set his oar into the trailer and then turned. Adam stood directly in his path back to the water. Martha could tell the moment he recognized Adam. His eyes widened, and he stopped short. Martha wasn't sure what exactly to do, so she took out her phone and opened the camera app and began recording the encounter, just in case.

"Hello, Evan." Adam's voice was strong and confident.

"Do I know you?" Evan sounded cocky, even in those few words. A few of his teammates had stopped to see what Adam was doing.

"I think you do," Adam said. "I think my name should be very familiar to you, considering you've been using it as your own for the past few years."

"I don't know what you're talking about. I don't know any Amish freaks."

Now that was just mean. Martha wanted to step forward and give this guy a piece of her mind, but she stayed back, recording the interaction. She noticed that Evan's teammates had stepped a bit closer.

"You stole my driver's license when we worked together at the vet clinic. Then you stole my social security number, and you used it to open credit cards and register cars and even when you got in trouble with the police." Adam's voice was calm and clear, lacking the hint of an accent he sometimes had when he was talking to other Amish.

Evan seemed to weigh this. A muscle in his jaw worked, and Martha saw his arms tense. For a moment, she worried he was going to hit Adam, and she prayed this would not turn physical. Adam was tall, and strong from daily farm chores, but Evan and his teammates were all ripped, and they outnumbered Adam and his two middle-aged companions.

But then, Evan did something she didn't expect. He laughed.

"So you finally figured that out, did you?" He laughed again. "The Amish are even stupider than I thought. It took you more than two years to catch on. Idiots."

"You crashed into a buggy. You nearly killed the Mast family." Adam delivered this calmly, evenly.

"Those buggies should be illegal. They're a hazard. They deserved what they got for being so slow. Other people have places to be. That's why they invented cars."

Evan's teammates were now watching him with their faces scrunched up in confusion. Were they seeing a new side to their friend? Martha wasn't sure, but she did know she'd gotten the whole thing on video, and they now had all the evidence John and Officer Hooper needed to arrest him.

"She's recording this, bro." One of Evan's teammates, a guy with dark hair, said, gesturing toward Martha.

Evan looked over and saw Martha and Mary, apparently for the first time. He let out an expletive, and then he lunged forward and grabbed the phone out of her hands. Martha tried to hold it, but she was so surprised by the turn of events that she didn't react quickly enough, and Evan began running toward the parking lot.

Why was he running that way? Martha wondered, even as she tried to make her limbs start moving to go after him. She felt like she was watching the whole thing unfold through a sheet of glass. Wouldn't it make more sense for him to run toward the water and throw the phone into the lake? But he was running toward a car in the parking lot. Surely he didn't have keys with him under that skin-tight outfit.... But he just yanked open a door and hopped into a small black car. Mary was running toward the lot as well, following Adam.

"Keys!" Adam shouted. Mary dug into her purse and grabbed the keys and tossed them to Adam, who caught them easily.

"Come on!" Mary shouted, and Martha tried to force her limbs to obey. She ran after them and reached the car just as Adam cranked the ignition. What was happening? Adam couldn't drive. He didn't have a license.... How had this turned into a car chase? But they had to get her phone back. It contained the evidence they needed to stop Evan for good. All these thoughts raced through Martha's mind as she jumped into the back seat. Her door wasn't even closed when Adam backed the car up and pulled away, following the black car Evan was in. The pedestrians jumped out of the way as the cars raced toward the exit of the lot.

Martha remembered Rachel saying that Adam had liked to drive fast, and thought about Adam's trips to the racetrack.

She saw what they meant now. Evan must have been flooring the gas pedal as they pulled out onto the main road, but Adam was right behind him, keeping pace.

"So it *could* have been you that was driving that car that crashed into the buggy," Mary said.

"It could have been, but it wasn't." Adam didn't take his eyes off the road. "I like to drive fast, but I lack the wheels."

Martha wasn't sure if that was meant to be a joke or not, but she didn't have the energy to find out. How was this going to end? None of the scenarios her mind conjured were good.

"There's a curve up ahead," Mary was saying, and Adam nodded, his eyes focused on the car in front of him.

They had to be going at least eighty, but Martha couldn't bring herself to check. How long had it been since Adam had been behind the wheel of a car? She felt her stomach drop. This wasn't good. She was going to die in a high-speed chase in a car driven by an Amish man. The irony was almost too much to bear.

"Where did you learn to drive like this?" Mary asked from the passenger seat. She sounded delighted. Martha saw her life flash before her eyes.

"There are many back roads," he said, without shifting his focus from the car directly in front of him. If Evan stomped on the brakes now, there would be no way to stop in time. Fortunately—or not, depending on how you looked at it—he didn't seem to have any intention of slowing down. "I have told you that I was considering becoming Englisch. I did not tell you that becoming a vet was my second choice, behind race car driver."

She would have laughed out loud if she wasn't so afraid for her life. "Your mother mentioned a couple of speeding tickets."

"She was not telling the whole truth. It was more than a couple."

They made it around the bend in the road, and a few hundred yards up ahead was an intersection. Martha held her breath. Which way was he going to turn? Or would he go straight? They had a green light now, but it would certainly change by the time they got there, and Evan didn't seem like the kind to wait at red lights.

"You know what?" Martha tried to keep her tone light and jovial, but doubted she was succeeding. "I don't really need that phone anyway. Let's just stop this now, before someone gets hurt." She could enter new contacts. She'd lose the recent set of pictures of her grandkids, but weren't these things all backed up to the cloud anyway?

"That phone has the evidence we need to put a stop to this once and for all," Mary said. "Adam, you're doing a great job." Up ahead, the light was turning yellow, but Evan showed no sign of slowing down.

"He probably already deleted the video," Martha said.

"Not while he was driving like that." The light was turning red, but Evan gunned it. The light was fully red when he entered the intersection, and Adam followed a moment later after slowing down enough to make sure there were no cars coming,

"This is insane! We have to stop." Martha was panicking. Where were they even going? What was the plan here?

Adam didn't answer, but a moment later, the sound of sirens started up behind them. She had never heard such a beautiful noise in her life. The sirens got closer, and the flashing red and blue lights were gaining on them quickly. Surely he would—but no, Evan either didn't hear them or was simply ignoring them. He kept driving, racing toward who knew what. She supposed she should be thankful this was a fairly rural area and not a densely populated city.

The police car pulled up alongside them, veering into the lane for oncoming traffic, which was thankfully empty. It raced past them and caught up with Evan.

"Pull over," came a booming voice from the police car. Evan didn't listen, but Adam had already lifted his foot off the accelerator, and Martha said a silent prayer of thanks. The officer inside the car grew increasingly angry as he yelled at Evan to pull over, and Martha prayed he would listen. And then, she just prayed. She closed her eyes and asked the Lord to protect them on this insane errand. She asked that He would protect the innocent people around them, and that this crazy stunt would not endanger any other lives. She prayed for protection for the police, and she prayed for Evan, that he would be safe and that he would have a change of heart. She tried to tune out the shrill wailing of the police siren and the booming voice of the police officer saying something about a roadblock ahead.

A...what? Martha's eyes flew open. She saw that there, a few thousand feet down the road, a police car was parked sideways across a bridge, its lights flashing, blocking the road.

There was nowhere for Evan to go. Either side of the road was woods leading up to the bridge, and there was no way to cross the bridge without his slamming directly into the police cruiser.

Please, Lord, let it slow him down, Martha prayed, but for a moment, Evan didn't seem to slow down.

It wasn't until Evan's brake lights appeared that Martha let out a breath she hadn't realized she'd been holding. It seemed to take forever for him to stop, but his car eventually rolled to a stop just a hundred feet from the parked police car. A moment later, the other police car pulled up beside him and, over the loudspeaker, instructed him to step out of the car with his hands behind his head. Officers had guns drawn, aimed at the car.

Martha saw another policeman come up to their car, also with his gun drawn, and give them the same instructions. Martha pushed open the door, took in a long, deep breath, and then stepped out. Adam and Mary were also climbing out. In her peripheral vision, she could see that Evan hadn't yet opened his door. There was nowhere left for him to go. He should step out and face the music. But she turned back to the officer who was now standing beside Mary's car, staring at them, his mouth wide open. Whoever he'd been expecting to be inside the car, it apparently wasn't two middle-aged women and an Amish man.

Maybe it was the relief of finally being safe, and of knowing that Evan was finally going to be punished for his crimes. Maybe it was because she'd just realized how ridiculous the situation truly was. But for whatever reason, when she saw how stunned the officer was, Martha began to laugh. And once she started, she couldn't stop.

"I think we have some explaining to do," Mary said quietly.

"Yes," Adam said in his same calm, measured way. "I think you may be right."

CHAPTER NINETEEN

Martha had been inside police stations many times, but she'd never been in the position of the one being questioned. It took many hours of repeating the same story, over and over, to various officers of the State College police force, and many phone calls to the East Lampeter station before they were free to go. She, Mary, and Adam—all separated once they'd been brought to the station—had given the same story, and Officer John Marks had backed it up, though he'd clearly been less than thrilled to hear about their adventures of the day. Martha's phone was taken as evidence, and no amount of arguing on her part was apparently going to change that. The police officers here weren't swayed by her insistence that she needed it to pull together the details for an Amish bake sale that night.

"The Amish make do without phones. You can too," was the police officer's stern reply. Martha thought about pointing out that the Amish didn't actually do without phones, they just didn't have phones in their homes, and explaining about phone shanties, but she decided it wouldn't help her and would simply annoy the officer. The important thing was that they now had the video, which clearly showed Evan acknowledging his crimes. The police could not cite lack of evidence now. Surely he would finally face the consequences of his actions.

Finally, they were released, and Martha supposed she should be grateful for that. She had been worried that they would hold Adam, but once they'd heard the whole story, they must have seen that he wasn't a real risk and let him go home. They were instructed to report directly to the East Lampeter police department, where John and Officer Hooper would be waiting for them.

Mary drove on the way home. Adam insisted his driving days were truly behind him, and, now that Martha was safely out of the situation, she realized it was kind of a shame. He was actually very good.

The ride back was mostly quiet, each lost in their own thoughts, and when they finally pulled into the parking lot of the police station, Martha was almost disappointed.

There would be a lot of explaining to do.

But as Adam stepped out of the car in his Amish beard and hat, Martha knew that it had all been worth it. Adam was free. His record would be cleared, and he could go back to living a simple life with his wife and, soon, a baby. Evan was in police custody, and they had the evidence to make sure he stayed there for a good long time.

When Martha pulled into the driveway of the Fischer farm that evening, she couldn't believe what she saw. The yard had been cleared and swept, and a line of buggies was already forming along the fence, with horses tied up in the paddock. The door to the barn was wide open, and even from here, Martha could see strands of battery-powered twinkle lights draped from the rafters, lighting the barn with a lovely soft glow.

"Oh my." Martha couldn't believe it. Tables draped in elegant white cloths were set up throughout the open space in the barn, and battery-powered candles flickered in frosted votives, lighting up each table. Ivy and evergreen boughs were draped around the cakes and pies and breads that were already crowding the tables, and Amish women scurried back and forth, arranging the desserts and ferrying serving utensils and cash boxes. Propane-powered heaters, set up around the edges of the barn, made the space feel toasty warm.

"Martha. It is good to see you."

Martha turned and saw that Rachel had come up beside her, a stack of white cardstock in her hands.

"This looks incredible." Was this the same barn?

"I think it did turn out nicely," Rachel said. "Thank you for all that you did to make this happen."

"I didn't—" Martha didn't know what to say. This wasn't at all what she had envisioned. But it was so much nicer. "I can't believe it."

Rachel had the good grace to smile.

"Come set those down." She gestured toward a table, and Martha gratefully set down the carrot cake and two loaves of chocolate-zucchini bread she'd been holding. There was plenty more in the car. "Can you make labels for them?" Rachel asked, pulling a Sharpie from a pocket of her dress. She set the stack of cards down, and Martha noticed that there were handwritten labels in front of each dessert.

"Do you have the cash box set up?" Martha asked as she made the labels.

"Oh yes." Rachel gestured toward a table set to the side, where three cash boxes were already being set up by women that looked vaguely familiar to Martha.

"What about the beverage station?" They'd discussed having coffee and tea for sale. Rachel gestured to the table on the other side, where urns of coffee and hot water were already brewing. Women were carrying small pitchers of cream and setting out sugar.

"Parking?"

"Ephraim and Luke are directing traffic, and Matthew and Thomas are caring for the horses."

"Wow." Martha looked around, but she couldn't see anything that needed to be done. "What can I do to help?"

"Nothing. You can relax." Rachel gave her a wide smile. "I do not think that you know how, but you can try."

"I'm not great at it," Martha confessed. The place looked gorgeous. They had more desserts than she could have imagined. There were plenty of women ready to help out. Now all they needed was for people to show up.

But judging by the line of cars and buggies that was already snaking its way down the driveway, that wasn't going to be a problem.

They hadn't done it Martha's way. But it had turned out okay anyway. More than okay.

"I'm sorry I was trying so hard to control all of this," Martha said. "This turned out beautifully."

"It was a team effort," Rachel said. "You know how to put on an Englisch event, and I know how to make an Amish party happen. Together, hopefully, we can raise a lot of money for the Mast family."

The next hour was a blur of greeting neighbors and friends and selling slices of cake and muffins and whole pies just as fast as they could set them out. Martha chatted with people who had seen the signs in the businesses in town or seen the ads she'd placed online, but she saw just as many Amish families who had heard about the event through the mysterious Amish grapevine and brought the entire family out for the evening. People were laughing and catching up, and it was beautiful. She couldn't even begin to imagine how much they were making to support the Mast family. Though Miriam was home with Abel, Abner was there, talking with people, thanking them for coming.

"Martha?" Elizabeth came up beside her, touching her arm gently. Martha had seen her and Mary come in a while ago, but hadn't had a moment to say hello yet.

"Hi there." Martha leaned in to give her older sister a hug.

Elizabeth bit her lip. "Can I pull you away for a moment?"

"Sure." Something in Elizabeth's face made her nervous. "What's going on?"

"There's someone I want you to meet."

Martha followed Elizabeth, threading through the crowd, to a quiet corner of the barn near the horse stalls. Mary was already standing there, along with an Amish woman who appeared to be a bit younger than the Classen sisters.

"This is Loriann Hershberger. She's Susannah Fischer's granddaughter."

"Oh." The sound escaped before Martha could stop it. Elizabeth had already told them what she'd learned from Anke, so this couldn't be their niece. But...she was descended from Susannah.

"Hello." Loriann smiled kindly. "It is nice to meet you."

"You're really..." Martha wasn't even sure what she was trying to say.

"Yes," Loriann said with a laugh. "My mother was Susannah's firstborn, though my grandfather had three children from his first marriage when they married."

"It's...it's nice to meet you." Had she already said that? She wasn't sure. She had so many questions she wanted to ask, she didn't even know where to start.

"Anke wanted us to meet Loriann," Elizabeth said. "After I talked with Anke the other day, she spoke with Loriann to ask about her grandmother." Elizabeth seemed to be trying to encourage Loriann to say something.

"My grandmother passed away a few years ago," Loriann said.

"I'm sorry," Mary said, though Elizabeth had told them Susannah was gone after she spoke to Anke.

Loriann continued. "She lived in the dawdy haus behind my uncle's home for many years. When she passed away, my sister and I cleaned the house out. We found many things, most of them what you would expect. Clippings of her children's hair, that sort of thing. But there were a few things that we did not understand, at least not until Anke talked to us this week."

"What did you find?" Martha asked.

"There was a stack of letters, sent from a college far away," Loriann said. "Written many years ago. They were…they were love letters. From a man named Henry. It seemed that whoever this man Henry was, he loved her very much."

"That was Daddy," Mary said quietly.

"Yes, that is what Anke told me," Loriann said. "She also tells me that he has passed away."

"It was about ten years ago," Martha said.

Loriann nodded. "I did not know your father, but I do know that my grandmother loved him. She kept his letters until the day she died."

Martha felt tears sting her eyes. For some reason, it made her heart glad to hear it. She'd guessed that Daddy had loved Susannah, but it was somehow powerful and gratifying to learn that Susannah had loved him too. Both had gone on to marry other people, and Daddy, at least, had genuinely loved and cared for Mama, even if he never forgot his first love.

But there was still one question.

"Did…did your mother ever say anything about another child? One before her?"

"No." Loriann shook her head. "No, Mama never said anything about a baby. But Anke asked me the same question, and I think I know what happened there."

All three Classen sisters were looking at her, waiting for her to go on.

"After my second daughter was born, I lost a baby. It was early in the pregnancy, but still, I was devastated."

"I'm so sorry," Martha said.

"That's awful," Elizabeth agreed.

"Many people seemed to not understand why I was so upset. It wasn't as if I had lost one of the children I had birthed, they thought. I was not far along, and they seemed to think I wouldn't be attached to the baby at that point."

"It was your child," Mary said.

"I loved that baby, even though I was so many months from meeting it," Loriann said. "And it hurt that no one seemed to understand." She paused and took a deep breath. "Except Oma. She came to see me, and she held me, and we both cried. She told me that she had lost a baby once, many years ago. A baby she had loved deeply."

"Did she say when this was?" Martha asked.

"All she said was that it was early in her marriage," Loriann said. "I did not ask for more than that, and I am sorry about that now. I wish I could tell you. But I would guess... Well, early in her marriage means it could have been his, right?"

She didn't need to say who she was referring to. They all understood.

"Yes," Mary said quietly. "It sounds like it could have been."

There was no way to know for sure, but it seemed likely that that answered the question. Susannah had married Lloyd, but she lost the baby. There was no older sibling out there, but Susannah had never forgotten Daddy, just as he had never forgotten her.

"Thank you for telling us," Elizabeth said.

"I need to thank you. You have helped me understand my grandmother better, and for that I am grateful."

Martha felt the same way. She was sorry for Daddy, sorry that he had his heart broken, sorry that his early mistakes had caused so much hurt. But she was grateful to know about it. She knew more about her daddy than ever before, and she was glad for it.

After Loriann walked away, Mary slipped her arm around Martha's shoulder. Then Elizabeth wrapped her arm over her other shoulder. The three sisters stood like that, all together, for a few minutes in silence.

"It's really amazing, isn't it?" Mary finally said.

"Yes. To think that Daddy loved someone else, all those years ago," Elizabeth said.

"Well, yes," Mary said. "But I meant all of this." She gestured around at the fundraiser, which was really more like a party, with friends chatting and laughing and neighbors enjoying being together. "It's amazing to see the whole community come together for something like this."

"It is," Martha agreed. "It really is."

Martha looked around the barn and saw that Adam and Leah had come in, Leah cradling her belly. She was glad they'd been able to help Adam. It in no way made up for all the help and love and support they'd received from the Fischer family all these years, but it was some small way of repaying them, and it felt nice.

"They could have been family," Elizabeth murmured.

Martha realized that she was right. If Susannah's baby— Susannah and Daddy's baby—had lived, the Classens would be united to the Fischer family by more than adjoining properties.

"They kind of are like family, though, aren't they?" Mary said.

Martha thought about all that the Fischer family had meant to her family over the years. They had shared meals and tools.

They had cared for them when Mama and Daddy were sick, and now worked their land. Their lifestyles were very different, sure, but the Fischers were almost like family. Helping to clear Adam's name was nothing compared to all those things. But that was what family did, wasn't it? They took care of each other, and they didn't keep score. They loved, even when they disagreed. She glanced over at Rachel, smiling and laughing with Ruth Yutzy. They came together to care for one another.

"They really are," Martha said, and pulled her sisters in closer. "And I'm so grateful."

A NOTE FROM THE AUTHOR

Dear Reader,

This book is in so many ways about identity, and writing it brought back one of the times in my life when I was struggling to figure out who I really was. I was a freshman in college, 3,000 miles from home, and I had joined the university's crew team. I had never tried the sport before, but it looked fun, and I had been a swimmer in high school. The coach assured me that swimmers made good rowers.

It turned out, I was good. I was good enough that I started to think I didn't really need to be spending time at church and with the campus fellowship, because I was too busy with my new sport. I won't go into the details of what happened, but suffice it to say that it ended badly, and I was forced to confront the reality that I was not a rower first—I was a Christian first, and when I forgot that, life did not go well. It's a lesson that has stuck with me, even as I left rowing far behind.

Maybe you were surprised, like I was, to find out that many of the Amish have social security numbers. I had assumed that was one of the many things they had opted out of in choosing to live in their closed society. But once I discovered that they do have these numbers—mostly so they can opt out of social security payments, which they do see as insurance—I began to wonder what would happen if this personal information from an Amish person was misused.

For most of us, this nine-digit number is an important identifier, and we rightly guard it closely. If the number falls into the wrong hands, it can be used to steal our money and our data. However, as ubiquitous and important as these numbers are in our daily life, I find it important to remind myself that a number does not define me. My identity cannot be stolen if I define myself, first and foremost, as a child of God. No matter what happens here on earth, to my finances or otherwise, no one can take that away from me.

I hope you enjoyed reading this story as much as I enjoyed writing it.

Best wishes,
Beth Adams

ABOUT THE AUTHOR

Beth Adams lives in Brooklyn, New York, with her husband and two young daughters. When she's not writing, she spends her time cleaning up after two devious cats and trying to find time to read mysteries.

BARN FINDS

My husband and I love thrift shops, yard sales, vintage stores, flea markets, and rummage sales of all kinds. There is something so thrilling about searching through things someone else is discarding, looking for treasure.

When we traveled to Italy earlier this year, one of the first places we went was a Sunday morning flea market in Rome that was rumored to be great for finding interesting souvenirs. We drank several cappuccinos and headed out, and at one stall, we found a thick, heavy book with a cracked spine. Inside, we found architectural line drawings of the most important churches, infrastructure, and cultural sites in Italy. We did not want to carry the entire book home, but the man was willing to sell us individual pages.

My husband and I bought a page that showed the design of several important churches in Italy, including St. Peter's and the Duomo, to give to our friend who was graduating from seminary. We also took home a page of drawings of domes—most of them in the focal point and main structural element of famous cathedrals—for ourselves. The picture dome, beautiful in its simplicity, hangs on the wall of our home in Brooklyn, and it always reminds me of the joy of our trip, of the excitement of finding something special that no one else sees, and also of the beautiful and astounding churches built throughout the centuries for God's glory.

This is where the idea for the book Della Bradford brings into the shop came from, and I like to imagine that someone in Lancaster County will come into the shop and find it. I like to believe they will take it home to brighten their walls with images of the religious structures built to bring glory to God.

FRESH FROM MARTHA'S KITCHEN

German Chocolate Cake

Cake Ingredients:

4 ounces German sweet
   chocolate, chopped

½ cup water

1 cup butter, softened

2 cups sugar

4 eggs, room temperature,
   separated

1 teaspoon vanilla extract

2 ½ cups cake flour

1 teaspoon baking soda

½ teaspoon salt

1 cup buttermilk

Frosting:

1 ½ cups sugar

1 ½ cups evaporated milk

¾ cup butter

5 egg yolks, beaten

2 cups sweetened coconut
   flakes

1 ½ cups chopped pecans

1 ½ teaspoons vanilla extract

Directions:

In a saucepan, melt chocolate with water over low heat. Let cool.

Preheat oven to 350 degrees. Cream butter and sugar in large bowl until light and fluffy. Beat in 4 egg yolks, one at a time. Blend in melted chocolate and vanilla. Combine flour, baking soda, and salt, then add to the creamed mixture alternately with buttermilk, beating well after each addition.

In a small bowl, beat 4 egg whites until stiff peaks form. Fold a fourth of the egg whites into creamed mixture; fold in remaining whites.

Pour batter into three greased round baking pans. Bake 24 to 28 minutes or until a toothpick comes out clean. Cool 10 minutes before removing from pans.

For frosting, heat sugar, milk, butter, and egg yolks over medium-low heat, stirring constantly, until mixture is thickened and golden brown. Remove from heat, stir in coconut, pecans, and vanilla extract. Let cool. Spread frosting over each cake layer and stack the layers.

Read on for a sneak peek of another exciting book
in the Mysteries of Lancaster County series!

Beg, Borrow, or Steal
by Anne Marie Rodgers

Sunlight streamed through the tall, east-facing windows of
the Mount Zion Mennonite Church's fellowship hall, and
birdsong drifted in through the open sashes, weaving a charming counterpoint to the chattering crowd. It was an unusually
warm, mild April day in Lancaster County, Pennsylvania, and
Elizabeth clearly felt the pull of spring. Some of the women in
more contemporary garb had traded wool and warmth for
lighter fabrics, and the tables around the room sported vases
of sunny daffodils.

The fellowship time during the short reception between
Sunday school and church was always well attended, but today
was Palm Sunday, and there were even more people than usual
at the traditional morning service.

Several pots of hyacinths had been set on the long table
where baked goods and drinks were located, and Elizabeth
Classen could smell their sweet scent, though she stood some
distance away with her sister Martha and several of their friends
in the congregation. The bright colors of the spring flowers
were echoed by the lighter, brighter colors many of the women
in the congregation wore. Everyone seemed happy that spring

had arrived, and the bluster of March had finally given way to warmer spring temperatures across Lancaster County.

Elizabeth wore a blue-and-yellow flowered skirt with a pale yellow twinset, relatively new wardrobe pieces she'd chosen because she loved the colors. She felt a bit self-conscious. Sometimes she still felt as if she was calling attention to herself with her new style of dress, even as modest a change as it was.

As she listened to Martha discuss a recipe for Paska Easter bread with a friend, Elizabeth's gaze roamed the assembled people. Dozens were seated at the tables provided, enjoying snacks from the refreshment stand at the far end of the room. Mary was in front of the stand, exchanging a few words and a smile with the woman who was refilling drink cups. Ever casual, even on Palm Sunday, she wore a slim pair of jeans beneath a flowing pink-and-blue paisley blouse with a scalloped hem and bell sleeves. It was a slight departure from the oversized painter's shirts she often wore, but not drastic.

Elizabeth smiled, watching a young mother who appeared to be trying to dissuade her toddler from grabbing a handful of cookies from the dozens of baked goods. Words apparently were not working, because the child began to wail loudly. The mother, looking mortified, quickly snatched him up and carried him through the double doors into the hallway beyond. As the doors slowly closed, the sound of his tantrum diminished in volume.

At the far end of the refreshment table sat several bowls holding fruit. A slender teenager placed an apple from one of the fruit bowls into the pocket of her oversized tan jacket. The teen's back was to the room, and all Elizabeth could see was shoulder-length, rather curly and wild-looking black hair and a pair of faded jeans with a ripped-out pocket and frayed hems that were significantly less dressy than most of the other young people in the room wore. The girl at the table stood out because of the shabbiness of her clothes.

The teen picked up a banana and stuffed it into another pocket. Then Elizabeth saw her take another apple. What on earth...?

It appeared someone else had noticed the unusual behavior. Geraldine Goertz, a large woman who wore a conservative plain blue dress with a small lace prayer cover affixed to her hair, stepped up to the table and addressed the girl. Elizabeth saw the slender figure startle, but the teen apparently responded, and Geraldine said something else. Then, before Elizabeth could even process what had happened, the girl turned sharply, took several almost running strides, and slipped through the exit leaving a trail of crumbs behind. Perhaps she had some cookies in her pocket as well. Geraldine frowned after the girl for a moment, shrugged her shoulders, and then meandered along the table and picked up a cookie.

"Did you see that girl?" Elizabeth turned to her sister Martha, lovely in a soft lavender sweater set and a matching flowered skirt that swished around her calves. Her middle sister was a beauty, Elizabeth thought, admiring Martha's brown hair and the light in her blue eyes as she chatted animatedly with a fellow chef in the crowd.

But Martha was still talking recipes with Essie Baldwin. Both women looked at her as one. "What girl?" they asked in unison.

Elizabeth shook her head, smiling. "Never mind."

Mary approached. "That's good lemonade," she said. "Would you like me to get you some?"

"No, thank you," Elizabeth said. "Did you happen to notice the girl who was standing near you in the oversized jacket?"

Mary glanced around the room. "No. What girl?"

Elizabeth gestured. "She was at the other end of the table from you. It was really odd. She was filling her pockets with fruit."

"That is sort of strange." Then Mary shrugged. "Or maybe not. Kids do weird stuff all the time. Maybe she was taking some for friends."

"It certainly caught my attention," Elizabeth said. "She didn't eat any, just started loading her pockets with apples and bananas. She had plenty of room in that big jacket she was wearing. And then she left abruptly."

"Where'd she go?" Mary looked around as if she might be able to spot the teen.

"She ran outside."

When Mary's eyebrows shot up, Elizabeth elaborated. "Geraldine Goertz noticed what she was doing too. Geraldine walked over to speak with her. And about six seconds later, the girl bolted out the exit just behind the end of the table."

Mary's eyebrows rose even higher. "What on earth…? Seems like if she was doing something innocent, she wouldn't have run away like that. What do you suppose Geraldine said to her?"

"To whom?" Martha had finished speaking with Essie, who was turning to greet someone else. She raised her eyebrows inquiringly.

Elizabeth repeated what she'd told Mary. "I'd give a lot to know what Geraldine said that made that child take off like that," she concluded.

"Well, why don't you just ask her about it?" That was Martha, always sensible.

"I think I will," Elizabeth said.

But before she could look around and locate Geraldine, Mary tapped the face of her watch. "It's time for church."

Elizabeth followed her sisters to the sanctuary, promising herself she would catch Geraldine later.

Entering the sanctuary, they were greeted by the usher teams for that Sunday and given bulletins with the order of the service and this week's relevant announcements. As they made their way into their pew, they exchanged greetings with the familiar families who sat around them.

Shortly after the sisters took their seats in the pew the Classen family had been sitting in since the sisters' grandparents first attended Mount Zion, the prelude began. When it ended, the organist began to play a lovely piece of music composed by Jean Baptiste Faure that had been a staple of the church's Palm Sunday celebration since Elizabeth's own childhood. One by one, the children of the congregation slowly carried palms to the front of the church, where they were received by elders and pastors and piled before the altar. As the refrain began, Elizabeth felt her throat grow tight and tears sting her eyes. She and her sisters had been among those children many years before.

"Join all and sing His name declare,
Let ev'ry voice resound with acclamation,
Hosanna! Praised be the Lord!
Bless Him, who cometh to bring us salvation!"

The final word was drawn out into roughly seven syllables.

For the past several years, the "palms" had consisted of plentiful local grasses scythed in the fall and stored throughout the winter, as members of the congregation had become more aware that ordering palms from Central American countries, where they were harvested with little regard for the damage done to the ecosystems of the surrounding forests, was not an environmentally friendly practice.

As the choir and congregation sang, and the grasses piled up, Elizabeth continued to feel moved by the beauty of the moment. It was a lovely ritual, made even more poignant when she contemplated Jesus's entry into Jerusalem. Palm Sunday preceded a week of somber reflection on His tragic death less than a week later. Throughout the coming week, they would mourn. But today, Christ had made a triumphal entry into the Holy City accompanied by an enthusiastic crowd. She felt herself relaxing into the joy of the moment.

A bit later, she listened attentively to Pastor Nagle's message, which focused on his visions for ministry in the community, for his anticipation of his eventual face-to-face meeting with his Lord. How would each of them react when Christ asked for an accounting of how they had responded to those who asked for assistance, whether in monetary form or otherwise? Would assistance have been conditional, based on a personal decision about how worthy they had judged the need to be? As he moved on to discuss Christ's knowledge of what He was about to face after the celebratory crowd embraced Him, expecting salvation from their overlords, Elizabeth's attention strayed, caught by the question.

How would she have reacted earlier if she had been the one to speak with the girl in the tan jacket who had been stuffing her pockets with fruit? She had an uncomfortable feeling her first question would have been along the lines of why the girl needed all that fruit, and she wondered if that was what Geraldine had said.

Surreptitiously, she looked around the congregation. The girl did not appear to be among her fellow worshippers. It was possible she hadn't stayed for church or was helping out with the youngest children in the church nursery. But Elizabeth couldn't recall ever having seen that particular girl before. Was she a church member at all? And if not, what on earth could have led her to attend the social time between Sunday school and church? Surely she hadn't come only to pick up some fruit and possibly some cookies. That was just too strange to contemplate.

After the service Elizabeth and her sisters filed out of the sanctuary, speaking to friends along the way. She blinked as she, Martha, and Mary stepped out into the bright sunshine. Scanning the sidewalk, she located Geraldine Goertz chatting with several members of her extended family a short distance away. She hadn't forgotten her desire to ask Geraldine about the conversation she'd had with the teen.

Elizabeth smiled warmly as she approached the other woman. "Good morning, Geraldine."

"Good morning, Elizabeth. Blessings to you on this Palm Sunday." Geraldine smiled.

"Thank you. And to you." Elizabeth cleared her throat. "I saw you speaking to a young girl during the fellowship time. I didn't recognize her, and I wondered who she was. Did you know her?"

Geraldine snorted in a good-natured way. "There wasn't much speaking going on. I saw her putting fruit and crackers in her pockets. Did you notice that?"

Elizabeth nodded. "I noticed the fruit. Did she say what she was going to do with it?"

"I don't know. I mentioned that the fruit was a much better snack than cookies, and she agreed with me." Geraldine's eyebrows rose. "And then she asked if I had twenty dollars she could borrow! Can you imagine such a thing? She said she'd pay me back when she was able."

Elizabeth felt a shock of surprise. "What did you say to her?"

Geraldine shrugged. "I didn't know what to say, to tell you the truth. I asked her to tell me her name and why she needed twenty dollars. And the next thing I knew, she turned around and hurried out the door like a pack of wild dogs was on her tail."

Elizabeth had to chuckle at Geraldine's description. But concern niggled at the corners of her mind. The girl had appeared slender. Was she hungry? "What did she look like?" Elizabeth asked. "I could only see long, curly, kind of wild dark hair from the back. Is she a member of the congregation?"

Geraldine shook her head. "I'd never seen her before. I'd remember those eyes."

Eyes? "What about her eyes?"

"She's got a thin little face," Geraldine said. "But she has these great big eyes of a very light color. Not blue. Perhaps greenish. The color is not what struck me. It was more that her eyes are the most memorable feature of her face."

"I don't believe I've ever seen her before either," Elizabeth said. The two women fell silent for a moment.

Then Geraldine shrugged. "I guess it's just going to be a little Palm Sunday mystery."

"I guess it is." Elizabeth chatted a little bit more before returning to her sisters. They had stopped to speak with others on the way to the parking lot. After joining the group, Elizabeth recounted the incident with the unknown girl, sharing Geraldine's close-up description of the girl's memorable eyes. "Does that sound like anyone you might know?" she asked the group in general.

Rella Wiens, who had overseen the guest book for today's services, cocked her head to one side. "I don't recall any young person coming in who fits that description exactly, but it could be Tammy McClain's daughter, Brittany. She has long dark hair, and she's in the youth group. I'm not sure I'd describe her hair as wild, but that's sort of a subjective term, isn't it? She hardly ever comes to church, but I believe she came in the side door with her mother today."

"You know," Mary said, "there's a girl with shoulder-length black hair who plays the guitar at the evening service. She looks like an older teen to me, and her hair's definitely what I'd call wild. In fact, it often has a streak of some color or other in it."

Elizabeth almost never attended the evening service. She couldn't bring the guitar player to mind at all. The girl she'd seen today hadn't had any noticeable color in her hair, but a streak could have gone unnoticed, especially from a distance. "Do you know her name?"

"Sorry." Mary shook her head regretfully. "I've never actually met her."

"That's Sheila Canner," said someone behind Elizabeth. She turned to find Minerva Helman, the head librarian at the Bird-in-Hand Free Library, standing at her left shoulder. "Sheila's a bit of a wild child." Minerva smiled to take the sting from her words, shaking her head fondly. "It would not surprise me to find Sheila sneaking off with her pockets filled with goodies."

"But it was fruit and crackers, not cookies," Elizabeth said. "I think I'd understand it more if it had been goodies."

"Well, nothing would surprise me," Louise Schott said. Her mouth pursed. "That child has been poorly supervised her entire life. I remember when she was just a toddler, she yanked on one of the table legs and pulled an entire table of salads over at a potluck dinner. And I've seen her sneaking handfuls of extra cookies from the dessert tables any number of times. I wouldn't be surprised if that's who you saw."

But why had she asked Geraldine for money, Elizabeth wondered, if that was who it had been? Twenty dollars wasn't insignificant. She hadn't mentioned the monetary request to the group, and she wasn't inclined to after hearing Louise's pronouncements. She resolved to try never to be so judgmental, no matter how old she got.

Mary tugged at Elizabeth's elbow. "Are you ready to go? Don't forget I have to be home to take that puppy this afternoon. I want to have time to grab some lunch."

Mary had volunteered to foster a beagle puppy for a rescue. The young dog was a new intake, and the foster family that was going to care for him couldn't take him until they returned from vacation next week. Mary, after checking with her sisters, had felt that for such a short period, she could handle the extra work that caring for a puppy would require.

Elizabeth snapped her fingers. "Sorry, I forgot. Yes, I'm ready."

"Elizabeth?" A voice behind her stopped her as she began to move toward the car. Mary and Martha went on ahead.

"Good morning, Frannie," Elizabeth said, stopping to speak with the woman who had hailed her.

Frannie Bartel was a church member who volunteered at a food pantry along Route 30. "There's a girl who stops into the food pantry that fits your description, although I didn't see her here today, and I don't know that they've ever attended church. Her name is Ellie Pearce." She hesitated. "I don't want to be known as a gossip, but there are things you should know if Ellie turns out to be the girl you saw."

"I won't pass on anything you share with me in confidence," Elizabeth promised. "Well, I might discuss it with my sisters," she added honestly, "but none of us will spread it around. I was concerned when I saw the girl taking fruit from church today, and I suppose I felt led to offer help if she needs it."

Frannie looked relieved. "The Pearce family is known to be in what my mother used to call 'reduced circumstances.' The father lost his job, and I don't believe he's found another one yet. Ellie's mother works two jobs to keep food on the table. People suspect her husband beats her when she doesn't bring home enough in tips from waitressing. The mother comes into the food pantry sometimes, and once she had a black eye. I've heard he drinks a great deal."

Elizabeth made a sympathetic murmur. "That's sad for all of them."

"That's not really gossip," Frannie said. "It's a pretty well-established fact, and I'm only telling you because I'm a little concerned for your safety if that's the family you become involved with."

"I understand." Although Elizabeth didn't expect to be doing anything that would put her in danger.

"The girl is very quiet," Frannie added, "but if she's the one you saw, she could be trying to protect the mother by bringing food home."

"Thank you. If it was Ellie Pearce, perhaps I can find a way to help the family that isn't obvious," Elizabeth said. "Have a good week, Frannie."

"You too," Frannie said, as Elizabeth hurried off to join her sisters for the drive home.

She was almost to the car when she saw Pastor Abraham Nagle and his wife heading for their own vehicle. "Pastor?" She hailed him.

"Hello, Elizabeth." Pastor Nagle was a pleasant man who was fitting in well in his new position, having only come to Mount Zion not quite a year ago. "How can I help you?"

"I just have a quick question." She mentioned the Pearce family, and Ellie in particular.

The pastor shook his head. "I'm not familiar with the family, I'm afraid, and I was not introduced to anyone by that name today. But Palm Sunday and Easter are services that draw a lot of unfamiliar faces, and they could have been in attendance today without my knowledge."

Or the girl could have slipped into the fellowship time expressly for the purpose of foraging, Elizabeth thought. Aloud, she said, "That's true. Oh, by the way, do you and Maida have plans for Easter dinner? Because if you don't, my sisters and I would love to have you join us."

"That's very kind of you," Pastor Nagle said. "We're going to be taking communion to some of our members who live at Morningside Nursing Home after church. We'd love to eat with you if we won't hold up your meal too much."

"Not at all," Elizabeth said. "Shall we say two o'clock? Will that give you enough time for your visits?"

"I think that would work nicely," the pastor said. "Thank you for the invitation."

Finally, Elizabeth climbed into Martha's car. The engine was already running, and they pulled out immediately.

"Sorry to rush you," Mary said. "I just don't want to be still having lunch when the rescue person arrives with the dog."

"I'm the one who's sorry," Elizabeth said. "But I stopped to invite the Nagles to have Easter dinner with us next Sunday."

"Oh, what a nice idea," Mary said. "Are they able to come?"

"Yes, after they take communion to the church members at Morningside who can't attend the Easter Sunday service. I told him two o'clock, and he said that would work."

"That was a very thoughtful thing to do," Martha said. "Oh, boy, a bigger group to cook for! What shall I serve?"

"Ham," Mary said immediately. "We always have ham for Easter. Why would you even think of doing anything differently?"

"I didn't mean I wouldn't serve ham," Martha said with a chuckle. "Relax. I was just thinking about what dishes I should serve with it."

"Some kind of potatoes, some kind of vegetable, and rolls," Mary replied promptly.

Martha rolled her eyes and sighed. "Mary, you're a food philistine."

"No, I'm not," Mary said. "I'm neither hostile nor indifferent to your cooking and baking, which is what I'd be if I were a philistine. I only know that whatever you serve will be so scrumptious I won't care what it is."

Martha laughed. "Oh, well done. Compliment me so I can't insult you anymore. Elizabeth, do you have any opinions on side dishes for Easter?"

From the back seat Elizabeth said, "I really love those four-cheese scalloped potatoes you make. Would they go well with ham?"

"Oh yes," Mary said. "They'd be perfect. Good idea."

"What else, Elizabeth?" Martha asked.

"What? Oh, I don't know." Elizabeth's mind had already wandered back to the mystery girl.

"What's on your mind?" Martha asked. "Since it's clearly not on Easter dinner."

"There was something about that girl I saw during fellowship time today," Elizabeth said. "The one I saw hiding fruit in her coat. She really caught my attention. It seemed like such a strange thing to do, and it's equally odd to me that hardly anyone noticed her. Even weirder, I think, not a single person recognized her."

Mary spoke from the front passenger seat. "Definitely odd. So Pastor Nagle didn't know her either?"

"Well, he didn't see the girl when I did," Elizabeth admitted, "so we didn't really discuss that. I asked him if he knew Ellie Pearce or her family."

"Who's Ellie Pearce?" Martha wanted to know.

"A girl Frannie Bartel mentioned. Her family goes to the food pantry. That's where Frannie knows her from. And she fits the description of the girl I saw today."

"A slender teenage girl with long dark hair," Martha said with a chuckle. "That only describes about two-thirds of the teen girls in Bird-in-Hand."

Elizabeth sat back with a sigh. She knew what Martha said was true. There were scores of teenage girls in town who had long dark hair and who were perfectly fine. But Elizabeth knew in her heart she had to find this one. This one needed her help.

A NOTE FROM THE EDITORS

We hope you enjoyed this volume of the Mysteries of Lancaster County series, created by the Books and Inspirational Media Division of Guideposts. We are a nonprofit organization that touches millions of lives every day through products and services that inspire, encourage, help you grow in your faith, and celebrate God's love in every aspect of your daily life.

Thank you for making a difference with your purchase of this book, which helps fund our many outreach programs to military personnel, prisons, hospitals, nursing homes, and educational institutions. To learn more, visit GuidepostsFoundation.org.

We also maintain many useful and uplifting online resources. Visit Guideposts.org to read true stories of hope and inspiration, access OurPrayer network, sign up for free newsletters, download free e-books, join our Facebook community, and follow our stimulating blogs.

To learn about other Guideposts publications, including the bestselling devotional *Daily Guideposts*, go to ShopGuideposts .org, call (800) 932-2145, or write to Guideposts, PO Box 5815, Harlan, Iowa 51593.

Find more inspiring fiction in these best-loved Guideposts series!

Secrets of Wayfarers Inn

Fall back in history with three retired schoolteachers who find themselves owners of an old warehouse-turned-inn that is filled with hidden passages, buried secrets and stunning surprises that will set them on a course to puzzling mysteries from the Underground Railroad.

Sugarcreek Amish Mysteries

Be intrigued by the suspense and joyful "aha" moments in these delightful stories. Each book in the series brings together two women of vastly different backgrounds and traditions, who realize there's much more to the "simple life" than meets the eye.

Mysteries of Martha's Vineyard

Come to the shores of this quaint and historic island and dig into a cozy mystery. When a recent widow inherits a lighthouse just off the coast of Massachusetts, she finds exciting adventures, new friends, and renewed hope.

Patchwork Mysteries

Discover that life's little mysteries often have a common thread in a series where every novel contains an intriguing mystery centered around a quilt located in a beautiful New England town.

Mysteries of Silver Peak

Escape to the historic mining town of Silver Peak, Colorado, and discover how one woman's love of antiques helps her solve mysteries buried deep in the town's checkered past.

To learn more about these books, visit Guideposts.org/Shop

Sign up for the
Guideposts Fiction Newsletter
*and stay up to date on
the books you love!*

You'll get sneak peeks of new releases, recommendations from other Guideposts readers, and special offers just for you . . .
and it's FREE!

**Just go to Guideposts.org/Newsletters
today to sign up.**

Guideposts.

**Visit Guideposts.org/Shop
or call (800) 932-2145**